Anja de Jager is a London-based native Dutch speaker who writes in English. She draws inspiration from cases that her father, a retired police detective, worked on in the Netherlands. Anja worked in the City for twenty years but is now a full-time writer.

Also by Anja de Jager

A Cold Death in Amsterdam
A Cold Case in Amsterdam Central
Death on the Canal
A Death in Rembrandt Square
A Death at the Hotel Mondrian
Death at the Orange Locks

Death in the Red Light District

Anja de Jager

CONSTABLE

First published in Great Britain in 2023 by Constable
This paperback edition published in Great Britain in 2024 by Constable

1 3 5 7 9 10 8 6 4 2

A CIP catalogue record for this book
is available from the British Library.

ISBN: 978-1-40871-899-5

Typeset in Bembo by Photoprint, Torquay
Printed and bound in Great Britain by Clays Ltd, Elcograf S.p.A.

Papers used by Constable are from well-managed forests and other
responsible sources.

Constable
An imprint of
Little, Brown Book Group
Carmelite House
50 Victoria Embankment
London EC4Y 0DZ

An Hachette UK Company
www.hachette.co.uk

www.littlebrown.co.uk

To my parents, who recently celebrated their sixtieth wedding anniversary.

I'm grateful that you continue to share your stories.

Death in the Red Light District

Chapter 1

The large advertising hoarding that covered most of the office building on the Singel, one of Amsterdam's oldest canals, screamed that this was a rare opportunity to lease such a substantial property on such an amazing location. However, the weather-frayed edges of the cardboard gave away that it had been on the market for months. The property was still vacant, and Detective Lotte Meerman knew that the reason for her presence here was only going to make it harder to find new tenants.

She checked her watch. The woman from building management was taking her time. She stopped waiting at the front and went back inside. Most of the site was ready for anybody to move in at a moment's notice, but one corner of the smart downstairs floor was as incongruous as a museum exhibit. It seemed like a modern art installation formed of empty jenever bottles, stubbed-out cigarette ends and a dirty sleeping bag, all visible through a makeshift wall of upended empty wooden pallets.

Thomas Jansen, Lotte's colleague, joined her. His dark hair was neatly styled, as if he had to make an appearance in the in-house police magazine. Lotte thought he spent more time on his looks than she did on hers. He wore a blue shirt under a thin jacket. She was still wearing her winter coat, but regretted that decision. Even with the zip completely undone, she was too warm. Early April was the time of year when the changing weather meant you always wore the wrong clothes.

He looked around him at the pile of rubbish. 'He was homeless, then?'

'He was squatting here, I guess,' Lotte said. The contrast between the discarded rubbish and the otherwise pristine but empty office made the junk appear carefully curated. She wondered if the presence of squatters had delayed the lease. The council would step in if they didn't get tenants soon.

'Same difference. Looks like he was drunk or drugged up and fell off the walkway.'

She pushed open the door to the back and entered the green oasis that ran the width of the building. It was a feature of Amsterdam's seventeenth-century canal houses that they had secret gardens. They were completely hidden from view and nobody walking along the canal ever knew they existed. Normally peaceful, today the garden was a hive of activity. It was filled with uniformed police officers buzzing around like angry wasps in their dark blue jackets with fluorescent stripes.

Lotte skirted a rhododendron and followed the gravel path around a marble statue. She paused at the clearing at the edge of a large rectangular pond. Bordered by man-high reeds and towering bamboo, the water feature dominated this garden.

The sightline was meant to be picturesque, but instead it

offered her a clear view of the body of a dead man floating face-down in the water.

On the narrow grey walkway crossing the pond, four forensic scientists tried to capture as much evidence from the scene as they could before they lifted the corpse. A photographer eternalised the body's exact position. All in case this enormous garden turned out to be a crime scene.

Lotte felt distanced from the busyness, because she hardly mattered. She wasn't important. It was all going to come down to what forensics would find. The anonymous person who had called it in from a landline inside this building, but who hadn't hung around, had spoken of a drunk man and an accident. The victim had already been dead for hours by the time the police arrived.

Charlie Schippers, the third member of their team, strode across that same walkway, past the bamboo and reeds. His reddish hair shone in the afternoon sunlight. He was always active, as if he were a spaniel and his job during the hunt was to move around and disturb the game. The grey path was only just wide enough to let two people pass, and Charlie had to step over a kneeling figure in a white coverall to get across. The dead body implied that this was a dangerous procedure, but the water was probably only waist deep. There was no sign of a 'Deep Water' health and safety warning.

'It's a beautiful place to die,' Thomas said.

'Quite morbidly so.'

'Makes a difference from a normal drowning.'

Lotte nodded. She'd expected the body to be in the canal at the front of the building. That this man had instead drowned in the wide, shallow pond in the garden at the back was the main reason why they'd hesitated to immediately write it off as an accident.

'They measured it,' Thomas said, as if he could follow her thoughts, 'and it's only a metre deep.'

It was such a needless way to die. You had to have drunk yourself into oblivion, she thought, to drown in such shallow water.

'I'm sorry it took me so long.' An elderly black woman in a trouser suit rushed up the garden path. 'I'm Julie Flissen,' she said. 'We spoke half an hour ago.'

'You're the building manager?' Lotte asked.

'That's right. Hold on one second.' The woman leaned a hand against a birch tree to catch her breath. She threw a glance at the pond and immediately looked away again. 'Oh my God, poor Teun.'

She must have known him really well, Lotte thought, to identify him from the back, especially as she'd only seen the body for a second or so. From where they were standing, all that was visible was the matted grey hair and a dark-green coat. The rest of his body was hidden from sight by the reeds.

'You recognise him?'

'Yes, that's Teun. Teun Simmens. He's been here for two months or so.'

Lotte took a note of the name. There had been no ID amongst the pile of rubbish.

'You know what the squatter's called?' Thomas sounded incredulous. Normally building management worked to move these people to somewhere else as quickly as possible;

they didn't socialise with them. 'Did you know him before he moved in?'

'No, I'd never met him before.'

'You spoke to him after he started squatting here?'

'The owner of the building has given us strict instructions to let these people live here in peace while the property is empty, and to treat them with respect.' Julie rubbed a hand over her short hair and shook her head as if to say that she hadn't made those rules and didn't agree with them. 'He was a squatter himself once, and active in the squatter movement during the eighties.'

'What's his name?' Lotte asked.

'Gerard Klaasen,' Julie said.

'There was never any threat to remove this guy, then?' Thomas asked.

'Well, at one point there were ten people living here. That was too many and put off potential lessees. Mr Klaasen agreed that if they limited it to five, he'd let them stay until there was a new occupant of the building.'

'No sign of that?' Thomas asked.

Julie shook her head. 'Commercial real estate is slow at the moment, but we'll find someone. We wanted to get one company to take over the whole space, but now we're going to parcel it out. It'll be fine.' Despite her words, she looked concerned. 'We still have two months before the six-month deadline.'

Any building that stood empty for longer than six months, be it a private dwelling or an office block, was compulsorily rented out by the council at rates that they decided. Lotte tried not to think about how long it was since she'd been to her own flat. She could only hope that nobody reported it as vacant.

'You said five people lived here now?' she asked. 'There was nobody else when we got here.' And when the police had searched the building, they had only found one sleeping bag. One pile of junk.

Julie shrugged. 'Not always five. We agreed five at most, but you know what it's like: people come and go.' She handed Lotte her card, said to contact her if she needed anything else. It was clear that she was keen to leave.

Most people didn't want to hang around the site of death.

Lotte let her go, because this was going to take a while. They could easily call her in if they couldn't locate any next of kin and needed her to formally ID the man.

Thomas and Charlie returned to the police station on the Elandsgracht two hours later, but Lotte remained next to the water feature as forensics bagged up the body. When they lifted him, she crouched down to take a careful look at his face. He wasn't bloated like the victims who'd been in the water for a long time. His grey hair stuck to his cheekbones and he hadn't shaved in weeks. His face was fallen in, thin and deeply lined. She guessed he was sixty or so, but it was always hard to judge the age of those who'd been living rough for a long time.

She stayed until forensics were finished. They indicated that death had taken place the previous night between 1 and 3 a.m., but they would give her a better indication with the full report tomorrow.

She walked back to the police station in dazzling sunshine. The weather seemed too bright for this death of a lonely homeless man, and entering the station at least brought her relief from that. She took her coat off as she walked up the stairs to the team's office.

'There's a Teun Simmens in the police database,' Thomas said as soon as she got in.

She wasn't surprised. Many homeless people had been in contact with the police at some time or other. But when she pulled the record, the Teun Simmens in the photo was someone her age, with a healthy rounded face. The image on the screen looked nothing like the dead man. 'I don't think that's him,' she said.

Either Julie Flissen had misidentified him, or he had given her a false name. Lotte sighed. Now they had to start the complicated task of identifying the dead man without any papers.

'Are you looking at the old photo? Check out the more recent one,' Thomas said. 'Looks like him to me.'

She noticed the date on the police record on her screen. This was ten years old, when Simmens had been arrested for money laundering and sentenced to five years in prison. Thomas was right, there was a more recent record. She pulled it up. He had gone back to jail three years ago for GBH whilst under the influence of alcohol. Since his first arrest, he had lost a lot of weight. The rough life had taken its toll and he no longer looked healthy. In this photo, his face was framed by long matted grey hair and largely covered by a matching straggly beard.

There was no doubt that this was the dead man they'd found today.

Lotte looked through the rest of his history. After his initial release, he had been in and out of homeless shelters and mental health institutions. It was a downward trajectory that she found sadly familiar. His death could as easily be suicide as an accident caused by intoxication. Without a note, they'd rule it as the latter.

The only shock was that the man was only seven years older than Lotte herself. Within ten years, prison, alcohol and homelessness had transformed Teun Simmens from a healthy, successful-looking man into someone whose death by drowning didn't surprise anybody.

Chapter 2

31 March 1980

Piet Huizen's hard-shell suitcase was so heavy, it felt he'd packed his entire life in it. 'I'm going,' he said softly into the empty corridor full of the detritus of his family's daily existence. He ran a hand over the wall. He was proud of his house and of owning a property. He rummaged for his keys on the hallway shelf, which was covered with discarded toys and old shopping lists. When he'd bought the place six years ago, he just hadn't known that he'd end up living in the small two-bedroom house with his wife, his daughter and his brother.

He smiled at the sight of Lotte's toy, a small pink wooden figurine that fell slack when you pressed the base. It had been a firm favourite last year, but now lay abandoned on its side. On an impulse, he picked it up and stuck it in his pocket. It was hard to believe that his daughter was already going to kindergarten. Soon she'd have swimming lessons, and for her fifth birthday next month, he was going to get her a bicycle.

Footsteps stumbled overhead. Piet considered dashing out of the front door and avoiding the contact, but he put his luggage down and waited. He felt conspicuous in the wide jeans and white Adidas trainers that his younger brother, Robbie, had persuaded him to buy for this trip. There definitely was an advantage to working in uniform: you never had to think about what to wear. That uniform was now packed in his suitcase.

Robbie came down the stairs in his pyjamas. He scratched his head and made his already unruly hair stand on end. Piet wanted to slick it back with a wet comb, as he'd done with his own this morning, but his brother called that old-fashioned. That was what having a wife, a child and a job did to you; responsibilities made you outdated when you were still only thirty.

'I'm sorry about last night,' Robbie said. 'I shouldn't have argued with her, not on the evening before you left.'

Rehashing grievances from the previous night was the worst way to start a morning. 'I have to go,' Piet interrupted his brother, and picked up his luggage again.

'I'll make you breakfast.'

He glanced at his watch. 'My boss will be here in five.'

His brother put a hand on his shoulder. 'I'll look after them,' he said. 'Don't worry.'

'Thanks.'

'And you should pay me for that.' Robbie took his hand off Piet's shoulder and stretched it out, palm upwards. The grin on his face took the edge off the request for a hand-out enough that they could both pretend it was just a joke. 'It will be a really hard job.'

'Don't push your luck.' Piet thought about going back upstairs to see his daughter one more time before leaving, but his brother effectively blocked the narrow corridor. He collected his peaked cap from the hat stand and tucked it under his arm with a smooth, practised movement that hours of drilling had perfected. 'Don't argue with Hilda while I'm away,' he said. 'Please?'

Robbie nodded his agreement, but Piet knew he'd forget about the ceasefire at the first provocation, probably in an hour or so, before they'd even finished breakfast. He was suddenly anxious to leave, and Robbie reached past him and opened the front door.

Piet stepped out into the quiet Alkmaar street and without looking back walked to the corner, where his superior officer was due to pick him up. It was already light. Because he had a couple of minutes, he rested against the lamp post, lit a cigarette and blew the smoke into the morning air. Inspector van Merwe, his boss, had given up smoking a month ago, so this was the last chance of a nicotine hit before getting in the car. He shivered. The morning carried a definite touch of chill, even though it was officially spring.

He was certain he'd forgotten something. Hilda had helped him pack, but neither of them was all that clear what was expected. He hadn't been keen to go, but she had urged him. It was extra pay, after all, and they definitely needed the money. A discussion about their finances had escalated into that row last night. He knew it was why she'd stayed in bed this morning and let him leave without saying goodbye.

But was it so inconsiderate that he had suggested she could look for a job now that Lotte was going to kindergarten? Yes, it was his responsibility to provide for his family, but even if she just stacked shelves in the local Albert Heijn supermarket, that would make things easier.

He took a long drag from his cigarette. He shouldn't have put it like that. Hilda had countered that it made more financial sense for him to give up smoking, or for his brother to get a job. Some things were impossible to implement but were effective arguments to shut him up. Even more so as his brother had been right there and of course kicked off straight away.

A blue Citroën 2CV turned the corner and stopped beside Piet. He took a last drag, then dropped the butt on the ground and crushed it under his shoe. Inspector van Merwe opened the car door. His heavy jowls and the deep bags under his eyes reminded Piet of the bulldog he'd had as a kid. Van Merwe looked at Piet's luggage and got out of the car with a sigh. The bulldog had been a grumpy dog.

'Good choice,' he said.

'Sorry?' There was nothing special about the suitcase.

The inspector indicated Piet's clothes. 'You're dressed like a tourist. Who knows what we're going to get ourselves into.' He unlocked the boot. 'Stick your stuff in there.' He stepped aside.

Piet fitted his case carefully next to the boss's brand-new Samsonite. 'Thanks for giving me a lift.' It was a good thing he didn't have a bigger bag, because it was a tight squeeze, and he didn't want to scratch van Merwe's property.

The inspector shrugged. 'You're on my way.' Otherwise he wouldn't have bothered.

'What are we going to be doing?' Piet said as he got in. The briefing had been vague.

'Whatever's needed.' Van Merwe started the engine. 'They must be desperate. They really just need bodies, and anyone will do. Even someone like you. Have you been to Amsterdam before?'

'A couple of times,' Piet said. 'Once on a school trip. We saw the museums.'

'It's not a school trip now, but just do your best.'

'Yes, sir, I will do.' He felt as if he was back at school, though, and was a mild disappointment to the head teacher, who already had low expectations of him.

'Magda wasn't too pleased,' van Merwe said. 'My wife doesn't trust me on my own for a month.'

'But we'll be back on weekends, won't we? Who knows, maybe it'll only be for a week.'

The inspector shook his head. 'This will go on until Beatrix's coronation,' he said. 'It won't stop until the end of April, at the earliest.'

Queen Juliana had announced in January that she would abdicate on 30 April, Queen's Day, and her daughter, Princess Beatrix, would ascend to the throne. It wasn't a popular change, especially since Beatrix was married to a German. Her husband, Prince Claus, claimed he hadn't fired a single shot during the war, but that didn't change the fact that a Nazi officer was now going to sit as prince consort on the Dutch throne.

'What made you change your mind, Huizen?' he went on. 'I know you weren't keen at first.'

'They need more police in Amsterdam, so isn't this our duty?' Piet hadn't wanted to leave his family on their own.

He hadn't wanted to be away from his daughter, his wife, his brother.

'Was it the extra pay?' Van Merwe grinned. 'Whenever people talk about duty, they want to hide that they mean cash.'

It was disturbing that his boss knew him so well. There was a lot he was willing to do if that meant keeping his family afloat. There were too many people relying on him, and all these people cost money.

'Anyway,' his boss said, 'I'm sure they'll find you a job that even you are capable of. Put you in charge of parking tickets or something.'

'They still give tickets? Even now?'

Van Merwe laughed. 'You're so stupid, Huizen. Honestly.'

Piet stared out of the window as they hit the motorway. There were four lanes of no traffic. Everybody must be avoiding Amsterdam right now. Nobody wanted to visit the capital city, which looked like a war zone on the evening news. The worst violence since the German occupation, a journalist had said last night. Linking the coronation so openly to the Second World War was controversial, but it was undeniable that the riots had intensified as the coronation day drew nearer. The battles between protesters, squatters and the police had escalated to the point that they now absorbed the entire Amsterdam police force.

The 2CV wasn't a car for speed, but on the empty roads it only took them forty-five minutes to reach the capital. In the early-morning light, the place looked pretty. Peaceful. The boss pulled up on one of Amsterdam's canals. This seemed far away from any trouble.

'I'm seconded here.' Van Merwe pointed to a large square building. He had found himself a comfortable position at the main police station. No surprise there, then. 'You know where you're supposed to be?'

Piet nodded. Last night, before the argument with Hilda had broken out, he had once more looked up his designated police station and double-checked the map. He opened the boot and collected his suitcase, then tucked his uniform cap back under his arm.

Van Merwe examined the metal parking meters that lined the canal. 'Sod that,' he said, and fished a book of parking tickets from his jacket pocket. He filled one in and stuck it under the windscreen wipers of the Citroën. 'That'll do for today. Don't embarrass us,' he added as he headed off towards the police station, abandoning Piet like an unwanted and potentially unruly puppy.

The city was waking up. This was a good time to walk around: rioters and protesters weren't out of bed at 8 a.m. A few people cycled along the canal, but otherwise it was quiet. As he followed the water's edge, it dawned on him that he hadn't arranged with his boss to get a lift back on Friday, and that the map he'd consulted last night was at the bottom of his suitcase. He was alone in an unfamiliar city, not certain of his actual location and close to the front line in the war between rioters and police.

As he walked, his main thought became that he was also in a city where he didn't know anybody, and where – more importantly – he was a stranger to all of them too. Worry evaporated in the cool morning air. At home in Alkmaar, anybody who'd ever gone to the same school as him saw him as that boy who was so stupid he'd been held back a year.

He turned a corner and came to a street that seemed twice as wide due to the sudden lack of parked cars. On a boarded-up window someone had spray-painted a likeness of a police officer in full riot gear. The figure was mainly made up of the rectangle of his shield, and only the top of his helmet and the toes of his boots identified him as a person. So that was how his colleagues were seen here: barely human, threatening and violent. The helmet with the visor down gave the riot police the same anonymity that Piet himself had gained purely by going to another city.

As he followed the graffitied street, he came upon the first roadblock. On either side of the makeshift barricade, some-one had piled bricks into stacks of ammunition with sharp edges. The barricade was built mainly out of chairs and tables, reinforced with paving slabs, planks of wood and sheets of MDF. Where the bricks had been taken from the street, bare earth was visible like a scar. On the news every night he had seen his colleagues battling to hold back the rioters, who were hell-bent on aggression and destruction.

'Are you lost, mate?'

Piet looked up abruptly at the voice that came from above him.

A man stared down from a second-floor balcony, smoking a cigarette. 'Don't go that way. It's all blocked up.' Through the railings of the balcony, Piet saw a pile of bricks at the man's feet. The safety of the empty morning street was now a threat.

He was stupid not to have taken notice of the boarded-up windows and the anti-police graffiti. This was obviously one of the squats that formed the rioters' base. He was suddenly acutely aware of the peaked cap tucked under his left elbow. As the squatter was on his right, the man only had a view of the hand with the suitcase. Inside enemy territory, looking like a tourist was as good a disguise as he was going to get. He mentally thanked Robbie for the jeans and trainers.

'I'd avoid Dam Square if I were you,' the man said.

'Thanks for the advice, mate.' Piet mirrored the squatter's earlier words with a dry mouth.

'Just go back that way and then take a left.' The man pointed with the cigarette.

Piet knew that turning around would expose his police cap to the squatter on the balcony, but what choice did he have? He couldn't clamber over the barricade. For a fleeting second, he considered using his suitcase as a riot shield and transforming himself into one of those graffiti policemen. He didn't do it. He just walked away and hoped that the man had lost interest.

No such luck. Jeering laughter rained down on him. 'You've brought the wrong hat, copper,' the squatter shouted after him. 'You're going to need a helmet!'

Piet flinched, but made himself continue at the same speed with his cap clenched against his side and his shoulders tensed in anticipation of a brick.

It didn't come.

Ten minutes later, he arrived at the safety of his assigned police station on the Western Canal Ring. The building was a wide office block with only a blue plaque with the word *Police* to identify it. It fitted in neatly, as if trying not to draw attention to itself.

'Here's another one,' were the duty officer's words of welcome before Piet even told him who he was. He was a thickset man with a mop of curly sandy hair and a bushy moustache. 'And now we're finally complete,' he said. 'You're the last one to turn up.'

'My boss dropped me at the other side and—'

'Don't worry about it.' The officer cut him short. 'I'm Bouma. Let's have a quick chat. I'll get the others and you follow him.' He pointed at a wiry man in his late thirties with huge sideburns and a cigarette between his fingers.

The man stuck out a hand and gave a wide smile. 'Welcome, partner, I'm Wim van Buren. From Arnhem.'

Chapter 3

Lotte ate her lunch in the canteen of the police station, which overlooked the wide water, and was blissfully by herself. Outside, on the canal, a group of young people were messing about in a flat-bottomed boat, rowing with delighted ineptness, more joy in the splashing of water than in moving the boat towards its destination. She bit into her cheese sandwich and drank a glass of milk. There was comfort in eating the same thing every day, as there was in her solitude in the otherwise buzzing canteen. It was a sign of ageing, she thought, that she needed to be by herself for at least half an hour a day or she'd go nuts. She stopped looking out of the window and paged through the forensics report on Teun Simmens' death, which had landed on her desk that morning with the expected 'accidental death' ruling.

There was only one thing in the report that bothered her, and she had to think about how to deal with it.

The legs of a metal chair scraping on the floor jolted her out of her concentration, and she looked up. A man in uniform, roughly her own age, sat down opposite her. She recognised the guy and sighed. She couldn't fathom why he wanted to sit with her, especially as a quick scan of the canteen told her there were plenty of empty tables.

'Hi, Lotte,' Rick van Buren said. 'How are you?' He didn't have a tray of food, so he wasn't here for lunch.

She didn't think they were friendly enough to exchange pleasantries like this. She hadn't talked to this guy in years and would have been happy if it had been twice as long.

'I only found out this morning.'

What was he talking about?

He took his police cap off, revealing his completely bald head. He put the cap on the table between them.

Oh great, so he was planning on staying.

'I came as soon as I heard.' He rubbed a hand over his smooth pate. 'I looked for you in your office, but you weren't there. Your colleagues told me where I'd find you.'

'Right.' It was more than five years since she'd last worked with him. 'It's been a while,' she said. He was based in a different Amsterdam police station, so she hardly ever saw him.

'Ah, so you remember!' A sad smile split his deeply lined face. His blue eyes were watery. Was he trying not to cry? Was he drunk?

During their last case together, he'd reeked of alcohol most days. He'd been so drunk on the job that he'd messed up the case by bagging up evidence incorrectly. It had got the whole team a stern reprimand from the prosecutor, and because of that, Rick had been demoted from CID. He was still in uniform. At least he was sober this time. As far as she could tell.

'It must have been such a shock.' He reached for her hand.

What the hell? She pulled it back quickly. Maybe he was drunk after all. She put her plate and glass on her tray and grabbed her handbag. A hasty exit was called for.

'We see death all the time,' he said, 'but it's still different when it's someone you know, isn't it?'

'I have no idea what you're talking about.'

'Teun Simmens,' Rick said. 'When was the last time you saw him?'

'Teun Simmens?' The homeless man they'd found dead yesterday. She put her bag back on the floor. 'I've never seen him before.'

'*I* knew him.'

Must have been a drinking buddy. 'I see.'

'You knew him too,' he continued. 'You must remember. We used to play together.'

'We did?' She frowned.

'Yes. You, me and Teun. When we were young.'

Lotte shook her head. 'We never did.' The drink must have messed with Rick van Buren's brain.

'Didn't you say you remembered me?'

'Oh, I remember you. From the Chugong case.'

He grimaced. 'Ah yes. I messed that one up. But don't you remember when we used to get together as kids?'

Lotte shook her head. 'You've got the wrong person. From what I remember of the report, Simmens was seven years older than me.'

'Exactly! He was the oldest. Always the one suggesting which games to play. Don't you remember how he used to love being in control?' Rick was so adamant, so pleading, that Lotte almost wished she *could* remember him and Teun as children.

But she didn't.

She had been a bit of a loner as a child, especially after her parents divorced when she was five. She hadn't found it easy to make new friends at primary school when her mother had moved to Amsterdam a few years later, and so she definitely would have remembered a group of childhood buddies. 'Seriously, that wasn't me,' she said.

'It doesn't matter,' he said. 'What did forensics say?'

She could suggest he sit next to her and read the report, but she didn't want to get that close. Instead, she gave him a brief summary. 'Water in his lungs, no sign of any struggle. Plus he had high levels of alcohol in his blood. So it's officially an accidental death caused by drowning.'

All this talk of childhood friends made her think of the swimming lessons in the first year of primary school, which focused just as much on how to survive if you accidentally fell in as on the fastest way to complete a length of the pool. To get their first swimming certificate, she and her classmates had to jump in fully clothed, employing the technique to keep their heads above water at all times, tread water for one minute and then cross the pool widthways. Some of her fellow pupils had cheated by wearing lightweight plastic shoes. She had worn last year's shoes, which were a size too small by the time she jumped into the pool in them. Those childhood lessons were so instilled in her that she could replicate them on autopilot, and it made her wonder how drunk you had to be to fall into a garden pond face-down and not try to get out.

Rick sighed deeply. 'It's sad,' he said. 'What about the other people in the squat? Did they see or hear anything?'

That he knew where Teun had lived made her give up any idea of leaving the canteen. 'When did you see him last?' she asked.

'A couple of weeks ago. I checked in on him every now and then. I'd been trying to get him to go to AA meetings with me, hoped every time that he'd acknowledge his drinking problem, but he wouldn't. He knew he had a problem, but he didn't want to face it. Couldn't see a way out, you know.'

'I talked to Julie Flissen from building management, and she told me that people came and went. How many people lived in that building the last time you saw Teun?'

'There were two others. A man and a woman.'

'Do you know their names?'

Rick shook his head. 'I never talked to them. They stayed indoors while Teun and I had a chat outside in the garden.'

'An anonymous man called it in from a landline inside the building. That could have been the other guy. The other squatter, I mean.'

'I can check with social services for you. They might know.'

'Thanks,' Lotte said, 'but you really don't have to.' It was an accidental death, it didn't matter.

'I owe you one for the Chugong case. And I owe my friend too.'

'Your friend? So you've kept in touch with Simmens since you were kids?' Rick van Buren might just be the person to solve her conundrum.

'Yes, we met on and off. I don't know why. Teun was older than me, but we just got on. He always liked bossing me around. It petered out a bit after his father passed away. I guess our fathers were the main reason we kept in contact.'

Or it had petered out because Teun was in prison.

'Then I bumped into him again a couple of years ago,' Rick continued, 'and I was shocked at the state he was in, to be honest. I hadn't seen him in ten years or so, and back then he'd been this successful guy: good job, wife, kids, big house, nice car. You know the type: the ones with the perfect life that all the guys are jealous of. Well, I was jealous anyway. And if I'm honest, that's why we drifted apart.'

She didn't understand why he was telling her all this. It was more personal information than she needed to hear about this failed colleague. 'And then he drank his perfect life away?' She said it flippantly.

But Rick paused for a few seconds to consider the question. 'From what he told me, I think it was the other way around: he lost it all and then started to drink heavily,' he said. 'And once he did that, he couldn't get his life back. I don't know the exact ins and outs, but he told me that he lost his job first, then made some stupid decisions to stay financially afloat – he didn't tell me what they were, he was cagey about that.'

'Money laundering,' Lotte said, remembering what she'd read in the police database.

'Anyway, he went to prison, got divorced and lost the house, and when he got out, it was impossible to get a job even close to what he used to have. So he drank the time away and then became unemployable.' Rick shrugged. 'You know the spiral.'

Sure, she'd seen it often enough. 'You're still in touch with his family?'

'Yes, Vicky, his ex-wife, called me this morning to tell me that Teun had passed away yesterday. That's why I came to talk to you.'

Lotte nodded. 'That's good.'

'Good? Why?'

'There's something in the forensic report that I feel she needs to know. When the pathologist did the post-mortem, she noticed that, along with the advanced liver cirrhosis from prolonged alcohol abuse, his body was riddled with cancer. It was late-stage bowel cancer. His family ought to be told about this.'

'Maybe that's why he looked so terrible, and also why he was drinking so much,' Rick said. 'He must have been in a lot of pain.'

Or maybe he was drinking so much that he'd never even noticed.

'I'll call Vicky,' he said. 'It's kind of you to point it out, and I think it'll bring her some comfort.'

'Comfort?' Lotte frowned. 'Hardly. Bowel cancer can be hereditary. His children need to get screened.'

'I see. I'm going to have to give them bad news on top of bad news.' He sighed. 'But it's okay, I want to do that for Teun. Plus, like I said, I owe you one for that Chugong case.' He got up, then added, 'Say hi to your dad.'

Chapter 4

31 March 1980

Sergeant Bouma, the duty officer, stood in front of a map of Amsterdam. 'We're here,' he tapped on the location of the police station, 'and this area here,' he pointed to the east of Centraal station, 'is District 2. The Red Light District. It's a square kilometre of misery. A thousand bars, two thousand prostitutes, drugs, gambling, violent crime, you name it. Stay away from District 2. Especially in your spare time.' He scanned the faces of the four men in front of him as if trying to decide how much trouble they were likely to cause.

'This zone here,' he continued, indicating the area around Dam Square and the Nieuwe Kerk, 'is where Princess Beatrix's coronation will take place. Fifty-nine royals from all over the world are coming. Nine of them are deemed vulnerable to attacks and will get extra protection. The IRA, Baader-Meinhof, ETA,' he counted them off on his fingers, 'all these terrorist groups have people in Amsterdam and it's highly likely that one of them will try something. Between you and me, we're especially concerned about an IRA assassination attempt on Prince Charles. Special forces are dealing with that.

'These places here,' he tapped on four locations near the centre, 'are the squatters' bulwarks. We might leave them alone, or the riot police, which is everybody these days, may clear them out with appropriate levels of violence. Not your problem. Your area is here.' He indicated a section west of Centraal station mainly made up of concentric canal rings. 'Singel, Koningsgracht, Keizersgracht, Herengracht, Prinsengracht.' He flicked a finger against each of them in turn. 'That's where you'll be working. Stay in this section of the canal area and you'll be fine. Your hotel is in this zone too, just around the corner, so you'll get familiar with this part of town.'

This information would have been useful before he got here, Piet thought, as he recognised at least one of the spots that Bouma wanted him to stay away from. It was the squat he had walked past this morning, nearly ending up with a brick in the back of his neck.

'With all personnel pulled in to deal with the riots, the squatters, the terrorists and the coronation, we have to make do with you lot seconded from all over the country for the regular police work in our zone. You're Team 4, and you're on the early shift, eight a.m. to four p.m.' He threw a pointed look at Piet. 'Going forwards, be on time. Apart from that, it's normal everyday work for you, just in a different location. It will be overwhelming, as we're so short-staffed, so prioritise. Public drunkenness, traffic issues, parking tickets, ignore all of that. Luckily, the drug use and dealing is contained in District 2, so that won't be a problem. Only theft and robbery spills over into here. Your job is to give the impression of business as usual to the locals. We don't want them to feel unsafe. The madness should finish with the coronation, so we've just got one more month to keep it all together.' He scratched his head. 'I wonder if Queen Juliana knew what mayhem she'd unleashed when she announced her abdication back in January, giving us only a few months to prepare for the chaos.'

In the distance, a phone started to shout shrilly for attention. Bouma got up. 'Right,' he said, 'I hope you've got it from here.' He disappeared, leaving the four men alone.

'Eelke Wieringa. Groningen,' one of them said solemnly, as if he wanted to underline that he came from the north.

'I'm Barry Simmens. From Overveen.' Barry was the oldest of the four of them.

Piet thought he was the youngest, even though he and Eelke seemed close in age. 'I'm Piet Huizen. I'm from Alkmaar.' He mirrored their way of introducing themselves, which put as much importance on their home location as on their name. At least nobody introduced themselves by rank. Not that Piet was embarrassed at still being a constable after almost ten years in the police force, but he had the distinct impression that Barry Simmens was much more senior than him. Being away from home made rank less important, he guessed, but it was good that there was someone with more experience.

'Follow me,' Wim van Buren said, and set off down a corridor. He opened a door on the right to an area with space for ten people. Only three of the desks were currently in use. 'We decided to sit together,' he said, 'but there is a choice. Plenty of empty desks over there if you decide you don't like us. But then we'll need a report in triplicate to explain why.' He pointed at the electronic typewriter that stood ready next to a pile of empty forms and carbon inserts.

'Oh no, I'm happy to sit with you.' Piet put his uniform cap on the empty desk that Wim indicated and placed his suitcase beside it. Signs of the desk's previous occupant were still visible. A mug, a half-smoked packet of Marlboros, pens. He opened the bottom drawer and found a bottle of cognac. He quickly shut it again.

'We all got here last night,' Barry said, 'and stayed in the hotel they've allocated us. It's nice, but we're the only ones there. A bit like this police station.'

It would have been easier if Piet had also come last night. Then he'd have been settled in like these temporary colleagues. He would also have avoided an argument at home. 'I'm sorry I only arrived now,' he said. 'My boss gave me a lift down from Alkmaar and he insisted on going this morning.'

'It really doesn't matter. I'll show you where the hotel is at lunchtime and get you checked in,' Wim said. 'It's right around the corner anyway. The manager is happy to have us. At least the city is paying him some money after scaring away all the tourists.'

'Thanks.' Piet felt he'd been thrown into the deep end and had to do his best to swim. Let's not drown, he thought, even if I'm way out of my depth.

'Eelke and Barry are one team, we're the other. I don't know what I said last night but neither of them wanted to work with me.'

'I met some of the guys in Team 3 last night when I

arrived,' Barry said. 'They do the weekends. They told me it's been nuts.'

'I didn't know weekends was an option. They'll get triple pay,' Eelke said. He must need the money as much as Piet did. 'My boss said the main thing I should do is pray that nobody gets murdered while we're here.'

'Can you imagine,' Wim said, 'being part of a murder investigation in another city? That would be a disaster. My plan is to do as little as possible.

'But think of the extra hours we'd work,' Eelke said. 'Lots of overtime pay.'

'Let's not get ahead of ourselves,' Barry said. 'We need to keep things ticking over, and the less these phones ring, the better it's going to be.'

'I'll pocket the extra pay for being seconded here,' Wim said, 'and then go back home happy in four weeks. Well, partner,' he clapped Piet on the shoulder, 'we're in Amsterdam now. This is going to be fun.'

As if on cue, the radio in the corner crackled and the voice of Duty Sergeant Bouma came through. 'Team 4, Team 4, assistance required at a suspected domestic on the Reestraat. I repeat, assistance required at a suspected domestic on the Reestraat.'

'We're on our way,' Barry responded. He and Eelke dashed out of the room.

'It's early for that,' Wim said. 'Who wants to fight with their wife at ten o'clock in the morning? You'd better get changed.'

Piet nodded. As he unzipped his coat, his fingers found the little figurine, Lotte's toy, which he had stuck in his pocket this morning. He took it out and placed it next to the previous occupant's packet of cigarettes. Now this desk was marked as his. It was a visual sign that he was going to stay. He opened his suitcase and found his light-blue uniform shirt and dark-blue trousers. They were barely creased, so he hung them over the back of his chair and dug for the dark-blue jacket with the flame of the police force on the arm. Instead, his fingers found the metal of his gun, which he had hidden out of sight as much as possible. Best to put that away in the drawer of his desk for the time being.

He gathered his uniform over one arm, as he liked to get dressed where he had a mirror. It was important to appear respectable when he was in uniform, and he needed the confirmation of a mirror to tell him he looked the part. But before he could ask Wim where the toilets were, the radio crackled again.

'Team 4, Team 4, urgent call: an ongoing robbery at the jeweller's at the Boomstraat. I repeat, a robbery at the jeweller's at the Boomstraat.'

'Shit,' Wim said. 'That's us. Let's go.'

'But I'm not wearing my uniform,' Piet said.

'Just put the jacket on. It'll do.' Wim headed for the door.

Piet thought this was all wrong, but he had to follow his colleague. He dumped most of his uniform back over his chair and shrugged on his police jacket so at least he was visually identifiable as a police officer. Then he quickly strapped his gun around his hips – you never knew how a robbery might play out – and planted his uniform cap on his head. At least his top half was passable. He dashed after Wim, who was just disappearing down the stairs.

At the entrance, Bouma handed them car keys. 'Do you know where you're going?' he asked. He threw a withering glance at Piet, which made Piet only too aware that he looked a mess wearing his cap and uniform jacket over the jeans and Adidas trainers.

'Boomstraat,' Wim said. 'Jeweller's.'

'Do you know where that is?' the sergeant repeated. He clearly had experience with people coming from outside the city. He stepped out from behind his counter and pointed at the large map of Amsterdam on the wall. 'We're here,' he indicated, 'and the Boomstraat is here. The jeweller's is at this location.'

Without looking too closely, Wim was already out of the door and rushing towards the car. Piet quickly memorised the route and sprinted after him.

He saw with a sense of relief that their car was a Volvo. At least something was the same in Amsterdam as in Alkmaar. Wim took the driver's seat and Piet got in the other side. 'You can drive next time,' Wim said. He switched on the siren with obvious glee and turned the key in the ignition. Then he reversed the car out of the parking spot at high speed and screeched to the right. The siren sent the few pedestrians scrambling out of the way. He took a left. A helicopter hung threateningly in the air ahead of them. It was a strategy that the Dutch had copied from American crowd control during anti-Vietnam protests. There was nothing so intimidating as the air blasted from the rotor of an army helicopter. It was a clear indication what lay in that direction.

'We can't go that way,' Piet said. Even in a police car,

with the siren blaring, it was not a clever idea to mix it with a riot.

'I can't turn around here,' Wim said.

A minute later, they were left with no choice as they hit a roadblock. Wim took a right turn into a narrow cross street. They hadn't gone far before that street turned into a T-junction with a canal. 'Shit,' he said. 'Right or left?'

Piet had lost track of their route three turnings ago. 'We want to go in that direction,' he said, pointing ahead. 'Let's go right and then directly left.'

'Okay partner.' Wim followed the instructions. They seemed to go in the correct direction for a bit, but then they hit another canal. He took a left and they crossed over a bridge that rattled in protest at being taken at high speed. The street sign said *Herengracht*. They followed it until it became suddenly one-way. Wim slowed down. 'I have no idea where we are,' he said. He stopped and pulled up the handbrake. 'Let's look at the map.'

Piet cursed. His map was still in his suitcase back at the police station.

'There should be one here somewhere,' Wim continued. 'Check the glove compartment.'

Piet opened it and found only two bags of sweets and a packet of cigarettes. He checked the slot in the door. Bingo. He unfolded the map.

'Right,' Wim said, 'so where are we?'

Piet wished Wim would turn off the sirens. It was mortifying that they were standing still and were completely lost. At least the huge map concealed the fact that he was dressed in only half a uniform. 'Herengracht. I found it. We're here.'

'Are you sure? That doesn't seem right.'

Piet agreed, it didn't. He looked closer at the map. That canal ran from east to west. 'Ah. We're anywhere between here and here.' He ran his finger along Amsterdam's entire canal ring. He felt sick.

'That doesn't really narrow it down.'

He tried to remember the route they'd taken so far. 'I think we must be somewhere around here.' He pointed at the map. 'We should turn round.'

'We're along a canal,' Wim said. 'Unless you think this car will float, a U-turn is going to be tricky.'

'I'll ask for directions.' Piet was trying to stay calm. They were lost, and there was still a robbery going on somewhere. A woman with dyed red hair came up behind them on a bicycle. He rolled down his car window. 'Excuse me,' he said, 'how do we get to the Boomstraat?'

She stopped. A cigarette dangled from the corner of her mouth. 'Not from around here, are you?' she said with a sneer. 'It's all one-way, so it's quickest to leave your car here and walk.' She looked at the map in his lap, then reached through the open window and stabbed with her finger at a point somewhere near his thigh. 'You're here.' Piet squirmed. 'And you want to be—'

'We get it,' he interrupted to stop her from prodding him anywhere more intimate. 'Thank you.'

She pulled her hand back. 'Idiots,' she muttered as she cycled away.

Piet rolled up the window again and Wim started to laugh. 'This is a joke,' he said. 'We're terrible!' His whole body was shaking and he hid his face in his hands. 'They'll never let the two of us get in a car together again!'

His laughter was infectious and Piet chortled too. The tension escaped from his body like air from a punctured balloon. When he had himself under control again, he grabbed the radio. 'Dispatch,' he said with a smile in his voice, 'we're lost.'

He heard the man sigh. 'Where are you? Roughly?'

'Herengracht.'

'How did you manage to get there? Okay, you need to turn around, so go right over the bridge and then right again.'

'Got it,' Wim said.

'Avoid Squatter Central,' dispatch cut in. That must be where the helicopter was. 'Cross the next bridge before the second right. You need to be on the other side of the canal.'

Even with detailed instructions, it took them twenty minutes before they were at the jeweller's. The robbers had long gone. The large window at the front was smashed and all the stock from the display had been taken.

The elderly proprietor was sweeping up shards of glass. He threw one look at Piet in his uniform jacket, jeans and trainers and shook his head. 'Are you having a laugh?' he said to Wim. 'Is this guy even a real cop, or did you just bring one of your mates along? You're lucky nobody got hurt. The only useful thing you guys ever do is write up a report to give to the insurers.'

Chapter 5

'I'm home,' Lotte said into the hallway as she took off her too-warm winter coat. That coat could be put away in the cupboard, she thought. Her cat, Pippy, didn't bother to rush to the door any more to greet her. The smell of fried onions and tomatoes told her that both her partner and the cat were most likely in the kitchen. She followed the lure of food and then paused. Mark was humming to himself with his ear-phones in and Pippy was at his feet, staring at him adoringly, as if showing him lots of love would get her fed sooner. It probably worked.

'I'm home,' Lotte repeated more loudly.

Mark turned around and took his earphones out. 'Sorry,' he said, 'I didn't hear you come in.'

'Because you were singing,' she said.

'It makes the food taste better. Trust me.'

'I'll take your word for it.'

'Dinner will be ready in ten minutes.'

Some days she felt guilty for being such a lousy cook, but most days she was just grateful that Mark cooked for them. She planted a quick kiss on his cheek and then popped upstairs to get changed.

It only took her five minutes to strip from office wear to slob wear, and that was all she needed to switch from police detective into normal person mode. Downstairs again, she told Mark about her day without getting into the details a normal person would find disturbing or revolting. Normal person mode meant focusing on the people who were still alive rather than the dead ones. She'd mastered the tightrope of telling Mark about what she did during the day without overloading him with crime and making him as jaded and cynical as she sometimes thought she was.

'It was weird today,' she said, leaning against the work surface in the kitchen and trying hard not to give Mark the same *I love you, now feed me* look that her cat did. 'This guy came to see me and said he knew me.'

'And did you know him?'

'I'd worked with him, but he said he knew me from when we were kids.'

'What's his name? Maybe *I* know him.'

'Just because we went to the same school doesn't mean you know everybody who knew me. We weren't even in the same year.'

'Exactly. Maybe this guy was in my year.'

That was a fair point. 'His name's Rick van Buren. He said we used to play together.'

'Rick van Buren?' Mark shook his head. 'No, doesn't ring a bell at all. He probably made it up and dines out on the story of how he used to play with the now-famous detective.'

'I doubt it. He also said we used to play with a guy who drowned yesterday. An alcoholic homeless squatter.'

'An alcoholic homeless squatter: you kept the best company,' Mark said.

Deaths from drowning were a sadly regular occurrence for Amsterdam's police force. On average, someone drowned in the city every other week. Eighty per cent of victims were male, many with alcohol or drugs in their bloodstream, some of them homeless or with mental health issues.

Teun Simmens ticked all those boxes.

If you lived in a country with this much water, accidents were always going to happen. In many of the cases, the chain of events was only too clear: when the body was dredged out of the water, it still had its flies undone. The man had been boozing in a café, needed the toilet and went outside to relieve himself. The sudden cool air caused dizziness as he peed from the canal edge, and he lost his balance and fell in. A police spokesman had once officially stated that the number of drownings would substantially fall if men didn't try to take a leak in a canal but instead used the facilities provided. On the other side of that argument, the father of a drowned Swedish tourist had lamented that if Amsterdam had placed railings along all the canals, his son would still be alive. There was no way the council was going to do that, but in the last few years they had installed emergency metal steps at drowning hot spots.

'Can you lay the table while I finish this?' Mark asked.

Lotte grabbed the cutlery and some water glasses and put them out.

'And then feed your cat,' he said, 'or she'll be pestering us as we eat.'

'Poor Pippy-puss, did your owner make you wait?' She

crouched down and rubbed the cat's soft little black-and-white head. She was unsure whom she meant by 'your owner': herself or Mark. She opened a packet of Felix and put it in Pippy's food bowl. The cat threw a glance at Mark as if reluctant to leave his side, then decided that cat food was preferable to human food and strolled over to eat her dinner.

Mark carried two plates of couscous and vegetable tagine to the table and Lotte joined him. 'This is nice,' she said after the first bite.

'Glad you like it. Hey, listen,' he said, and threw her the kind of glance through his wire-rimmed glasses that she knew only too well.

'Out with it,' she said. She shovelled more couscous into her mouth and didn't bother to hide that she was starving.

'I was just wondering . . . maybe we should make things official.'

The couscous went down the wrong way and caused a coughing fit. She reached for her water and washed the food down with big gulps. 'Make what official?' she said when she could breathe again.

'The fact that we live here together. That this is our house.'

'I don't live here, I just stay here. I have my own flat.'

Mark grinned. 'When you move your pet into someone's house, you're clearly living with that person.'

'That's because I couldn't go back and forth all the time. It was such a hassle.' But she had felt bad about how much she was leaving Pippy by herself, only popping home every day to quickly feed her before work. It hadn't been right.

Both cat and owner were much happier with the current arrangement.

'You're always here,' Mark said, 'and Pippy is also here, and I like it. A lot. The only thing I don't like,' he looked down at his plate, 'is that your flat is empty. It's been vacant for a while.'

'I know,' she said. 'I was thinking about this only yesterday. We found that drowned man's body at the back of an empty office block, and that reminded me of the six-month rule.'

He laughed. 'I love that our conversation makes you think about dead bodies.'

'He was a squatter and—'

'I know, only joking. But think about it, okay? I don't want to pressure you into anything, but maybe consider renting out your flat. It's such a gorgeous space and it shouldn't stand empty. It's been much longer than six months since you slept there last, let alone really lived there. Someone could report you.'

A few years ago, a foreign university lecturer had brought a court case after the council had rented out her flat on her behalf. She had argued that it was only empty for more than six months every year because she worked in two different countries. She claimed the laws discriminated against foreign nationals. The court ruled against her, saying she could get short-term tenants in for those six months and have them move out when her job at the Dutch university began again. She could easily rent out her flat.

Like Lotte could rent out hers.

She couldn't even remember exactly when she'd been

there last. The thought of someone else living in her old home made her slightly nauseous with nerves. It was her safety net. But it was also illegal and immoral to leave it empty. Houses were for living in, not for standing vacant. 'I'll think about it,' she said.

'Where was this dead person? You said in an empty office block?' Mark was a property developer and as interested in real estate as Lotte was in crime. 'Which building was it?'

'It's on the Singel, two doors down from the furniture museum.'

'I know the one. It has an amazing garden at the back.'

'That's where we found him.'

Mark nodded. 'It'll be more difficult to rent that out now.'

'They were talking about parcelling it up.' Lotte liked these moments when her job and Mark's overlapped.

'I might give them a call. See if they want some help.'

Pippy finished her food, curled up on the sofa and watched her two owners with a contented look, even if her eyelids were closing every now and then.

Chapter 6

31 March 1980

'We were useless,' Piet said as the four members of Team 4 ate an Indonesian meal together an hour after Team 2 had come in to relieve them. 'Utterly useless.' He took a gulp of his beer and surveyed the table full of food. Wim van Buren had ordered for all of them, and as this was going on expenses, he hadn't held back.

'It's not our fault,' Wim said. 'We did what we could. If you want to blame anybody for what happened today, blame the squatters. If there were no riots, we could all do our normal jobs.'

Piet looked across the table at Barry Simmens to get the older man's take. He was more concerned with spooning nasi onto his plate than with joining in the conversation.

'Wim is right,' he finally said. 'Top brass clearly panicked at the riots and just got people in from everywhere.'

'Exactly. Piet, you're taking this too seriously. We'll be gone in a month or so,' Wim said. 'We're not responsible.'

Not responsible.

Nobody had ever said that to Piet before. He had been responsible for everything all his life. He was responsible for his wife and daughter. He was responsible for the part of Alkmaar that was his beat. And he had been responsible for his brother since they'd been kids, even before the death of their parents. Naturally, Robbie had been Piet's best friend before he started school. They were only a year apart and they mostly got on.

Now he was in a strange city, his wife and brother were in another town, and unless he called them, they had no way to contact him. Even his work was not his responsibility. He filled his plate with more food. God, this felt good.

That thought immediately scared him.

'I blame those canals,' Eelke said. 'They drive me crazy. It's so hard to find anything.'

'I'll do some homework tonight,' Piet said to Wim. 'I'll study the map. If I know my way around, I'll do a better job. Trust me, within a week I'll be a top navigator.'

'We're not a rally team,' Wim muttered. 'Take it easy.' He looked around the table. 'Anybody want to swap? Take Keen Guy off my hands? I'll buy you drinks for the rest of the week! On expenses, of course.'

Piet grinned. It was also nice not to have to worry about money. He slept in a hotel and ate in a restaurant that was all paid for. Being Keen Guy was fine. It wasn't the worst nickname he'd had. In fact, he liked it.

Wim was still joking about that as they walked back. He even offered Barry and Eelke some of his own money to team up with Keen Guy instead.

'Are you coming for one more drink?' he asked when they got close to their hotel. 'The night is still young.'

'I won't,' Piet said. There were things he still needed to do.

The others also declined, and with a shrug, Wim strolled off by himself.

Piet went inside. Up in his room, he luxuriated in his double bed for a few minutes. There was a cigarette burn in the bedspread that made him feel at home, and the blue carpet only had a couple of scuff marks where the wheels of the chair by the little desk had rubbed it. He had never been in such a nice hotel before. Then he admonished himself. He mustn't fall asleep yet. He sat up, picked up the phone at the side of the bed and called home.

'Hilda Huizen,' his wife answered within two rings.

'It's me,' he said.

'Finally! I was getting worried.'

'I'm sorry. It's been crazy.' That wasn't a complete lie, but if they hadn't argued last night, he'd have called sooner.

'What do you mean, crazy? Is it dangerous?'

'Not for us,' he joked.

'What do you mean?' Her voice rose with worry.

'I'm kidding. I'm just doing normal police work. There's nothing to be concerned about.' He thought of the conversation he'd had with his brother this morning. 'How's Robbie?' he asked. 'Has he been helpful?'

'How can that be the first thing you ask about?' she said. 'Why didn't you call when Lotte was still awake?'

'I know, I should have called earlier.' He should have called her before the team had gone out for dinner. 'I'm sorry about that.'

'And *I'm* sorry that I didn't make you breakfast this morning,' Hilda said. 'It was childish of me.'

'It was because I was going on about money again,' he

replied. 'I shouldn't have.' The distance created by the phone line made their apologies easier.

'How's Amsterdam?'

'I met my colleagues, found a desk and checked into my hotel. There are four of us here, all from different parts of the country. How are you coping?'

'It will be Friday soon, and then you'll be back.'

That she avoided answering his question told him all he needed to know. 'Yes,' he said, 'it'll be Friday before we know it.'

'I've been thinking a lot after our argument yesterday. What you said about me getting a job. It made me realise what I really want to do.'

'What's that?' Piet smiled and wondered what career his wife had in mind. He'd been worrying for nothing.

'I want to try for another baby.'

His smile froze on his face.

'But let's talk about it more on Friday.' Her rapid voice filled the silence. 'Piet, Piet? Are you still there? Piet? Let's talk on Friday, okay?'

'Sure,' he said. 'Sure, we'll talk.'

The yoke of responsibility settled back on his shoulders as if it had never left.

Chapter 7

Lotte was back at the police station when she received an email from Rick van Buren with the address of a homeless shelter in Amsterdam Noord.

'What's with this guy?' she said to Thomas Jansen, who had the desk opposite her. Charlie Schippers had the day off, as he and his girlfriend were moving to a new apartment. It was the second time this year. She could offer him her flat, Lotte thought, but then immediately shuddered at the image of Charlie sleeping in her bed. It was better to rent it out to a stranger.

'Which guy are you talking about?' Thomas said without looking away from his computer screen.

'Rick van Buren.'

'Ah yes, he came looking for you.'

'And you helpfully told him I was in the canteen.'

'He seemed upset. It was unlike him.'

'You know him?'

'So do you: we worked together on the Chugong case,' Thomas said. 'You can't have forgotten that.' They had been in the same team for many years, and even if they hadn't always got on, they had this shared memory, like an old married couple who had made it through a rough patch in their relationship.

'Of course, but that was years ago.'

'I see him around every now and then, especially since he got demoted. He has this happy-go-lucky attitude and insists on talking to everybody. When you bump into him in the street, ten minutes go by before you can escape. The opposite of you, really.' He gave Lotte a wink.

'Very funny. But when you spoke to him, did he say weird stuff? Like that he knew you as a child?'

'Is that what he said to you?'

'Yes, that he knew me and also Teun Simmens.'

'The dead tramp?'

'He said they were childhood friends.'

'Friends? That explains why he was upset.'

'And then he said that I was their friend too, but that doesn't make any sense. He said it must have been a shock for me to see the body of someone I knew.'

'I would hate that.'

'Right. But this wasn't someone I knew. I didn't know Teun Simmens. I'd never met the guy before. And now Rick emails me the temporary location of the two other squatters who lived in that building with him. Daan and Gemma, they're called. No surnames. I don't know what he wants. This was an accidental death, so there's nothing to follow up on.'

'He wants you to talk to these people who knew his friend,' Thomas said. 'And whether or not you knew the guy, surely you can do that for a colleague?'

Lotte sighed. 'The colleague who once screwed up our case.'

'We all screw up now and then,' Thomas said. 'Plus, it was a long time ago.'

Sure, Lotte had screwed up, but not from being drunk all the time.

'Where are those squatters now?' he asked.

'Amsterdam Noord.'

He stood up and grabbed his coat. 'The weather is nice, the sun is shining, let's get out of the office.'

Lotte was familiar with the hostel where the two people who'd squatted with Teun were temporarily housed. The communal areas were clean and the staff did their best to help the people who came through their doors. That help sometimes included stopping the police from entering the place, but Lotte made it clear to the man at the entrance that no crime had been committed and she just wanted to have a chat with the pair because Teun Simmens had died. The man told her that Teun had stayed there for a month last year. He was a decent guy when sober, he said, but unfortunately that hadn't been often. A belligerent drunk, he called him, who didn't get on with many people. And they'd find Daan and Gemma outside by the canal.

They were exactly where the guy said they'd be, huddled together on a bench as if they were each other's only comfort in a largely unkind and unwelcoming world. Gemma nearly disappeared in a thick green parka, and her red hair was tied back with an elastic band of the type that posties discarded. Daan was one of those guys who might be attractive if he had a wash, a shave and a haircut. Or maybe not. It was hard to judge. Neither of them was young, and they were marked by many years of rough living. Around her age, Lotte thought, give or take a decade or two.

'They only need a dog to complete the pity picture,' Thomas muttered. 'Or maybe they had a dog but it died.'

'Their friend died,' Lotte said.

'I bet they're more upset about losing their comfy location than their mate.'

Their feet were so close to the canal's edge that a wobbly step in that direction could easily make them fall in. Lotte suddenly had some sympathy for the Swedish father's request for railings.

If Thomas had seen this as a fun outing, Daan and Gemma were less happy with the police turning up. Lotte's initial hello was greeted with hostility.

'What do you want?' Gemma asked.

'I'm Detective Meerman,' Lotte introduced herself, 'and this is Detective Jansen. We wanted to tell you that we found the dead body of your friend Teun Simmens two days ago.' She didn't enjoy informing people of the death of someone they knew. She hadn't been the one to notify Teun's next of kin. Even if your ex-husband or your father was an alcoholic squatter, his death still came as a shock. She looked for shock on the faces of the pair in front of her but saw none.

'Teun Simmens died,' she repeated, to get any kind of reaction.

'Yes, we know.' Gemma confirmed her suspicion.

'Did you call it in?' Thomas asked.

'No.' Daan's dark eyes were bloodshot, and he squinted in the April sunlight. He looked at Lotte, but then his eyes drifted off to something to the side of her face. 'Mr Owner said he'd do it.'

'Mr Owner?'

'Klaasen. He was there,' Gemma said.

'He was there when Teun died?'

'He found him,' Gemma said. 'We were still sleeping.'

'The more responsible guy made the call.' Daan bared a row of yellowed teeth in a vague semblance of a smile.

'The one with money,' Gemma added. 'With a fixed address.' She giggled.

Someone they'd lived with had died two days ago and she was giggling. Lotte had initially thought they'd lost a friend, but Gemma didn't seem all that upset. Then she remembered that the guy who worked in the hostel had called Teun a belligerent drunk. She could imagine that these people he'd shared a dwelling with had seen the alcohol-induced anger plenty of times. They might even have been on the receiving end of it. Perhaps they had lost not a friend but an aggressive housemate. Someone with a prison record for GBH under the influence.

'Was Teun ever violent towards you?' she asked.

Gemma shrugged. 'He was fine as long as you knew when to stay out of his way.'

As if living with someone violent on a short fuse was normal. But then if you lived rough like these two, it probably was.

'Thanks for coming to see us, Detective Meerman,' Daan said. 'It answered a question.'

'What question is that?'

He just shrugged.

There really wasn't anything else to talk about, and she'd done what Rick van Buren had wanted her to do, so they left the two of them on their bench.

Even though Gerard Klaasen had money and a fixed address, he had still called the police anonymously. He hadn't wanted to be involved in the squatter's death. A squatter who had died in the garden behind his building.

'We should pay Mr Owner a visit,' Thomas said, as if he'd read her mind.

Chapter 8

1 April 1980

Desk Sergeant Bouma greeted the team on arrival the next morning with buckets and brooms. 'You guys have the lightest shift,' he said, 'but it does involve cleaning.' The first people in were the ones to deal with the debris from the night before. Traces of blood and vomit covered the floor.

'What a mess,' Piet said as he assessed the area. This was only Tuesday morning, but it was like a Friday in Alkmaar. He did plenty of cleaning back at home. Apart from walking his beat, it was the chore that his boss deemed him most suitable for. He'd once overheard the inspector say that unfortunately Piet Huizen wasn't much sharper than his dim-witted brother.

Bouma went back behind his desk, lit a cigarette and took a deep drag. 'Team 2 had a non-fatal stabbing and a fight,' he said. 'There are four people in the cell downstairs. We're only keeping them in overnight and will kick them out in an hour.'

'I'd rather arrest people than mop the floors,' Wim van Buren sulked, but he grabbed a broom. The others had had breakfast together, but Wim had only joined them at the last minute, when they were just about to leave.

The four of them had everything cleared up before the first phone call came and Barry and Eelke headed out.

Piet and Wim hung out with Bouma and chatted for a bit. He filled them in about the guys in the cell. One drunken man sleeping it off, one habitual carjacker who was here roughly once a month, and two of the men involved in the fight. Piet asked him if they needed to follow up on anything – the stabbing, for example – but Bouma laughed and told him everything was under control. Wim joked that if there was a spare baton lying around somewhere, he'd happily help out and beat up some squatters. That was better than standing around doing nothing. Then the phone rang again and the busy day started for them too.

They were occupied with a stream of carjackings, pick-pockets and bicycle thefts. They rescued a man who'd fallen into a canal, fishing him out to the delight of a local photographer who eternalised the moment. It showed the other side of the police force, the photographer said: even during this time of violence, there were still moments when officers were helpful. The man they rescued wasn't all that happy. Obviously confused, he screamed and swore at Piet, and refused to go back with him to the police station to dry off.

It continued like that, with hardly time to eat a sandwich at lunch, until a lull at 3 p.m. When there was finally nothing to do, even all the reports typed up, Piet stared out of the window and an unfamiliar feeling came over him. He stood there for ten minutes and nobody asked for his time or attention. An orange balloon drifted aimlessly past the window. The colour suggested that it had escaped from a pre-coronation celebration somewhere. Even though he was in uniform, which normally anchored him, he was weightless just like that balloon. He could float off and nothing would fall apart. Happiness spread from his stomach. It was light and bright, this sensation.

He looked away from that tempting balloon and instead stared hard at the desk sergeant's phone, as if willing it to ring. The phone didn't comply with his wishes, but as if on cue, the front door flew open and a woman rushed in. 'My child!' she screamed. 'My son is missing!'

Piet suppressed the thought that this emergency was the answer to his prayers. 'Where and when did you last see him?' He planted his cap firmly on his head. Action. This was what he needed.

'When I went to work this morning. He was sick and couldn't go to school, and when I came home, he was gone!'

'He was at home alone?' Piet frowned. He hadn't thought about what happened when a working mother's child was ill. He'd only thought about the extra money Hilda would make if she found a job. Either way, he shouldn't judge this woman. They had to rush, because time was of the utmost importance when locating a missing child. 'Let's go to your home and I'm sure we'll find him.' He anchored himself with that promise.

'We live on the Singel,' she said. 'Number 247.'

'Best to walk,' Bouma said. 'Just follow her, but it's left from here and then immediately right.' He muttered the directions under his breath, as if he didn't want to disclose that the two police officers didn't know their way around.

Piet and Wim rushed after the woman towards the Singel.

'I'm so worried,' she said through streams of tears. She was older than him, Piet guessed, and extremely well dressed, in a narrow skirt and a green trench coat. 'He's never done anything like this.'

'Is he alone a lot?' Piet asked.

'Hardly ever!' the mother said. 'I take him to school every day and pick him up again.'

Piet's daughter, Lotte, wanted to walk to school by herself next year, when she was – according to her – a big girl. He found it worrying to imagine her doing that, even if she only had to cross two streets to get there. But then every parent worried, he was sure, and he dreaded the upcoming confrontation. It was best to let Hilda deal with it.

They arrived on the Singel. The mother turned the key in the lock and opened the door to the communal hallway. A kid's bike rested abandoned against the wall. They went up one flight of stairs. Piet hoped that the child was back home, but the mother opened the door to an empty apartment.

An entirely empty apartment.

'Leon? Leon?' She called out her son's name, but there was no response. 'You see,' she said, 'he's gone.'

But so had everything else. There wasn't a single piece of furniture. The walls were bare, and not even a light bulb dangled from the ceiling.

'What the hell?' Wim said behind him. 'Are you moving house?'

Only now did Piet notice the stink of alcohol coming from his colleague. Had he been drinking at lunchtime? How was that possible? They'd been rushed off their feet. Then he remembered the bottle of cognac in his desk drawer, and wondered if Wim had found one in his too.

He stepped inside. He had assumed the child had just let himself out to buy sweets or something and got lost. Or that he'd woken up confused and headed out to find his mother. But this stripped-bare apartment was deeply eerie.

'When you left to go to work this morning,' he said, mentally feeling his way around the situation, 'did you have furniture?'

'Yes, of course I did,' she said. 'I came back and they'd taken everything. They even stole my child.'

Would someone steal a child? But clearly something had happened here. 'Which room is his?'

The woman opened a door to the left. Another completely empty room. There were no toys, no clothes, no books. Piet had once heard of a carjacker who'd nicked a car with a baby in the back seat, but surely nobody stole a bed with a child still in it. He went into the kitchen, which had no pans or plates. He opened cabinets where there was no food. His footsteps echoed. Even when he had moved into his own house, it hadn't been this empty. There had been some bits and pieces that the previous owners had left behind: a couple of mugs and a pot plant. Here there was nothing. There was something really wrong.

'Where is your husband?' Wim asked. 'Could he have done this?'

Piet understood that Wim must think it was the start to an acrimonious divorce. Then at least the kid was safe.

'Of course not!' The woman dashed their hopes. 'I called him immediately, but he's as in the dark as I am. He's on his way back from work.'

'Do you have a photo of your son?' Piet asked. 'Did you say his name is Leon?'

The woman nodded. She opened her wallet and got out a small photo of an adorable child of about six or seven. He was the right age for that bicycle in the communal area. He had dark hair that fitted around his face like a helmet and looked seriously at the camera. He was only a couple of years older than Lotte.

'I'll call it in,' Piet said, 'and then we can have all cars look out for him.' At least those that weren't dealing with squatters. He tried to forget their disaster in a car yesterday. 'Let me take your details. What's your name?'

'Patricia Martens.'

'Piet, hold on a second,' Wim interrupted him. He was standing in the doorway. 'Let's check with the neighbours first.'

'Okay,' Piet said. 'We'll be right back.'

Patricia sat down on the bare floor with her back against a bare wall.

'The neighbour upstairs just opened her door and beckoned me up,' Wim said softly. 'I think she's seen something.'

'Great,' Piet said. 'That's great.'

The neighbour was a different type to the smartly put-together Patricia Martens. She was young, dressed in a T-shirt and jeans with Dr Scholl clogs. Piet recognised the brand because Hilda had the same ones. 'I'm surprised she went to the police,' the woman said. 'Her son did this.'

'Her son?' Piet said. It took him a couple of seconds to process that. 'Oh, there's an older brother?'

'No, they've only got the one son. Leon, he's called.'

'The child is missing.'

'Child?' The woman huffed. 'He's not a child. Leon is twenty-one.'

'He's twenty-one?' Wim was incredulous. 'Her son is an adult?'

'Yup. And I just know he did this. Cleared out his parents' flat. To be fair, can't say I blame him.'

'You saw him leave?' Piet asked.

'No,' she said. 'I came home half an hour ago, just before Patricia did. But look.' She pointed down into the hallway. 'That's my daughter's bike. Nobody who even took the light bulbs would leave a bicycle. Unless it's personal. The son did it.' She lowered her voice. 'Unless it was the husband, of course. She came here to borrow my phone to call him. Are they getting a divorce?'

'Thank you,' Wim said. 'That's very useful.' They went back down the stairs. 'Who needs the police,' he muttered to Piet, 'when you have nosy neighbours.'

'Mrs Martens,' Piet said when they were back in the downstairs flat, 'let's talk about your son. He's twenty-one?'

'Yes,' she said. 'He's in trouble,' she sobbed. 'He's never left home before.'

'You can't report an adult missing,' Wim cut in, 'until he's been gone for twenty-four hours.'

Piet shot him a glance. He wasn't comfortable with the situation at all. He looked around him for signs of forced entry, but he didn't see any. 'Did you leave the door ajar when you left?'

'No, I closed it behind me, I'm sure.'

'Our best course of action,' Wim said, 'is to report Leon as the suspect for the burglary. Then we can start looking for him straight away.'

'Leon a suspect? He didn't do this!' his mother suddenly shouted. 'How dare you even suggest that?'

'It's either that,' Wim said, 'or we wait twenty-four hours to report him missing.' He looked at his watch. 'Twenty-two hours, to be precise. What do you want to do?'

The front door to the house suddenly flew open and a man stormed up the stairs to the first floor, barging Piet out of the way. Must be the husband. They looked like a matching couple. 'I told you there was no point in going to the police,' the man said.

'Do you have a recent photo of your son?' Piet said. 'Then we can keep an eye out for him.'

'We'll file a report about the burglary, but you need to come back to the police station to sign it,' Wim said. 'For the insurance if nothing else.'

'That's exactly what I expected from you,' the man said. 'You care about possessions, not people. Just go. Leave. Find some squatters to beat up or something.' He forcefully shoved Wim out of the apartment. Piet didn't make an attempt to stop him, but followed his colleague out.

'Some people!' They walked back along the canal and paused at the bridge. Wim lit a cigarette, and after a moment's pause handed Piet one too. 'You were hilarious: that gesture with which you put your cap on. You totally meant business. So serious!'

'I've got a daughter,' Piet said. 'She's almost five. I automatically assumed that the woman's child was young too.' He was an idiot.

'Five? Roughly the same age as my boy, then. He's six. It's a good age, isn't it?'

Piet nodded. 'What's your boy called?'

'Ricky. Your daughter?'

'Lotte.'

'You know,' Wim said after another drag of his cigarette, 'I don't want to write up this burglary. I'm applauding Leon on his thoroughness in his bid for freedom.'

'Are you sure that's what it is?'

'Aren't you? Didn't you hear what that woman said? She walks him to school and back every day. He's twenty-one, for crying out loud. School is probably university or something. Can you imagine how embarrassing that must be? No,' Wim said. 'I'm sure they were just keeping him too close, too protected, and he needed to rebel against that. Ricky was so proud when we let him walk to school by himself! He had the biggest smile on his face.'

'My daughter was talking about that,' Piet said, 'but it's different with girls, don't you think? We're going to wait for a year or so.'

'What you want to do,' Wim said, 'is team her up with another kid in her class. Then they're not by themselves but still feel independent. That's important for kids. Or so my wife tells me,' he added with a wink. 'I'm not really involved in all that. Anyway, well done, Leon.' He raised his cigarette to the sky in a salute to the runaway. 'Long may your freedom – and your money – last.' He took a final drag, then flicked the butt into the canal. Piet hesitated before mirroring the gesture. They walked back to the police station.

'False alarm,' Wim said when he passed the desk sergeant. 'Her child was a grown-up.' He didn't mention the burgled flat. 'I've brought a camera,' he added to Piet. 'We should take a photo outside to commemorate freedom.'

Chapter 9

A quick call to the building manager, Julie Flissen, gave Lotte the address of the man who owned the property on the Singel where Teun Simmens had died. Gerard Klaasen lived in an apartment in the Kinkerbuurt, not far from the Vondelpark. The houses here had all been rebuilt in the early 1980s, and Klaasen's block was bright-red brick with glass-edged balconies. Lotte and Thomas climbed the three flights of stairs.

The man who opened the door was in his late sixties. His long white hair was tied back in a ponytail, and a neat greying pencil moustache adorned his upper lip. Even though they'd called beforehand, he grimaced at the badges they held out as identification. 'You'd better come in, I suppose,' he said.

This place wasn't what Lotte had expected. 'We asked for your office,' she said, 'but the building manager gave us this address.' On the wall was a framed A4 poster, printed in orange. *My Kingdom for a House* screamed in large black letters above the image of the former Queen Beatrix. It was one of the slogans used during the 1980 coronation riots. It wasn't what usually adorned the wall of someone who owned a number of buildings in Amsterdam, but she remembered that Julie had told them Klaasen had been active in the squatter movement back then.

'I don't need an office,' Klaasen said. 'It's a decadent waste of space. I've worked from home all my life, even before it was trendy.' That the man was a former rebel squatter turned property magnate was also signalled by his clothes, as he combined his Barbour bodywarmer with an Arafat scarf.

'We heard that you called in the death of Teun Simmens,' Thomas said.

'Yes, I did. Is there a problem?'

'We're just curious why you did that anonymously. You didn't use your mobile phone, but called from a landline in the reception area of the building.'

'Yes, that's right.'

'But you didn't wait for the police to turn up.'

'I saw a dead body and I reported it, as I believe I'm legally obliged to do. I'm not obliged to wait for you lot to arrive. Calling anonymously isn't a crime.'

He was correct, but still it didn't sit right with Lotte. It wasn't humane or respectful to leave a dead man floating in a pond in a garden. 'You knew the deceased?'

'I met him once or twice, but that's it. I wasn't shocked at his death; he seemed hell-bent on drinking himself into an early grave. And he managed it.'

'Julie told us you were remarkably tolerant of squatters.' She nodded towards the framed slogan on the wall. 'I guess that's the reason.'

'It's what we fought for,' Klaasen said. 'In the war with you lot.'

'Us lot.'

'The police.'

'Right.' She had been four years old at the time. 'But now you own property yourself. Isn't that hypocritical?'

'There's no problem with owning property,' Klaasen said. 'There is, however, a problem with owning property for speculation and not renting it out.'

'Your building on the Singel is empty,' Thomas said.

Klaasen shook his head. 'It wasn't empty, and it won't be as soon as you guys leave.'

Lotte didn't think there were still any police officers at the property after the death had been ruled accidental, but she didn't correct the man.

'Daan and Gemma will come back,' he continued, 'and there will be others, right up to the point when we rent it out.'

'But there are no tenants.'

'True. If you want to be entirely accurate about it, the building isn't vacant, but I'm not earning money.'

'You must regret it now,' Thomas said, 'those annoying laws that say buildings can only be unoccupied for six months.' He just loved needling people. 'Wasn't that what the squatters achieved?'

'Those laws are there because we won. The squatters won.'

'But you have a problem if you don't find tenants within the next couple of months and Teun's death is going to make it worse. The garden that was a selling feature is now a place of death. Was that why you called it in anonymously? To keep it quiet for as long as possible?'

Klaasen huffed. 'If I'd wanted to keep it quiet, I could have called a few guys to remove the body and drop it in the canal at the front.'

The thought sent chills down Lotte's spine, but she knew that if you paid enough money, you'd find people willing to move a homeless man's body.

'You wouldn't be here if I'd done that,' Klaasen said casually, as though this was an everyday occurrence. 'You would say that it was just a dead drunk in the canal. But I didn't. I was respectful towards Simmens. I called you guys. Sure, I didn't wait around, but I don't see what the problem is.'

'For someone who's trying to rent out a building, you're very kind to those homeless people who live there. You were honestly fine with them?' Lotte asked.

'I was. I am.'

'I just don't get it,' she said.

'I'm not surprised. The police often don't get it, do they? Let me explain it to you like this and see if it clarifies things for you.' His voice was sarcastic. 'Imagine I run a restaurant. I make a profit from selling food, and I do my best to buy exactly the amount I'll sell every day because that's how I make the most profit. But some days I'll have food left over at the end of the evening. Should I throw that away, or should I give it to the homeless guy sleeping outside? I'd give it away. That's the moral thing to do, isn't it?'

'Right. But to stay with this analogy, when word of the free food gets out and your restaurant attracts more and more homeless people, it will damage your business.'

'So what? Should I throw away perfectly good food and

let people starve just because I might help too many people for free? Of course not.'

'Thanks for the moral economics lesson,' Thomas said. 'But when you saw that Teun was dead, why didn't you wait for the police? Why not make an official statement?'

'I hate the police.' Klaasen's mouth twitched as if he'd bitten into a lemon. 'Going to the station, making a statement, it brings back all the trauma.'

'Trauma.' Thomas repeated the word with deep irony.

'I was unarmed on a barricade and your lot drove a tank into me. A tank! I still dream of it at night.' Klaasen closed his eyes for a second. 'My grandson would say that for me, talking to the police is "deeply triggering".' He stood up and walked out of the room.

Lotte and Thomas looked at each other. 'A tank?' Thomas said. 'When did we use tanks?'

Lotte shrugged.

Klaasen came back with a glass of water. It wasn't surprising that he didn't offer them anything. 'Fine,' he said. 'I'll tell you exactly what happened. When I arrived at the building that morning, it was quiet. Everybody else was still asleep. I looked out of the window and saw the body face-down in the water. I could tell it was Simmens because he wore the same clothes every day. I rushed out, but he was obviously dead and I knew I shouldn't move him. I went back inside, woke up Daan and Gemma and asked if they'd heard anything. They hadn't. They packed up and left. I called you guys and then I headed out too. That's it.'

'The other two left immediately?'

'Why wouldn't they? It's bad for them to have to deal

with the police. Daan's been in prison and he's not keen on talking to you either.'

He hadn't seemed all that bothered this morning.

'I hope that answers all your questions,' Klaasen said, 'and that you won't come back.'

'Unless—' Lotte started.

'Teun Simmens' death was unfortunate but an accident,' Klaasen interrupted her. 'You're harassing me for no reason.' His voice rose.

'Harassing?' Lotte repeated. 'We were only—'

'I don't like to talk to the police and you should respect that. I'm in constant pain because of what you did to me. The injury to my back will never go away.'

'In the same way that you're doing your best to be a responsible property owner,' Lotte tried to mollify him, 'we're trying to be responsible police officers. Times have changed.'

'Things have changed because we fought for it,' Klaasen said. 'But those fights always come at a cost.'

'It was lucky nobody died,' Thomas said. 'Weren't you scared?'

'When you fight for something important, you can't worry about dying,' Klaasen said. 'If you worry about dying, you shouldn't even get in a car.'

'Thanks for your time and for your statement,' Lotte said, as Thomas wasn't making things any better. She got up.

'I had a call from a property developer this morning,' Klaasen said as he walked them to the door. 'He said he could help me divide the site into smaller units to make it easier to rent out. A guy called Mark Visser.'

She should have told him not to contact Klaasen.

'I know him, of course. I worked with him a few years ago. I even went to his house back in the days when he used to show it to potential clients as an advertisement for the work he could do. It's nice,' Klaasen said. 'Much bigger than your flat, I think?' With that, he shut the door behind them.

Lotte cursed under her breath as she and Thomas walked down the stairs.

'I think you made a friend,' Thomas said. 'Please tell me your flat is rented out.'

'None of your business.'

Back in the office, Lotte googled the footage of the 1980 riots. She found the tanks that Klaasen had mentioned and called Thomas over to have a look.

She couldn't even imagine using tanks against people armed only with bricks. The historical footage of the riots made Amsterdam look like the Gaza Strip, with protesters hurling stones at the police. The tanks reminded her of the iconic picture of Beijing's Tiananmen Square, but these ones didn't stop. Scenes she had assumed only happened abroad had taken place right in the centre of Amsterdam. She read that the mayor at the time had insisted that the cannons at the front of the tanks were removed to make them less lethal.

The cannons might have been dismantled, but a Dutch tank still mowed down a fragile figure dancing on a barricade.

Chapter 10

1 April 1980

The other team relieved them at exactly 4 p.m., and Team 4 strolled back to their hotel after wishing their colleagues a quiet evening.

'I'm definitely not going to have a quiet evening,' Wim joked as they got their room keys from the hotel manager, who also acted as the receptionist. The place was so empty that he was the only employee most of the time. 'Meet back here in half an hour for a heart-starter?'

'I'll join you at the restaurant,' Piet said. 'There's something I want to do first. Where are you going?'

'Not the same place we went yesterday,' Wim said.

'The place next door to the one we went to yesterday,' Barry said. 'We'll eat our way down the street. Five thirty?'

'Okay,' Piet said, and opened the door to his room.

'Don't be late,' Wim said. 'I'm starving.'

'I'll be there,' Piet said, 'but if I'm late, start without me.'

In his room, he called home before changing out of his uniform. He wanted to talk to his daughter, and this was the perfect time: after she got back from school but before dinner. Hilda answered the phone. She was careful not to bring up yesterday's conversation or complain about his brother. Reduced to banalities, her words were just a stream of sounds. In the background, he heard his daughter say, 'Is that daddy?' and he asked Hilda to put her on. Lotte regaled him with a tale of colouring flowers blue and yellow, and then informed him that blue and yellow were her favourite colours. It made him smile. Blue and yellow, like a summer's day.

After the call, he had a shower and got dressed in his jeans and trainers again. He checked his watch. Not even five o'clock yet. It was still too early to join the others. Talking to his daughter brought Leon, the missing guy, back to mind. It wouldn't surprise him if he'd come home by now with his tail between his legs. His parents would be upset but would welcome him with open arms. That was what you did with your kids. It was even what Piet had done with Robbie all those times he'd got into trouble.

He walked to the Singel, but when he reached number 247, he hesitated. He wasn't sure the parents would be that keen to talk to him again. Instead, he pressed the doorbell of the upstairs neighbour. She would know what was going on.

The woman didn't buzz him in but came down. 'Let's go around the corner,' she said. 'I don't want them to see me talking to you. I'm Anna, by the way.'

'Did Leon come back?' Piet asked.

She shook her head. 'Not a sign of him. I know that I said he did this, but I'm worried.'

Piet was glad he wasn't the only one.

'I went downstairs to talk to Patricia, but she got angry

with me. She gets angry a lot. They had flaming rows, her and Leon. That's why I'm not surprised he ran off.'

'What's Leon like?'

'What's he like?' Anna repeated his words. 'Hard to describe. A bit naïve maybe for someone his age, but he is smart. He's at university.'

'His mother said she walks him to school.'

'Yes, can you believe that woman? Dropping her son off at university, waiting for him after classes. His fellow students are squatting in a house down the street, manning barricades and fighting for housing rights. I'm not saying that what they're doing is right, but his mum accompanies him everywhere he goes. I'm sure it makes him a laughing stock. She treats him like a baby.'

Piet's father had reproached his mother for the same thing when Robbie's initial excitement about going to school like his big brother had lasted only three days. On the afternoon of day four, Robbie withdrew to his favourite corner, and when Piet asked him to play football outside, he refused to come. Over the next week, he became quieter and quieter and sat in his corner more than before, and when he spoke, it was to accuse Piet. 'You lied to me,' he said. 'School isn't fun at all. I don't want to go any more.'

'Look what you've done,' their dad said to their mother. 'You've mollycoddled the boy too much.'

Later that evening, his mother pulled Piet aside and asked what was going on at school. Piet didn't know. At break he had been playing with his friends and thought Robbie was playing with his.

'You need to look after him,' his mother said. 'He isn't strong like you.'

Piet nodded. It was why he regularly let Robbie hit him. You don't hit people weaker than you, his mother had told him.

'If someone is weaker, you protect them,' she added. 'That's your responsibility as an older brother.'

Piet had understood what she meant.

Maybe Leon was a bit like Robbie, but he didn't have a bigger brother to protect him.

'She wants to keep him out of trouble,' he said to Anna, because his own mother hadn't been overprotective either.

'She wants to feel needed. She wants to control her son's life, I think. Or at least that's what they were rowing about the other week. That's what he accused her of.'

Robbie had thrown those same words at Piet: that Piet was controlling him.

'Some people are more independent than others,' he said.

'Sure,' Anna said. 'Sure. Anyway, I brought you a photo. It's from our annual house garden party. It was taken six months ago.' She handed him the picture. 'The tall guy in the centre, that's Leon.'

He was handsome, with clothes that Robbie would no doubt describe as old-fashioned, and dark hair that Piet could picture his mother, Patricia, slicking back with a wet comb, as Piet always wanted to do with his brother's. 'You said he's at university?'

'Yes, the UvA.'

'Where is that?'

Anna raised her eyebrows. 'You're not from around here?'

'I'm just filling in. I'm normally based in Alkmaar.'

'Ah, the cheese city. Well, welcome to Amsterdam. Just cross the bridge to the next canal, turn left and keep going. You can't miss it. Keep the photo.' With a friendly wave, she went back inside the house.

Piet followed her directions to the university. Banners hung from the front, screaming slogans like *Kein Haus, Kein Claus*, referring to Prince Claus, Princess Beatrix's German husband. The number 8488 was written all along the street. A large group of students were milling around outside. Huddles of kids always made him suspicious, ever since primary school. He wondered if Leon was being bullied, as Robbie had been.

The group outside the university weren't bullying anybody, but they were probably plotting another protest. Piet would never have gone to university. People in his family didn't do that. Plus, he was the stupid guy who was held back in the last year of primary school. He could never be one of those students who had time to fight against the police. He had to look after his brother, and then his wife and daughter, and that was enough.

Only when he was standing here looking at this building did he remember the smart kid he used to be. Or maybe he had never been that clever, because being stupid had come only too naturally. Not paying attention in class, not doing his homework, getting into fights every now and then, getting a reputation for not being all that much brighter than his brother – it had been easy. Knowing what the right answer was to a maths question and writing down the wrong number, until he couldn't tell any more if he'd ever known how to do those things. And it didn't matter, because he was doing the responsible thing. His mother didn't need a smart son, she needed a trustworthy one.

He checked his watch. It was coming up to half past five. He should go to the restaurant if he wanted to have dinner with his team. He'd come back to the university tomorrow and ask about Leon, he decided. In his head, he tried to picture the quickest route to his hotel. He turned left into a side street and then right into a wider cross road. But a little further down, he came across a group of squatters erecting a makeshift barricade just like the one he'd seen on the morning he first arrived in Amsterdam. He must have gone the wrong way and drifted into one of those areas that the desk sergeant had marked as a spot to avoid.

'Give us a hand!' A guy in a leather jacket and a red motorcycle helmet was struggling to lift a table. 'Quick, before they come.'

Piet shook his head but moved a long plank aside to keep the pavement free.

Then he heard the noise of engines roaring and wheels squealing.

'Oh fuck!' Leather Jacket guy shouted. 'There they are. Run! Run!'

Six dark-blue buses filled with Piet's colleagues came hurtling down the street. Piet stopped in idle curiosity. The back doors opened and they streamed out, all armed with helmets and shields, just like the graffiti had depicted them.

Afterwards, he was astonished that it hadn't even entered his mind to follow the squatter's words and run for it. Even when everybody else around him ran as if their lives depended on it, he stood and watched. If not quite in admiration, then at least in professional appreciation. Weren't these people on his side? Weren't the squatters the enemy?

Even when they fitted their masks, he didn't run. Even as they charged in his direction, with batons raised, he didn't run.

When it finally dawned on him that they had no way of knowing that he was a police officer, it was too late. They were on him like a horde. Tear gas filled the air and attacked his eyes. I'm a cop too, he wanted to shout, but he couldn't drag enough air into his lungs to get the words out. Through tear-clogged eyes, he saw an officer wearing a mask covered with German words. The Germans provided the gear for this war between police and citizens. The Germans. Even though Piet had been born a few years after the occupation, he knew this was wrong. The man lifted his baton high and crashed it down on Piet's arm with a shout that was muffled by his protective gear. All Piet could do was turn away and protect his face with his hands.

Bricks flew from the direction of the barricade and distracted the officer for long enough that Piet could scramble away and find protection in a nearby doorway. His eyes and nose were streaming and he could barely see. He huddled against the door. Every inhalation was agony. As if to show him that there was no safety anywhere, the door suddenly opened and he crashed to the ground.

A hand clasped his wrist and someone dragged him inside.

Chapter 11

Lotte stared at her screen, at the email that she'd sent a week ago. She still hadn't received a reply. 'This guy, seriously,' she said. 'He was the one asking me to get in touch with the other two squatters, which we did, but when I tell him about it, he doesn't even bother to get back to me.'

'What guy?' Charlie was back in the office. His flat move had gone well and he sounded eager for something to do.

'Rick van Buren.' Lotte was sorry it wasn't anything more exciting than her personal annoyance.

'But what is there to say?' Thomas asked. 'Didn't you just tell him that we followed up with Gerard Klaasen, which clarified everything?'

'I don't know. A thank you, maybe?' Lotte's voice was sarcastic, but in the email she had also asked him if he'd talked to Teun's widow about his cancer diagnosis, and it was strange that he hadn't replied to that. Unless he didn't want to admit that he hadn't done it yet.

'He said he was Lotte's childhood friend,' Thomas said to Charlie, 'so now she's annoyed that he's got better things to do than be polite to her. He's a police officer, Lotte, he's probably busy.'

'He could be on holiday,' Charlie said, 'or moving house.'

'Don't you check your emails when you're away?' Lotte asked.

'Not really. If something is urgent, you call or text me. If you email me, that means it can wait until I get back.'

'I called him yesterday,' Lotte said, 'and it went straight to voicemail. He still hasn't called me back.'

'That is odd,' Charlie said.

'Right? It is, isn't it? I'm not the only one thinking that.'

'What if he's embarrassed?' Thomas said. 'You made it clear you weren't his childhood friend at all. He messed up one of our cases in the past. Now he's ghosting you.'

Lotte didn't think Rick van Buren was the type to be embarrassed about anything, but he wasn't the first person to avoid her. Unfortunately for him, though, she knew exactly where he worked. She needed to know if he'd talked to Teun Simmens' family, and if he couldn't be bothered to answer her calls or emails, she had no choice but to find him in person.

She put her light summer coat on and strolled over to the new police station on the Burgwal, where he was based.

It was a miserable day. Rain soaked her umbrella, bounced off the pavement and drenched the bottom of her trousers. All this for a drowned tramp, she thought. All this, if she was honest, because it pissed her off that Rick van Buren had asked her for help and then subsequently ignored her; that he'd said he'd talk to the family because he owed his friend, and her, and then never bothered to do it.

She entered the police station. 'I'm Detective Lotte Meerman,' she said to the desk sergeant, whom she only knew by sight. 'I'm here to see Rick van Buren. Can you tell me where he sits?'

The woman stared at her.

'Rick van Buren,' Lotte repeated. 'Where does he sit?'

'Didn't you hear?' the sergeant said. 'He died.'

Lotte had to hold on to the desk to keep upright. 'He died? When?' It was hard to believe that she'd talked to him just a week ago and now he was no longer here.

'Two days ago.' There was an edge to the sergeant's voice that Lotte didn't quite grasp at first. Then she realised that the woman wasn't sad about her colleague's death.

'What happened?'

'He crashed his car in the Red Light District.' The sergeant's mouth twitched in distaste.

Even given officers' customary bluntness with their colleagues, it surprised Lotte that she didn't say he'd been in an accident. 'You didn't like him?' she said.

'I know you're not supposed to speak ill of the dead, but he got into his car with a gut full of booze and hit a kid on a bicycle before he crashed into a wall. The child is still in hospital with serious injuries. Van Buren died instantly.' The sergeant looked down at her phone. 'His funeral is tomorrow at eleven thirty if you're interested in attending. Most people aren't going to go.'

'Ah, shit,' Lotte said.

'The girl is only eight years old. Life-changing injuries. So yes, I'm not even going to pretend I'm sorry for anybody's loss.'

Lotte remembered that Rick had often come to work drunk. He'd once been legless during an operation and in a fit of alcohol-induced red mist had nearly hit a handcuffed suspect. She and her boss had had to step in to stop him. A few weeks after that, he'd messed up the Chugong case by mislabelling evidence, which had set them back months. She'd been incensed then, and delaying a case was nowhere near as bad as seriously injuring a child. She was appalled that he'd got behind the wheel of a car drunk.

'Do you want to know where the funeral is?'

She shook her head. She wouldn't go either. 'I totally understand your feelings,' she said.

She left the station and walked back through the pouring rain to Elandsgracht. Just as she arrived at the garden by the side entrance, an elderly man of around her father's age approached her from the direction of the bridge. Before he said anything, he looked down at a soaked newspaper he held in his hand, and then back to her.

'You're Detective Lotte Meerman, aren't you?' he asked.

'Yes,' Lotte said, 'that's me.'

'Can I talk to you? Maybe we can go for a coffee?' His black umbrella was bent at one side, and water drenched his shoulder.

'What's this about?' Lotte asked. She noticed tears in the man's eyes and added, 'How can I help you?'

'I'm Wim van Buren. Rickie's father. Rick van Buren's father,' he added, as if it needed clarification. 'My son's death, it wasn't an accident.'

Chapter 12

1 April 1980

With the tiny sliver of his brain that wasn't absorbed by the struggle to breathe and the agony of his burning eyes, Piet thought of fighting against the hand that dragged him up the stairs. But every step up made getting air into his lungs easier. The person was pulling him to safety like a lifeguard towing a drowning man back to shore.

A door clicked shut behind him.

'I need to get this stuff off you,' a female voice said. 'I think the shower is the quickest. Bear with me.' She let go of his wrist. Piet hadn't realised that his rescuer was a woman. A few seconds later, he heard the sound of water cascading down, and he was pushed into the bathroom. 'Sit here,' she said.

Blindly he reached behind him and found a plastic stool. As soon as he'd lowered himself onto it, lukewarm water began to stream over his face.

'Open your eyes if you can,' she said, 'and let me know if it's too hot or too cold.'

But he couldn't open his eyes, and he hardly noticed the temperature, as his only sensation was of blessed relief as the tear gas was washed from his skin. Having a shower had never felt this good. After a few minutes, he turned his face away from the water. 'Thank you,' he said. 'That's so much better.'

'Those fucking pigs.' She turned off the shower and handed him a towel. 'Stay here and I'll get you some dry clothes.' She clunked the showerhead in the sink.

His clothes were drenched and the bathroom floor was like an indoor swimming pool. He held the towel against his eyes. God, that stuff was nasty; he'd never thought he'd be on the receiving end of it.

The woman came back and handed him a T-shirt and a pair of jogging bottoms. Now that he could open his eyes again, he saw that she was roughly his own age. She was chubby and her clothes had a good chance of fitting him. He waited until she'd closed the bathroom door behind her, then stripped off his wet shirt and wriggled out of the jeans that were glued to his legs. He dried his hair until it stood on end and put on the stranger's clothes. Her grey T-shirt was the right size, and he could get the jogging bottoms over his hips even if they only reached down to his calves. The angry red welt on his upper arm showed where the baton had struck him. He touched it, as if that could make it magically disappear, but immediately stopped as it hurt like hell. As his clothes were soaked anyway, he used them to mop up the worst of the water from the bathroom floor, then he opened the door.

'Thanks for the T-shirt and trousers,' he said. 'I look like an idiot, but I appreciate it.'

She didn't correct him and barely suppressed her laughter. 'Give me your stuff,' she said. 'I'll fill your shoes with newspaper and spin your clothes. They'll hopefully be dry enough to wear again by the time the police are done and you can leave. You don't want to be seen dressed like this.'

He handed her his sodden clothes.

'Come through.' She pointed at the living room and then disappeared into the kitchen.

In contrast to what was going on outside, even with the background noise of shouting and roaring engines, his saviour's flat exuded calm. Although it was a cloudy April evening, the place was filled with light. There were plants everywhere, and soft-coloured throws. From the second-floor window, he had a perfect but surreal overview of the battlefield outside. Protesters armed with bricks fought riot police equipped with batons and tear gas. Most of the squatters had their faces covered with bandanas. They were obviously more prepared than he had been. He could just make out the doorway where he had sheltered, and he was amazed that the woman had gone down to rescue him.

When she came back, the half-smile with which she had looked at him earlier was gone. Now there was a deep frown on her face, and she kept her distance from him and stayed in the doorway between the front room and the kitchen. 'Who are you?' she asked.

'I'm Piet. Piet Huizen.'

'Are you secret service?' Her voice was tight.

'What? No!'

'I heard they're infiltrating the squatters' groups.'

'No, I'm—'

'I found this,' she interrupted him, and held out his police badge. 'It fell out of your pocket as I hung up your jacket.'

'Yes, I'm a policeman.'

'What the hell were you doing here? Are you trying to find squatter sympathisers? Because I can tell you now, that's the majority of the city.'

He raised his hands in a placatory gesture. 'I was only walking back to my hotel. I wasn't here on purpose.'

'This has been a clash point for days and you went for a walk here?' She was incredulous.

'I'm not from Amsterdam. I'm seconded here from Alkmaar.'

'I didn't know they were getting people in from outside.'

'I'm based at the police station on the Nieuwezijds. My hotel is around the corner from there. I'm definitely not secret service, I'm just a normal police constable helping out.'

'Helping out with what?'

She would make a good interrogator, Piet thought; she was picking up on his every word. 'Just ordinary police work,' he said. 'So far, there have been robberies, a burglary, drunken people, a missing man.'

The woman relaxed ever so slightly. 'I can't believe I saved a fucking cop.'

'As the fucking cop in question,' he said, 'I'm really grateful.'

She stared at the angry welt that was visible under the short sleeve of the T-shirt. 'I'll give you a bag of frozen peas to put on that to keep the swelling down. Also, I was just about to eat when my neighbour shouted that someone was being beaten up in our doorway. You're stuck here for the next hour or so, unless you want to risk getting gassed again by your lovely colleagues.' She sighed. 'I feel stupid offering this, but do you want some food?'

At the word *food*, his stomach rumbled. He should have been eating dinner with the rest of his team a while ago. 'Thank you,' he said.

'I'm Maaike, by the way.' She handed him the peas.

He pressed the bag against his arm. The cold numbed it enough to make the pain bearable. 'I'm Piet,' he said.

'I know,' she said. 'You told me. And it's on your badge.' But some of the anger had left her voice. She put dishes out on the table. 'It's nothing fancy, just some potato salad and chicken. Seriously, I deserve a medal for feeding a cop.'

It was uncomfortable having his back towards the window whilst outside shouting and mayhem ruled. He kept looking over his shoulder.

'Ignore it,' Maaike said. 'It will go on for another hour, then your lot will sweep the squatters from the house. They've only just moved back in and haven't managed to fully barricade the doors and windows yet.'

'You're well informed.'

'I'm a real-estate agent,' she said, 'so I know that building's been empty for over two years. The speculator who owns it doesn't even try to rent it out. He's just gambling that the new metro station will be built and the price will go up. The squatters have tried twice this month and the police have been quick to protect the property.' She pointed at the bruise on his arm, which was turning a nice shade of purple. 'You see how they're doing it. Violence against ordinary people to secure the capitalist rights of someone who's been buying up properties in this area and leaving them empty. It's disgusting.' She spooned some potato salad onto her plate, then pushed the bowl in his direction.

He helped himself. 'But if you're in real estate, isn't it weird that you're against people owning houses?'

'I'm trying to help people find a place to live,' she said, 'and it's impossible. Do you know how many people are looking for a house in Amsterdam at the moment? More than sixty thousand.' She answered her own question. 'And do you know how many empty houses there are right now that aren't on the market? Almost nine thousand. Eight thousand four hundred and eighty-eight.'

He finally understood the graffiti he'd seen outside the university.

'Now tell me that isn't morally wrong,' she continued. 'Houses are for living in, not for standing empty. And the harder it is for me to find a home for a young family with a child, the more sympathy I have for the squatters.'

'And you help them escape from the police if they're huddled in your doorway,' Piet said with a smile.

'You have my neighbour on the ground floor to thank for that. I only opened the door because she shouted that someone needed help. She's quite elderly, so I couldn't bring you to her place. What were you doing here anyway?'

'I'm looking for a young man who's missing. He's a student and I went to his university.'

'And then you turned a wrong corner and got caught up in your colleagues sweeping the street clean.'

'Exactly.' He thought this could easily have happened to

Leon too. Maybe he was in a police cell somewhere, or inside one of those barricaded houses. He remembered the guy in the leather jacket and the motorcycle helmet who'd asked him for a hand to erect that barricade. If he'd been a student, he would have helped just for the excitement of it.

But why had Leon's parents' apartment been stripped bare? The missing student and the cleared-out flat had to be related.

'How long has he been missing?' Maaike asked.

'Since this afternoon. His mother came home from work and he was gone.'

'And she called the police? That's odd.'

'She's very protective,' Piet said. 'I thought her son was a child at first.' He smiled at his own mistake. 'I have a young daughter, so I related to her panic. Then it turned out he's twenty-one.'

'Twenty-one? My parents would never have called the police if I wasn't home for half a day at that age.'

'I was working at that age,' Piet said.

'I was at university, but my parents would just assume I was at lectures.'

'He was ill at home, and then he had suddenly disappeared. I can understand that she's worried.' Piet defended the mother.

'Still! You'd assume he'd got better and didn't want to miss class.'

'His mother told me she walks him to school.'

'You don't say school, copper.' Maaike gave him a mocking look.

'I swear that's what she said. School. She said school.'

'That's weird. Sounds to me as if she's infantilising him.'

'My colleague is certain he's run away from his over-protective parents.'

'And you're not? I see his point.'

Piet shrugged. 'The whole thing just seems suspicious. If he's run away, he also robbed his parents' apartment.'

'Ah, I see,' Maaike said, 'so you think it's drugs? Could well be. The son of one of my colleagues skipped lectures to go to the Red Light District to score, before he finally dropped out. It's sad if that's the case.'

How embarrassing that drugs hadn't even crossed his mind. Alkmaar had far less of a drug problem than Amsterdam. He remembered the words of Desk Sergeant Bouma that drug dealing was concentrated in District 2. Also, Bouma had told everybody to stay away from District 2. The empty apartment suddenly made sense.

'If you're going to rebel, it's much better to join the riots,' Maaike said, 'than to get hooked on drugs.'

Her words annoyed him. 'Why rebel? You can just do what your parents want you to do.'

'Did you? I didn't,' she said.

'Yes.' Piet was thinking about how he'd looked after his brother all his life. 'I've done exactly what they wanted me to do.'

The day at school when he had seen his brother being bullied, he'd told the other kids to stop and the group had turned on him like a mass of small rodents who thought they were strong together. Piet knew he shouldn't hit them, because they were the year below him and therefore weaker than him, but when he punched the nearest one in the chest, the rest stopped. Suddenly, instantly, they froze. His violence was unexpected and broke through their fun.

'Piet Huizen!' he heard his teacher say sternly behind him. Her hand grabbed his arm and she dragged him away. 'I didn't expect that kind of behaviour from you!' Then she fell silent as she saw Robbie on the ground, tears in his eyes, his knees grazed and his nose bloodied.

Half an hour later, Piet was alone with the teacher in the staff room when his mother rushed in.

'He was fighting,' Mrs Bruin said. 'With first-graders! That's not what bigger boys should be doing.'

'Piet doesn't hit a kid for no reason,' his mother said. 'Where was Robbie at this time?'

Piet recognised his mother's angry voice and hung his head. Those kids had been smaller than him and still he'd hit one of them. That went against everything she'd taught him.

'Robbie was on the ground,' Mrs Bruin said.

'What? Where is he?' Piet realised her angry voice wasn't directed at him.

'He's back in class.'

'Where's the boy who hit my son?'

'We don't know exactly which kid did that.'

'My son is being bullied and you're punishing Piet for standing up for him?'

'You have to understand: Robbie is a bit slow. Kids pick up on things like that.'

Piet's mother got up. She put her hand on the back of Piet's neck. He expected punishment, but she gave him a squeeze. 'You did well,' she said. 'Unlike your teacher, you did well.' She stared at Mrs Bruin as if daring her to disagree.

Then she put her arm around Piet's shoulder. 'And if anybody has a problem with that, they have me to reckon with.'

'You can go back to your class now,' Mrs Bruin said to Piet.

'I'll cook your favourite tonight.' His mother kissed him on the top of his head.

And even though his teacher glared at him, Piet felt good. He had protected his brother. It was what his mother wanted him to do.

'You didn't even rebel slightly?' Maaike asked now. 'Get a motorbike? An unsuitable girlfriend? A job they hated?'

He shook his head at each of her suggestions. 'None of those. Is that what you did?'

'I ditched the motorbike and the girlfriend. That's a joke,' she added quickly. 'I didn't rebel too much. I only broke up with the boyfriend my parents loved, and I have a job they hate.'

'What's wrong with being an estate agent?'

'Ah, you see, my parents wanted me to do something meaningful, like cure cancer or fight for nuclear disarmament. Instead, I have this job where I earn more money than they're comfortable with.'

Typical left-wing parents, then. He thought they were wrong. There was a solidity to her that made her seem reliable. If he was buying a house, he'd want someone like her to organise the sale. Because he would trust her. 'Isn't finding someone a house meaningful?' he asked. 'When I bought mine, it definitely was important to me.'

She smiled. 'Can you call my parents and tell them that? Actually, no,' she corrected herself. 'Having a police officer call on my behalf wouldn't impress them in the slightest. Sorry, forgot about that.' She pushed her plate away. 'In all seriousness, my parents pretty much let me do what I wanted and I only mildly disappointed them. Don't you think that the more controlling you are, the more people rebel against you? Everybody should have the freedom to do what they want to do, as long as they don't hurt anybody else.'

Piet thought of his brother. He wondered what Robbie wanted to do. 'It doesn't work like that,' he said. 'Some people can't be given that freedom. They can't cope with it.'

'Spoken like a true cop.' She got up and grabbed his plate. 'I think you're done with that. It sounds as if your colleagues outside are done too. It'll be safe to leave. I'll check if your clothes are dry.'

He could tell she wanted him gone.

It was dusk by the time he shut the outside door of Maaike's flat behind him. The barricade that the squatter had been busy erecting was entirely pulled down. A single police van was parked outside the building the squatters had tried to occupy. Shards of hoarding littered the street where it had been torn from the building and demolished. Two officers in full riot gear patrolled outside.

Piet wondered if it was one of them who had struck him. He turned the other way and walked a different route back to his hotel. Around him, the streets were eerily quiet, as if everybody was holding their breath in anticipation of more violence to come.

Chapter 13

Lotte took Rick van Buren's father to the little café by the bridge, close to the police station. It was annoyingly busy with mid-morning coffee drinkers, and only one table, next to the window, was still free. It wasn't as far away from everybody else as she'd have liked. She hated it when others could overhear a potentially emotional conversation, but talking in this small café was a better option than taking him back to the police station. That would give this chat a formality she wanted to avoid. She told him to take a seat as she ordered two cappuccinos at the counter. She could see the similarity to his son in his completely bald head. He looked unwell. His eyes were red and puffy, and he kept wiping his nose with a big handkerchief. It was caused by grief, Lotte knew, but out of habit she reached for the security blanket of the hand sanitiser in her handbag.

'I should introduce myself properly,' he said when she joined him again. 'My name is Wim. Wim van Buren. I used to work with your father back in the day. But you know that already.'

Lotte didn't know any such thing and made a non-committal noise. She was glad when the coffees turned up so that she didn't have to admit how little she really knew about her father. They hadn't talked much about his past in the years since she'd reconnected with him. Even if she was curious, she didn't dare ask, because she knew that such a conversation automatically led to details about her parents' divorce. She knew that he'd cheated on her mother, as her own ex-husband had cheated on her, and she didn't want to hear the nitty-gritty. Facts forced her to take sides, whereas being blissfully ignorant let her keep the careful equilibrium that allowed her to have a decent relationship with both parents. It might not be perfect, but it was as good as it was going to get.

'Rick told me that he spoke with you,' Wim said.

'Yes, we met last week. I've only just heard what happened to him. I'm so sorry for your loss.' Rick had seriously injured a child before he died, but she could be kind to this old man. She thought he looked much older than her own dad. Grief aged people.

'His death wasn't an accident,' Wim van Buren said again, 'but nobody wants to believe that.'

'I heard that he died in a drink-driving accident.' Lotte chose her words more carefully than the desk sergeant had done. There was no reason to add that she'd also heard that he'd hit a child on a bicycle before he crashed into that wall.

'And you know as well as I do,' he leant forward to add weight to his words, 'that Rick didn't drink.'

An appalled cough burst out of her. She picked up her coffee cup and took a sip of the too-hot cappuccino to cover it. Rick van Buren had been a problem drinker and it was hard to believe that his father wasn't aware of it. But then parents never really knew the ins and outs of their children's lives. There was a thin line between not speaking ill of the dead and bare-faced lying, and she had to set him straight. 'I worked with Rick a few years ago,' she said, 'and I can tell you that he definitely drank.'

'Yes, of course, I should have said that he didn't drink any more.' He stressed the last word. 'It's what I'm most proud of, that he managed to kick the booze. He joined AA during lockdown.'

The stories Lotte had heard were mainly about how people drank more during lockdown.

'There were two things that made him seek help,' Wim said in answer to the disbelief that must have shown on her face. 'He injured a guy during the lockdown riots.' He rubbed a hand over his head in a gesture that was eerily reminiscent of Rick doing the same thing when he'd joined her in the canteen over a week ago. 'Police officers might have done things like that in the past, you know, gone in too hard with batons. But these days everybody films everything, and if you search on YouTube, you'll find it.'

He took a sip of his coffee. 'This is nice,' he said, as if Lotte had personally brewed it for him. 'Anyway, Rick said that ultimately it was good that it had happened. I wouldn't have seen it that way, I can tell you that. I would have been really pissed off with the rioter who filmed me. But Rick was shocked at how he'd behaved. Shocked at his own red mist, I guess, mainly because he didn't remember anything about it.' He was rambling, the words streaming from his lips as if he didn't want to think about what he was saying. 'That's how drunk he was at the time. He was suspended for a few months – he got off lightly – and during that time he had to stay at home, of course, and his wife, his kids, they saw how bad it was. How much he drank. They sat him down. What do you call that?'

'An intervention?'

'Exactly. That's the word he used too. And he did it. He stopped drinking. Went totally cold turkey. Lockdown helped, because there was nowhere he could go. His wife kept him company on his walks, so he couldn't pop into the supermarket and buy a bottle to drink on a park bench somewhere. Anyway. He'd turned his life around, so it wasn't a drink-drive accident.'

Lotte frowned. 'They must have done a full investigation.'

'They can't have done, because they got it all wrong. They knew Rick's reputation, made some assumptions and wrote it off.' He gave her a sad smile. 'Please look into it for me. Even if just because you and Rick were childhood friends.'

Not this again, Lotte thought, but she didn't correct the man. Instead, she nodded. It wasn't all that difficult for her to pull up the file and look into the exact details of the accident. She could do that much for her father's former colleague.

Wim quickly finished his coffee and left. He'd got what he'd come for. Lotte went back to the police station and walked up the stairs to her office.

Thomas gave her a stare as she came in. 'What happened?' he asked.

Lotte remembered Rick's words that it was different when the dead person was someone you knew. 'He died,' she said. 'Rick van Buren is dead. He crashed his car into a wall.'

'Oh, that was him?' Charlie said. 'I heard something about it from my former team.' He used to work in traffic police before he joined CID. 'They said a colleague had died in a drink-driving accident, but they didn't tell me who it was.'

'His father asked me to have a look, as he can't believe it.' That Charlie already knew it was a drink-driving accident gave credence to Wim van Buren's belief that the investigators had made assumptions. That didn't mean those assumptions were incorrect.

'I can get you the accident report,' he said. 'Give me a second.' He picked up the phone, eager to have something to do.

Lotte pulled up the forensic report on the central database. Whatever Rick's father might think, forensics had done a thorough job. She scrolled through the notes to find the item she was looking for, then swore out loud: his blood alcohol level had been extremely high. Any higher and he'd have passed out.

She pulled her hair back from her face with both hands. It was going to be rough telling Wim van Buren the truth. She didn't want to make that phone call right now. To delay the inevitable, she called her father. When he picked up, she heard from the background noise that he was outside. 'Hey, Dad,' she said, 'did I catch you in the middle of something?'

'We're out for a bike ride. It's a nice day.'

She was surprised that it was a pleasant day in Alkmaar, as it was still raining heavily in Amsterdam. Thirty-five kilometres didn't seem enough distance to have entirely different weather. Still, she could picture her father zipping along on his electric bike, and it made her smile. 'I won't disturb you then,' she said.

'It's okay.' He laughed. 'We've stopped now. What's up?'

She didn't often call him during the day. 'Do you remember Wim van Buren? I met him earlier today and he said he worked with you in the past.'

'Wim? Wow, that is a long time ago. We were both seconded to Amsterdam in 1980 during the coronation riots. Did you know that's when Maaike and I met?'

Solidarity with her mother brought an automatic angry retort to her lips, but she managed to push it down. She didn't have to fight her mother's battles, but she also didn't want to listen to her father reminisce about how he'd blown up their marriage. It had been a mistake to call him.

'Hey, Maaike,' her father's voice distorted as he turned his face away from his mobile, 'do you remember Wim van Buren? Lotte met him today.'

Maaike responded with something Lotte didn't catch.

Lotte could just imagine her own ex-husband boasting to his mates over drinks how he'd slept with his secretary. Unlike her ex-husband's mates, she wasn't going to egg her father on to tell her more.

'How is he?' her dad said.

'Not well. His son died a couple of days ago.'

'Is that why you called me? I—'

'Sorry, Dad, someone's looking for me. I've got to go.' She disconnected the call.

Chapter 14

2 April 1980

Leon Martens' parents returned to the police station exactly twenty-four hours after their son had gone missing. They insisted on speaking to someone more senior than Piet and Wim, and voiced their disappointment when told that only Barry and Eelke were available. Desk Sergeant Bouma told the team afterwards that sure, they could keep an eye out for the guy, but they shouldn't go any further than that. Leon was most likely living in a squat somewhere, he speculated, and would come back when all the rioting was over. This missing guy was very low on their list of priorities right now.

The week flew by in a pattern of busy days alternating with solitary evenings during which Piet familiarised himself with his corner of Amsterdam so that he didn't accidentally amble into a riot again. As families cleared up after their meals and children got ready for bed, he strolled along canals and down cross streets. He carried the photo of Leon in his pocket but saw no sign of him. His route occasionally took him past the Martens flat, but their lights stayed off. He enhanced his knowledge of the paper map with the reality of what the cobbles, bollards and houseboats looked like, and after a few days he knew every one-way street in their quarter. The many hours' walking paid off, because on Thursday afternoon, when he and Wim were called out to a robbery, they didn't get lost and made their first Amsterdam arrest.

On Friday, the hotel manager told them to leave as much stuff as they wanted in the hotel over the weekend as the rooms were theirs for the duration. Piet hung his uniform in the wardrobe after his shift; he wasn't going to make the mistake of carrying his policeman's cap in front of the squatters' bulwark this time. As he crossed Amsterdam on foot with a much lighter suitcase to meet van Merwe for his ride back, he congratulated himself on his new ability to avoid both squatters and riot police.

Looking for any topic of conversation to break up the car journey, he began to tell the inspector about their first arrest, but his boss cut him short. He was willing to give Piet a lift, but could he please stop talking. The words froze in Piet's mouth, and he felt like an idiot for sharing the story of such a minor success. The easy camaraderie of Team 4 had made him forget what van Merwe was like. All the way back to Alkmaar his boss was uncommunicative, and when he dropped Piet off outside his house, he simply barked that he'd pick him up again on Monday morning.

Within seconds of van Merwe driving off, the door opened and Lotte came running out screaming 'Daddy, Daddy!' He rested his hand on the blonde head that pressed up against his legs. Hilda smiled at them from the doorway and said he was just in time because dinner was on the table. Robbie waved over Hilda's shoulder.

Piet's worry shifted. It was good to be home.

When he'd told Maaike the other day that it was a big deal for him to own his first house, he hadn't said it to make her feel better; he had told the truth. From the striped wallpaper to the wooden sideboard, he liked everything about this place. If the decor was slightly eclectic, well, so was his family. On an evening like this, it all was right. Everybody was on their best behaviour. Hilda said that a roast chicken must be boring after all his exotic meals out in Amsterdam, and even though the meat was a bit dry, the pleasure of being home made up for it. He even enjoyed the sweet white wine that Robbie had bought to celebrate the fact that his brother was home. After dinner, Lotte sat down in front of the television to watch a cartoon about bears who lived on a boat. Piet watched it with her, but it was all a bit weird. As if she'd sensed her father's lack of enthusiasm, she demanded an extra-long bedtime story.

The day caught up with him and he was exhausted. In bed, Hilda reached for him and gave him a kiss. He kissed her back, but then her words about wanting another baby jumped into his mind. He held her hand, turned on his side and fell asleep. He dreamt about his house being stripped completely empty, scarily reminiscent of Leon's parents' apartment, and woke up with a jolt and his wife's gaze on him.

'I have it all worked out,' Hilda said. She must have been awake for a while, waiting for him to open his eyes.

'What time is it?' He scanned the bedroom to make sure the lampshades and the light bulbs were still there.

'I'll show you my calculations later,' she said, 'but I've been busy while you were away. I've been to a number of estate agents. If you get a promotion and a pay rise, we can afford a bigger house. We need three bedrooms, I think, or maybe even four.'

He rubbed the cobwebs of sleep and traces of dreams from his eyes and checked his alarm clock. 'It's not even seven yet,' he groaned.

'Lotte will be up soon and I wanted to talk before then. I know you'll want Robbie to continue to live with us, and I understand, but when we have another baby, we'll need a bigger house, don't you agree?'

'Can we discuss this later, Hilda? I need some coffee first.'

'I know you'll get that pay rise. Surely this stint in Amsterdam must help. I've seen it on the news, and look at that.' She pointed to the bruise that the riot police officer had left behind on his arm. 'It's obviously dangerous out there.'

'That was my own stupid fault.'

'You've been a constable for almost ten years now. You'll get that promotion soon, and then we'll buy a bigger house.'

'I'm not sure my boss agrees.'

She huffed. 'He must rate you, to drive you to Amsterdam and back. I've been thinking a lot while you were away, and I've decided I should look after our finances. You're working hard, plus numbers aren't your strong point, so leave all that to me. It's one less thing for you to worry about.'

He'd always thought he liked numbers, but she was probably right.

After breakfast, Piet needed a walk to lift the heavy feeling in his stomach. He had skipped last night's after-dinner stroll, his new Amsterdam habit, and that must have caused it. Hilda said she wanted to do the washing as it was a nice day, and Lotte was too busy drawing to even notice what her father was doing, but his brother came up to him just as he shrugged his coat on. 'Can I come with you?' he asked.

'Sure,' Piet said.

They walked side by side through the park, which was filled with people walking their dogs.

'It's been okay this week,' Robbie said. He patted a golden retriever that came up to greet him. Dogs always liked him. 'Hilda and I hardly argued. Only over the TV on Wednesday, and that wasn't important.'

'That's good.'

'I know why she was so angry with me the day before you went to Amsterdam.'

'Yeah?'

'And I think she's right. I don't want to be on the dole, I should get a job. I just didn't know what.'

Piet noticed the past tense. 'And now you do?'

'I made a list of what I can't do and what I really don't want to do. All the jobs that went wrong in the past, I wrote them down and thought about where I messed up.'

'That's impressive.' That Robbie had made a list of his failures was huge.

'I'm not good with people, I know that. Most people don't like me.'

'You've got friends,' Piet said.

'Just a small group. And it's okay, I'm used to that. I'm also not very good with words.'

'You can read and write.'

'Yes, I can, but I don't want to do that all day. Do you remember when I worked as a carpenter for a few months? I think I liked that job best of all of them.'

'But you quit.'

'That was because I didn't get on with the other people. If I had my own workshop, it would be great.'

'Robbie . . .'

'No, wait, I'm not saying you should get me a workspace. I like making things, but I don't like being with other people.'

Piet didn't think his brother was all that good with his hands. Any attempt at DIY around the house went slightly wrong, and they'd ended up with skewed shelves and uneven wallpaper.

'The other time I was really happy,' Robbie said, 'was when I did my military service.'

'Were you? I thought you hated it.' They'd done their eighteen months' compulsory service together as soon as they got their school leaver's diploma. What Piet remembered most about that time was Robbie wanting to go home but having to stick with it. He'd worried more about his brother defecting than the Russians starting World War Three.

'I was happy when I was driving that munition truck. All by myself.'

'Yes, you were good at that.' Surprisingly good, in fact.

'I even drove it with eight other soldiers in the back. Do you remember?'

'I do.' Piet thought Robbie had even shocked himself at passing the written part of the driving test at the first attempt.

'And I think that if I can be in a vehicle by myself all day, I will be happy. If I can also sleep in it, that's even better, because then I won't be in your way.'

'You're not in the way.'

Robbie gave him a look that was a gazillion years old. 'I'm not blind. Even though I already lived in your house before Hilda moved in, I know I'm in the way.'

Piet took a deep drag of his cigarette.

'I think I've found my perfect job,' Robbie continued. 'I'm going to be a truck driver.'

Piet immediately shook his head. He couldn't bear the thought of his brother out on the road all day, driving to foreign countries by himself. All alone, without Piet to look out for him. 'That's not a good idea,' he said.

'You never let me do anything.' Robbie sounded like a rebellious teenager rather than a man nearing thirty. 'You never help me.'

Piet had never done anything *but* help his brother. He remembered the last year of primary school. He had been excited to go to the big school because then he could learn new things. Ever since the fight all those years ago, the other kids had left Robbie alone. If anyone threatened to bully him, Piet just walked up to them, and that was enough to get them to back off. His reputation for violence preceded him, even if he hadn't hit anybody in four years.

And then, at the beginning of that final year, he got the flu. He was so ill that he was off school for two weeks. In the first week, it was fine, but the second week, Robbie was spending time in his corner again, facing the wall. Piet looked at his brother's arms. He was covered in bruises. With Piet away from school, the kids were bullying him again. Beating him when the teacher wasn't watching.

Piet was shocked. If his absence for just two weeks had this result, then what about next year, when he was in another school altogether? He couldn't let that happen. There was only one solution: he had to stay in this class for one more year. He had to be so bad at schoolwork, his grades had to be so terrible, that he would be held back. Then he and Robbie would be in the same year, the same class, for secondary school.

He made the decision that he and his brother would be together for the rest of their lives. He would shelter and protect him for ever.

And even if the teacher's disappointment at his star pupil's abysmal marks really hurt, he knew he'd done the right thing. He overheard the man asking his mother if his illness had affected his brain. Was it just flu, or had it been something more serious? The difference, he said, was striking. After that talk, his mother wrapped her arm around Piet's shoulders once again and told him he'd done well. He'd done the right thing. He'd helped his brother.

That evening, Piet read Lotte another bedtime story. He sat on the floor outside the extended cupboard where her bed was. The story featured aliens who could turn themselves into any shape they wanted to be. From the hallway, two sets of eyes were on him. In the small space, it made him feel claustrophobic that Hilda and Robbie were both watching him like patients in a doctor's waiting room, eager for their turn to come. If he were one of those aliens, he would split himself into three and keep everybody happy. His daughter's eyes fell shut. Piet was tempted to speak louder to keep her awake, but Hilda's hand had already reached over his shoulder and she silently took the book away.

It dawned on him that to get that promotion that Hilda wanted, he'd have to study and take an exam. He imagined a small corner of this house where he would sit with his books. He could put a desk in the bedroom and close the door behind him.

He was coming round to the idea.

When his boss called him on Sunday afternoon to say that he was going to drive up that evening instead of the following morning, Piet quickly agreed, and then mollified Hilda by promising that he'd bring up the subject of his promotion in the car.

Chapter 15

When Lotte had told Wim van Buren that his son really had been several times over the legal limit when he crashed his car, he had responded simply that he understood, and thanked her for looking into it. She'd thought that was the end of it, but he'd called her back two days later and asked if she could talk to his daughter-in-law. The funeral had been sparsely attended, and it would help her so much. He'd guilt-tripped her into agreeing before she had a chance to think about it. Mark questioned the wisdom of going to her disgraced colleague's house, but paying Rick's widow a private visit wasn't the same as the public support of attending the funeral.

So that was why Lotte cycled to Amy van Buren's house after dinner. She liked April, when the days were long but didn't stop you from sleeping yet, and it was nearly King's Day, the holiday to celebrate King Willem-Alexander's birthday. She parked her bike in the racks and chained it up. The front door opened before she'd even stuck her keys in her bag. The woman in the doorway was in her fifties, with short-cropped blonde hair that was fading to grey.

'I appreciate it,' were her words of welcome. 'I wouldn't

have blamed you if you'd stayed away.' Said without bitterness and as a pure statement of fact.

'I'm sorry for your loss.' Lotte followed Amy into the house and their combined footsteps echoed loud in the silence. There were a few photos of the family on the wall: Rick, his wife, and two young men. 'Are those your sons?' Lotte asked to break the awkwardness.

'Yes, my eldest lives in Utrecht and the youngest is at university in Maastricht. They kept me company all week but left this morning. I told them to carry on with their lives. Can I get you tea or coffee, or a soft drink? Have a seat.'

'I'll have a cup of tea if you're making one.' Lotte couldn't drink coffee at this time of the evening, as it kept her awake most of the night. Often with thoughts of death whirling through her mind.

Amy put the kettle on. The open-plan kitchen was pristinely clean. People dealt differently with loss. Some withdrew within themselves and let their house become a rubbish heap, while for others, cleaning gave a modicum of control whilst everything around them was falling apart. Lotte had seen both types of reaction. After her own baby daughter had died, she had immersed herself in work. She still found the death of a child hard to deal with.

Or the serious injury of one.

Charlie had been as good as his word and got the full report of Rick's accident from his former teammates in the traffic police. Lotte now had copies of the photos of the crash site in her handbag. She sat down on the sofa and put the bag on the floor. She didn't plan on showing Amy any of those images; they were far too distressing. The little girl Rick had hit with his car was still in hospital with a broken neck, and her outlook wasn't good. She kicked the bag out of sight under the wooden coffee table.

Amy came back with two cups of tea. She put one in front of Lotte.

'It was so hard for Rick to stop drinking,' she said. 'I know what it cost him, but he managed it every time.'

'Every time?'

'He had a couple of setbacks. But he always stopped again. As he would have done now. AA was such a big part of his life. Over the last couple of years, his sponsor became a good friend. And then for him to fall off the wagon and die.' She covered her face with her hands and her shoulders shook with the silenced sobs.

'Teun's death shocked him deeply,' Lotte said. 'That's probably what made him start drinking again.'

Amy wiped her eyes. 'At least you accept that he was dry for a while.' She took a Kleenex from a box on the table and blew her nose. 'I overheard two of his colleagues saying at the funeral that he must have been pissed most days. I don't blame them. He was good at hiding his problems.'

'I looked into his record before I came here. I didn't just take his father's word for it.' She might as well be honest. 'I saw how much his work had changed these last couple of years. He once messed up one of my cases because of his drinking. There were complaints about him, and then there was the suspension because of the violence during the lockdown riots. But since he'd returned, his work had been good. I believe the stats.' Though now Amy had told her that Rick had started and stopped drinking a couple of times.

'Between you and me, Wim drinks a lot too. Your father might have told you that.'

Lotte hadn't asked her father about him.

'Rick talked to him a couple of times about stopping too, but he just got angry. The alcohol levels in his blood . . .' Amy's voice trailed off.

Lotte paused for a second, but then reminded herself that Amy had asked her to come here so that she could hear the facts of what had happened. 'He was ten times over the legal limit.' There was no way of making it any better than it was.

'How did the accident happen?' Amy asked. 'Everybody else has only been giving me vague answers.'

'He was driving at high speed along the S100 before turning off along the Prins Hendrikkade. On the Zeedijk, on the northern edge of the Red Light District, he clipped a bollard, lost control of the car and crashed into a wall fifty metres further down.'

'Thank you for not mentioning the girl,' she said. 'She was coming from the other direction, wasn't she?'

'That's right.' Lotte picked up her tea to give herself time to get the image of the crushed car out of her head.

'Rick told me he saw you after Teun's death.'

'Yes,' Lotte said, 'we met the next day. Teun died on Thursday and Rick and I spoke on Friday.'

'How was he?'

'He was shocked. The death of his friend—'

'Was he drunk, I mean,' Amy cut in through Lotte's careful words.

'No, I don't think so. He said some odd things, but I didn't smell alcohol on him.'

'What did he say?'

'He thought that I knew Teun and that he and I were childhood friends.'

'He was sad that you didn't remember any of that. He was quite proud of his famous friend.'

'I had never seen Teun before.'

'I'm not surprised you didn't recognise him. He used to be such a handsome man,' Amy said, as if the confusion was on Lotte's part, not Rick's.

There were only so many times you could correct something.

'Hold on, I've got some photos. Teun came to our wedding.' Amy got up and rummaged through a desk that dominated one corner of the room. She found the wedding photos quickly.

There was something comforting about photo albums, Lotte thought. When someone sat down next to you and opened one up, it was going to be story time.

Amy pointed out Teun. He had indeed been handsome. This was what he'd looked like before he went to prison that first time. She picked up another album and found Rick's childhood photos.

'Look, here it is. That's the three of you with your fathers. See, that's Rick, and that's you.'

In the photo, four men stood behind three children. Lotte looked carefully at the little girl. She must be about five or six years old, and was standing between two boys. One of them was clearly older than the others. That must be Teun. She got her phone out. 'Do you mind if I take a picture?'

'Sure,' Amy said. 'It's a nice photo, isn't it?'

The girl in the centre of the photo was pretty, with brown curly hair and a wide smile. She was a happy child. 'That's not me,' Lotte said. 'I don't know who she is, but it's definitely not me.'

'But that's your father, isn't it?' Amy pointed at the man standing next to Rick's father, Wim. Both of them had had more hair then and more wrinkles now but were otherwise easy to recognise.

'Yes,' Lotte said, 'the one with the slicked-back hair is my dad.'

'Let me ask my father-in-law. I'll quickly text him.' Amy's fingers danced over her phone, then she waited until a beep announced Wim's answer. 'He's certain that's you,' she said. 'But if you have time, he can come over right away. He said he's got some more photos.'

'Sure,' Lotte said. 'I'll wait.'

Chapter 16

10 April 1980

On Thursday evening, after another day's work in Amsterdam, Piet went on his usual post-dinner stroll. Wim didn't even ask him any more if he wanted to go for a drink in the hotel bar, but joked that Piet was off for his necessary daily alone time. It jolted Piet that Wim was more astute than his joking demeanour suggested, or maybe his need for solitude was just that obvious. What had started off as a way to learn the street names in their district had become a routine that he enjoyed.

He paused on the canal's edge to light a cigarette and blew the smoke out over the water. A pair of ducks paddled alongside a moored rowing boat that was for hire by the hour. It was chilly, and he stuffed his free hand deep in his pocket. Spring was letting Amsterdam wait this year. The cold weather and drizzle should have deterred the squatters, but the skirmishes with the police were still ongoing. He followed the locations of the clashes more closely now, as he didn't fancy being on the receiving end of another baton strike. The bruise on his arm was now almost black, with green edges. In case he did get it wrong, these days he also carried a large handkerchief in his pocket to cover his nose and mouth against tear gas if necessary.

A car was parked illegally, but that wasn't his problem. He continued along the canal and crossed over a small bridge. A café on the corner was shut. Few places were open. The team had found a bar-café that only served three dishes, and were informed as soon as they'd come in that the kitchen was going to shut in an hour. The lack of choice had suited them well, and when they walked back to their hotel, Barry said they should eat there again one night next week.

Nobody doubted that they would still be here in a week's time.

Piet turned on to the Singel, past another bar with its lights off and shutters down, and made his way to number 247, where the Martens family lived. Just in case Leon had returned. Ahead of him, a woman struggled with a heavy cardboard box and plastic bags dangling off both arms. He sped up and called out, asking if he could help her. At the sound of his voice, she turned sharply, and then the worry on her face gave way to a relieved smile. He was surprised to see it was Maaike.

'If it isn't the cop I rescued the other day,' she said. 'Don't sneak up on people, you nearly gave me a heart attack.'

'Let me carry that box,' Piet said. 'It's the least I can do for my saviour.'

She passed it over. He gave an involuntary grunt when he felt the weight. It was filled with pot plants and heavier than he'd expected. 'Don't worry,' she said, 'we're nearly there.'

'Are you moving?' he asked. 'Getting away from the riots and into a nicer part of town?'

'Yes, all those police officers on my doorstep are getting me down.'

Piet grinned.

'Just kidding. I've been appointed to sell a flat,' Maaike said, 'and it's currently empty. I want to make it seem a bit more lived in, at least from the outside.'

'Don't want any squatters moving in,' he said.

'I don't think they would, but it's stripped completely bare. There aren't even any light bulbs.'

'No light bulbs? Are you selling number 247?'

She stopped. 'How did you know? You're really good.'

He kept walking, because the sooner he could put this box down, the better. He was impressed with how far Maaike had been able to carry it. 'Do you remember that I was looking for a missing student? Number 247 is his parents' apartment.'

Maaike hurried to catch up with him again. 'That's weird,' she said.

'Yes,' Piet agreed, 'it's really weird.'

When they got to number 247, Maaike opened the door to the communal hallway. Piet followed her up the stairs and put the box on the floor. 'Are you busy,' Maaike asked, 'or can you give me a hand? You're taller than me. I'm going to struggle with the light bulbs.'

'Sure,' Piet said. 'I have nothing else to do.' He was cutting his walk short, but it gave him another chance to look inside that apartment. She opened the door to the flat and he shoved the cardboard box inside with his foot.

'Was it already like this last week?' She handed him one of the plastic bags and indicated the missing bulbs.

'Yes, no furniture at all, and even the kitchen cabinets were empty. You must see places like this a lot, but I found it unnerving.' The plastic bag was filled with an assortment of Philips bulbs. 'I'll need something to stand on,' he said.

'There's a stepladder in the cupboard in the hallway, right next to the stairs down to the garden. I'll show you round the garden later. It's amazing.'

He found the cupboard and retrieved the little four-step triangular ladder. He set it up and screwed in the first bulb.

Maaike was arranging the plants on the windowsill. 'The owners are in a real rush to sell,' she said.

'Is that what they said?'

'I shouldn't tell you this, but I was tempted to buy it myself. It's a great apartment and I just love the garden. I don't have a garden at my place.'

'But you do have riots on your doorstep.'

'True, I would miss the excitement. But I'd need two months or so to raise the finance. She said she needed the money sooner.'

'Patricia Martens said that?'

'Yes, and she also said that she was willing to drop the price if that got her the sale. She doesn't need to; there are so many people looking that I'll shift it for her in no time.'

Piet sat down on the second step of his ladder. 'I'm really concerned,' he said. 'If your son goes missing, you don't move house, do you? You wait for him to return.'

'As long as Anna knows where they've gone, there's no problem,' Maaike said. 'The upstairs neighbour sees everything.'

Piet and Wim had already noticed that too. 'But you'd

want to be here, wouldn't you? If my brother ran away, I'd stay at home and wait for him. However long it took.'

'You live with your brother? How old is he?'

'He's twenty-nine. One year younger than me. I live with my brother, my wife and my daughter in a two-bedroom house.'

'If you ever need something bigger, let me know. I'm sure I can get you a good deal on a new property.'

'Are you always trying to sell?'

She shrugged. 'I like making money and I like getting people into the right place for them. Win-win.'

'I should put you in touch with my wife,' Piet said. 'Hilda definitely wants to get a bigger house.'

Why were the Martens family looking to rapidly raise funds? It didn't quite fit with Wim's theory that Leon had stripped the flat bare and run away. Piet remembered that Maaike had mentioned drugs the other day.

'Is it expensive,' he said, 'to put someone in one of those new drug facilities?'

'The addiction treatment ones, you mean? I have no idea. Nowhere near a quarter of a million guilders, that's for sure. I mean, they don't need to sell this place to pay for that.'

He screwed the last bulb into the last empty socket and flipped the switch. The apartment flooded with light that only emphasised how much was missing here. A feeling in the pit of his stomach told him that something was deeply wrong. 'You said there was a garden? Can you show me?'

Maaike turned around from arranging plants and knick-knacks on the windowsill and stared at him. 'You've gone into police mode,' she said. 'Should I refuse you entry without the right documents?'

'I'm worried about the missing son,' Piet said. 'You can understand that, can't you?'

She sighed. 'Okay, come with me.'

They went down the stairs and around a corner. Maaike unlocked the back door and opened it to an oasis. Piet was astonished. He'd never have imagined that something like this was here. To him, the area of Amsterdam that he'd walked through was just bricks and water. Houses, streets, pavements, canals, a tree here and there, but no gardens. Nothing like this verdant patch. He had to go down more steps to get to a small patio with a metal table and two chairs. He smelt cigarette smoke and it automatically made him reach inside his pocket to get his own. He lit up and then looked around him again. A tree close to him was just starting to sprout buds. He wasn't much of a gardener and had no idea what type of tree this was, but he liked the shape of the buds: all spiky, as if the tree was protecting the new leaves growing inside. Like a parent protects their child.

He followed Maaike down a path between shrubs. Hidden behind a tall bush with large leathery leaves was another sitting area.

'Hi, copper,' a woman with a cigarette said. It was Anna, the upstairs neighbour. 'Are you interested in buying a flat?'

'I'm just having a look around.'

'In case his parents buried Leon in the garden?' she mocked him.

Maaike chortled. 'He insisted I show him,' she said.

'If I ever killed someone,' Anna said, 'I wouldn't bury

them in my own garden. I'd go next door, through there.' She indicated a small iron gate that connected the garden to the neighbouring one. 'Theirs is huge. You should ask them, they might let you in.'

'Fine, make fun of me, but I'm worried that something's happened to Leon,' Piet said.

'He's enjoying himself at the moment,' Anna said, 'spending his parents' money.'

That's what Wim van Buren was thinking too. 'But they put their flat on the market,' Piet said.

'They always planned to do that,' Anna said. 'His mother wanted to move out of Amsterdam, away from the bad influences. Actually, she said *evil* influences.' She shrugged and exchanged a look with Maaike.

'She was worried about drugs?' Piet asked.

'Not drugs,' Anna said. 'Whores. Her word, not mine. She screamed that so loudly I could hear it over the sound of my TV.'

'Why didn't you tell me this last week?' Piet asked.

'Dreadful overprotective woman.' Anna took a deep drag of her cigarette and then stubbed it out. 'Now her son is having fun.' She gave Piet a stare that dared him to disagree with her. 'For once in his life.'

Piet knew that he was a provincial; he wasn't from a big city like Amsterdam. But if Robbie visited prostitutes, he wouldn't like it. He understood Leon's mother. Where previously it had seemed suspicious that they'd put their flat on the market, now he thought it was a sign of care.

When he got back to the hotel, it was just after nine o'clock and there was still some light in the sky. It was too early to go to bed. He took another look at the photo of Leon that Anna had given him a week ago. There was something in the way the young man looked at the camera that reminded Piet of his brother. As Leon was at university, he obviously didn't have Robbie's learning difficulties, but there was something equally open and vulnerable about his eyes. He wondered again if Leon had also been bullied at school and that was what made his mother so protective.

If Leon was spending his parents' money on prostitutes, it was obvious where he was: the Red Light District that Desk Sergeant Bouma had described on their first morning in Amsterdam as a square kilometre of misery. District 2, which he had urged them to stay away from. Wasn't it Piet's responsibility as a police officer to protect the vulnerable in society, regardless of what a desk sergeant told him? Regardless of the opinion of an upstairs neighbour in the garden that the young man in question was 'having fun'?

He checked his map for the best route to the Red Light District, avoiding all the main squats and potential flash-points. He stuck a few twenty-five-guilder notes in his inside pocket and put his wallet and police badge in the drawer for safety. He felt for his gun but thought better of taking it. He left the hotel key at reception and headed out armed only with Leon's photo.

Chapter 17

Wim van Buren arrived at his daughter-in-law's house ten minutes later carrying a small bag. He shrugged his coat off and dropped it over the back of a chair with the casualness of a regular visitor. When he sat down next to Lotte on the sofa, he was so close she could smell the alcohol on his breath. 'You must have seen these,' he said. 'They're all old photos of me and your dad.'

Lotte reached for them, desperate like an addict. The first picture showed two young police officers in uniform, younger than she was now, in front of the old police station on the Nieuwezijds. That was long gone and turned into an office block. It had been replaced by the new station on the Burgwal where Rick van Buren had been stationed. Her father looked dapper in his dark-blue uniform and cap. The silver flame of the police was clearly visible on his sleeve.

'I much preferred those old uniforms,' Wim said. 'I don't like the new ones with the fluorescent yellow stripes.'

As she leant in to have a closer look, she got another whiff of booze. Even his son's drunken accident wasn't enough to stop Wim from downing the alcohol. It reminded Lotte of a former neighbour who had been diagnosed with late-stage lung cancer but had still continued to smoke. Amy clearly knew that Wim was half-cut. She put a cup of tea in front of him with an angry clunk.

'When was this taken?' Lotte asked, to stop thinking about addiction and get back to the safer topic of her father's work.

'The first week we worked together, early April 1980, before it all turned into a mess,' he said. 'But you must know about that.'

'My dad and I don't really talk about the past.'

'We took that photo to commemorate freedom,' Wim said. 'I remember it well.'

'Freedom.' Lotte repeated the word with a bitter taste in her mouth. 'I think my dad took that a bit too literally.'

'Do you remember this? You must do.' The next picture showed the same four men, though this time they were engrossed in deep conversation around a table while the kids ran in a blur of motion to the side.

'Lotte says that's not her,' Amy said.

'This girl?' Wim pointed at the photo. 'That's definitely you.'

'No,' Lotte said, 'it isn't. When was this taken?'

'We had a team reunion on Queen's Day 1981 and got together with our families.'

'Who are the adults in this picture?' she asked.

'Your dad, me, Barry Simmens and Eelke Wieringa,' he tapped on each of the faces in turn, 'and our kids.'

'My parents were already divorced by then. My mother and I moved away and I didn't see my father until I was thirteen.' That was when the weekend visits to her father started. They weren't a huge success and didn't last long.

Wim scratched his head. 'Maybe Piet did come by himself. That's definitely not you?'

'Definitely. One hundred per cent certain. Rick thought the same thing, didn't he? That this was me?'

'The reunion pictures were up in my attic. When my wife passed away four years ago, we cleared everything out and found them. He recognised Teun, of course, but not the girl. I told him it was you.'

That was why Rick hadn't mentioned being her childhood friend when they'd worked together seven years ago; the misapprehension only started after his mother's death. She wondered if he'd been surprised when his father had told him that. Or shocked even.

Wim screwed up his eyes to look at the photo with more clarity. 'Was that Eelke's daughter, then? Must have been.'

'Doesn't Rick look just like Kevin did at that age?' Amy said. 'Kevin's our youngest,' she added for Lotte's clarification.

'Are you sure that isn't you?' Wim interrupted Amy. He clearly didn't want to let go of the idea. 'Maybe your parents divorced a year later?'

'No. What you said about that photo commemorating freedom, I think my father interpreted it as freedom from his wife and family. That month in Amsterdam blew up my parents' marriage. It was when he met Maaike and cheated on my mother.'

'I had no idea.' He frowned. 'I didn't think he was the type. He never went out drinking with me.'

He must have met with his lover instead of going drinking with his colleague.

'But then you never know what's going on in people's lives,' Wim added. 'As police officers we know that only too well.'

Lotte nodded. She'd seen too much of what went on behind closed doors.

'How did he have time? I'm really impressed. Sorry, sorry,' he added, 'I didn't mean it like that. Actually, there were a few times when he didn't join us for dinner. That must be when he met her.'

'I don't know when he met Maaike. I never asked.'

'Maaike? That name rings a bell.' Wim screwed up his face as he searched through his memories.

'She probably came to your second reunion. I'm surprised Dad didn't take her to the first.'

'Wait, is she that really chubby woman? Estate agent?'

Really chubby was unfair, Lotte thought, but she wasn't going to defend her stepmother. 'Yup, that's her.'

Wim turned towards her on the sofa. 'Her? He slept with her? If I'm thinking of the right person, I find that hard to believe. She really wasn't a looker.'

Lotte narrowed her eyes. It might be the alcohol talking, but this man really annoyed her.

'Wim, seriously!' Amy tried to shut up her half-drunk father-in-law.

'Sorry, sorry. I'm just shocked, that's all.'

That was why her father hadn't brought Maaike to the reunion. Even her mother had said that her father hadn't hooked up with Maaike for her looks. Lotte remembered the time she'd asked her about what had happened between the two of them. It had started as a conversation about money. Now her mother was remarried, but at that time, the contrast between her mother's life and her father's was just too stark.

They had been doing the dishes together when they had their one and only discussion about it. 'Mum,' Lotte said, 'we lived in relative poverty for years. You still have next to nothing. He has a huge house, a BMW parked outside the door, expensive holidays—'

'And you wish we'd had that too?' Her mother's eyes remained on the plate in her hand.

'No, I just want to know why we didn't. Why we didn't have some of that.'

'It wasn't my money to take. It was hers, OK?' She put the plate down.

'Hers?'

'That Maaike woman. His new wife.' She rested her elbows on the edge of the sink and wiped her face with the back of her hand.

'Why didn't you ever tell me this?'

'Tell you what? That your father left me for a richer woman? That the house he lives in, the BMW you so enviously describe, their holidays are all paid for by her? That the money he offered me to look after you was hers?' She straightened her back and pulled off her Marigolds. 'With your father it was all about the money.' She stepped away from the sink and leant against the side of the fridge. 'If he'd wanted money, I would rather he'd been on the take.' She laughed, a hard, sharp sound. 'Isn't that awful of me? I would have preferred it if he was corrupt. Instead, he was just sleeping with a rich woman.'

'Mum . . .' Lotte wrapped her arm around her mother's shoulder.

'It wasn't supposed to be like that. Marriage is supposed to be for ever. He was supposed to be responsible for me.' Her mother shook under Lotte's embrace as if fighting against it. 'You see, that's why it was different. Your husband left you for someone younger, someone prettier. Your father left me for someone richer. It was totally different.'

'I'm sorry that your parents got divorced,' Wim said, pulling Lotte out of the past.

Wim van Buren had said that Maaike wasn't a looker, and even if Lotte didn't want to think of her father as the money-hungry man that her mother described, it seemed to prove her mother's words. She couldn't decide whether it was worse if your husband dumped you for someone richer or left you for someone younger and prettier. Her ex had made a lot of money, so he could afford to trade her in for a newer model.

'That month was a total mess,' he continued. 'They seconded four people who hadn't a clue about what was going on in Amsterdam and then reprimanded us afterwards for not doing a good job. That's why we got together a couple of times afterwards, to blow off steam.' He must feel on safer ground talking about her father's work fuck-ups rather than his cheating. 'We messed up, sure, but I don't know what they expected. They were the ones who got us in from all over the country, but when the press turned us into a disaster, the top brass dropped us like a hot potato.'

'The press?' Lotte asked.

'Surely you've seen this.' He handed her a newspaper

clipping. In the foreground, squatters were throwing bricks at riot police. In the background, four officers in uniform were chatting, not even looking in the direction of the protesters.

It was a striking image of her father and his three mates utterly disinterested in maintaining any kind of order.

She understood immediately why the top brass, as Wim called them, had been unimpressed.

'Rick saw those photos, of course, as you must have done,' Wim said. 'I wonder if that was why he went in so hard during the lockdown riots. Wanting to prove he was nothing like his useless dad.'

Not wanting to be like your parents, Lotte got that. Unfortunately, she hadn't managed to avoid their example. She had a failed marriage behind her, like her mother, and her ex had been a cheater just like her dad. She took her phone out to snap the newspaper clipping and the photos. Then she thanked Amy and Wim for their time and headed out.

As soon as she was at her bike, she called her father and asked him if he was still up. She cycled home, told Mark that she was driving north to Alkmaar and might stay there overnight, and got into her green car.

She drove off with her partner's protests still in her ears.

Chapter 18

10 April 1980

A woman moaned and hugged her knees in a doorway, the rubber strap she'd used to make her veins stand out now discarded by her feet. A man with lank blonde hair was shooting up around a corner. In gutters and between cobblestones, used needles were scattered like fallen leaves. A Chinese man handed a parcel to two Surinamers and didn't even try to be surreptitious about it. On the next corner, a large café was open, busy but not selling food or drink. Instead, people dripped out one by one, pocketing the hit they were so desperate for. Two white guys as skinny as skeletons stood chatting in front of a shop, but fell in behind Piet as he walked past and trailed him too close for comfort. With his jeans, Adidas trainers and slicked-back hair, he couldn't be more conspicuous if he tried, bait to this pair of hungry piranhas. He didn't think they were armed, but he wasn't going to take any chances. He turned into a wider street and kept to the middle. They carried straight on, looking for easier targets and fatter wallets to steal.

When Bouma had described this part of Amsterdam as a square kilometre of misery, Piet thought he'd exaggerated.

He hadn't. Misery was here in every corner and every gutter, and nobody was doing anything about it; they neither upheld the law nor helped these people. The smell of dope hung heavy in the air. It was what the dealers were smoking while they sold heroin to their wretched punters.

His own section of Amsterdam had been unfamiliar when he first arrived, but the Red Light District was like a completely different country. Muttered strands of German, French and English caught his ear amongst the Dutch. It was busy. Addiction didn't care that there were riots going on. He came past women in bras and knickers standing in their windows like lifelike mannequins displaying what they had to sell. Alkmaar's brothels were different. Not just smaller, but also less hungry, less desperate. The thought of Leon in this cauldron of crime made him worry. The men who came for sex became the perfect prey for the addicted pickpockets trying to steal enough money for their next hit. The women in the windows were after that same money and could only hope that the men prowling the streets didn't get there first.

A prostitute in the nearest window, wearing nothing but see-through red underwear, gave Piet a glare in sharp contrast to her inviting pose. She could tell that he had no intention of coming in and thought he got his kicks from staring at women trying to sell themselves. Looking, looking, but not buying. He quickly averted his eyes.

He saw the blue sign of District 2's police station on the Warmoesstraat. It was a good place to start his search. The desk sergeant was calmly smoking a cigarette amongst the chaos. The place reeked of piss and vomit. On a wooden bench along the wall sat a Surinamer with his hands handcuffed in front of him, a prostitute with blood splatters all over her arm, a middle-aged man spouting nonsense with half his teeth missing, and a young man in a torn jacket covered in puke. A police officer in uniform stood next to the quartet and looked at them like an uninterested headmaster eyeing his unruly pupils. A fat drunken man with his jacket and shirt undone, showing his huge gut to the world, stumbled down one corridor. A rat raced across the other, its small paws rattling on the vinyl floor.

Piet could only count his lucky stars that he wasn't stationed here.

'Lost your wallet?' the desk sergeant said with a smirk.

'I'm looking for a missing young man.' Piet pulled down the zip of his jacket to get the photo out.

'Come back tomorrow morning,' the desk sergeant said.

'I'm a police officer, I'm seconded here from Alkmaar,' Piet said.

'Good on you. Has he been reported missing?'

'Yes, he—'

'This is our busiest time. Can't you see we're totally swamped?'

'He's been missing for over a week.'

'Then one night won't make a difference. What's his name?'

'Leon Martens.'

'Okay. We'll look for him tomorrow.'

Piet held out the photo, expecting the desk sergeant to take it, but then the phone rang and the man answered it. 'Where? Zeedijk? We'll be right there.' He opened a hatch to the side. 'Guys!' he shouted down the corridor. 'Fight!'

Within a minute, a stream of officers in uniform filled the doorway. Piet wondered where they'd been seconded from.

'Do you want to help out?' the desk sergeant said. 'I've got a spare baton here.'

He couldn't tell if the suggestion was serious or not, so he hung back next to the bench with the arrested quartet as his colleagues stormed out to restore order through violence. He wasn't going to get any help here. The reddish-pink twenty-five-guilder notes in his pocket would have to do the work instead.

He went back outside to walk the narrow path between the drug dealers and the pickpockets, the working girls and the users, the peeping Toms and the punters, looking for the guy who might be mired in this pocket of misery. In his head, he heard Anna the upstairs neighbour say that Leon was having fun. He wondered if she'd ever been here at night and seen these people who were only out to fleece others, to rob them of their money by offering one way or another of taking their minds off reality. That the streets were buzzing was more frightening than if they had been empty.

Whilst he was making sure that nobody was getting too close to him, he wondered where a sheltered twenty-one-year-old kid would go. Piet didn't think Robbie had ever paid for sex, but where would someone like him have gone at that age? Not to one of the prostitutes in the window, he thought, not if he was on his own. A young guy would not get the cold stare that Piet himself had received half an hour ago – even though he knew men for whom that would be the ultimate aphrodisiac – but a kinder glance, and a group of mates could have egged him on, especially if they were drunk, but it would be nerve-racking to step through the door by himself that first time.

Much easier to go to one of the peepshows to just have a look, or, even better, to a sex club, where you could tell yourself you were just going for a drink. He examined the front of one of the bars and was instantly accosted by a tout, who told him that he was lucky, it was Happy Hour, and with this leaflet he'd get two drinks for the price of one.

Robbie would freak out at that. This was not the right place.

Other establishments were made to look as if they were just normal houses, so that if you were seen going inside, nobody knew what you were here for. Or at least you and the person who'd seen you could both pretend. A sheltered kid might not be aware of what he was looking at. Not the right place either.

Then he came to a large venue on a corner. A sign saying *Casa Blanca* flashed in multicoloured lights. The walls were painted entirely white, to go with its name, apart from a large drawing on the wall of a barely dressed young girl happily sipping a cocktail with, in the background, someone who bore a vague resemblance to Humphrey Bogart. Piet found it amusing, even though he thought the actor would be less impressed. There were two bouncers at the door. They were big guys in suits, but one of them gave Piet an easy smile as he clocked him as someone from out of town. We're not here to keep guys like you out, that grin indicated, nor are we judging you. Their attitude was more protective than aggressive.

The kind of attitude that was tailor-made to draw in a kid

like Leon. Piet considered showing them the photo and asking if they'd seen him, but he didn't think he'd get far. Better to go in and use his money to buy information.

As expected, the bouncers opened the door for him at his approach and told him to go straight through. Unlike the booming drug trade outside, business was slow here. Only a few men sat in the booths that lined the wall, each accompanied by a woman who wore too few clothes for this time of year. At the far end was a bar where other women, working girls, sat by themselves. To the left was a wine-carpeted staircase. A man came down it and hurried outside, studiously avoiding making eye contact with Piet.

He selected the booth from which he could see the stairs and the door. He didn't like having his back towards either of them. The jukebox played 'Una Paloma Blanca' by the George Baker Selection. He wondered if it was a nod to the club's name. He ordered a beer from the waiter. A minute later, one of the girls from the bar joined him. She was older than him, and wore make-up that was thicker than her top. 'Buy me a drink?' she said with a smile. He didn't see any needle tracks along her arms, but her heavy eyes implied a liking for dope.

'Have you seen this guy?' He slid the photo across the table.

She glanced down at it but didn't pick it up. 'Might have seen him around. Why are you asking? Are you a cop?' The smile lingered around her lips. 'His dad?'

He stuck the photo back in his pocket. 'Bit too young to be his dad,' he said.

'Anything in it for me? Always happy to cooperate with the boys in blue. Or should that be men?'

He was pleased with himself for having found the right place immediately. He pushed a folded twenty-five-guilder note towards her. She tapped two fingers on the table. He passed her a second one and gave himself a mental reminder to fill in an expense form as soon as he got back to the hotel.

'I haven't seen Leon here in a week or so,' the girl said. 'You want Katinka, but she's busy right now. Want to wait? Buy me a drink?'

'Don't think I can afford it,' Piet said. 'You're expensive.'

She leaned towards him and passed him a card. *Katinka*, it said, and a phone number. As he reached for it, he was aware out of the corner of his eye of a man coming down the stairs. A man he recognised. Before he could duck out of view, the man looked over his shoulder and clocked him too, and winked.

The wink didn't sit naturally on his boss's fat bulldog face and the effect was disquieting. It tore away the pride that Piet had felt at correctly identifying the place that Leon frequented.

Before he could get up to explain his presence here, Inspector van Merwe was out of the door.

Chapter 19

It was coming up to ten o'clock in the evening and the last of the daylight was finally leaving the sky when Lotte turned off at Alkmaar's roundabout and arrived at her father's house. She parked her car behind the sky-blue Tesla that he and Maaike had bought last year. The white triangle of the house had solar panels on the left-hand side of the roof, and the warm-yellow motion-detection light that came on as she walked up the path had been charged by daylight. Last month, when she'd been here for dinner with Mark, he and Maaike had talked about energy-efficient houses all evening. Maaike had sold her real-estate business and now invested in living as carbon neutral as possible. It was as good a reason to buy that Tesla as any.

Lotte rang the doorbell. Her father had offered her a key, but that felt strange, especially as this was more Maaike's house than his. As her mother had told her, Maaike's money had bought this large property, not her father's policeman's salary. He greeted her with a wide smile that gave him a youthful aura, even if his short-cropped hair was white and getting sparser by the month. He looked better than Wim van Buren, Lotte thought. Not someone aged by grief and possibly heavy drinking. He gave her a hug and she stood still and let it happen. He hung up her jacket as she took her shoes off and put them underneath the coat rack. She was embarrassed to see that there was a new hole in her right sock. Last time, Maaike had offered to buy her some slippers to leave here; she should have taken her up on that.

'Can I get you a drink?' her father asked.

'No,' she said, 'I'm driving back.'

There was disappointment on his face, and Lotte regretted mentioning leaving as soon as she stepped through the door. Especially as it was really the memory of Wim smelling of alcohol, his son crashing his car drunk and Teun Simmens drinking himself to death that made her refuse the glass of decent wine that her father had on offer. How weird that she felt the need to make an excuse rather than just say she preferred a soft drink. She could have stayed overnight if she'd wanted to and driven back to Amsterdam in the morning; she'd told Mark that was what she was planning to do.

'I'll get you a glass of water,' he said, and moved towards the open-plan kitchen. When she saw him walk, he seemed older. The slope in his back, the upper half rounded and steeped forward, was especially ageing.

Maaike was reading an architectural lifestyle magazine on the large L-shaped brown leather sofa. Two empty wine glasses stood on the table. Blood-red dregs clung to the bottom. Apart from that, the place was pristine and had that lemon smell Lotte associated with her father's house. Wim van Buren had described Maaike as a 'really chubby woman'. Lotte had hated her for breaking up her parents' marriage and in the past had used harsher words than that. She had once described the new wife as 'gross' to one of her friends. She wouldn't say that now.

Maybe there was a statute of limitation not just for murder but also for how long you could harbour hatred.

'Hi, Lotte,' Maaike said. 'No Mark tonight?' She put the magazine aside. She'd no doubt hoped to discuss an article with him and was disappointed that he wasn't here. She was probably thinking that a conversation with her stepdaughter was a poor substitute for talking shop with someone on her wavelength. If Lotte was being fair, she had to admit that Maaike had aged well. She wasn't skinny like Lotte's mother, but these days she wasn't overweight either. When you got older, those few extra kilos looked good, and she came across as solid and grounded rather than frail and brittle. 'I guess this is about work then,' she added.

It was no surprise that she and Mark got on so well, Lotte thought. They both had their feet firmly planted in reality. 'Not really work,' she said, 'but it is police related.'

'I'll leave you to it,' Maaike said.

'You can stay.'

'No, it's fine, you two chat.' Maaike lowered her voice. 'You know how much your father enjoys it. I don't need to be in the way.'

Her father came back with water for Lotte and an open bottle of Rioja to top up their wine glasses. He sat down next to Maaike on the sofa and held her hand. Physical affection was like cake: there was only a thin margin between sweet and cloying. 'Is this about Wim van Buren?' he asked. Maybe the hand was there to stop Maaike leaving and to signal that he wanted her to be part of this conversation.

'Wim showed me this photo.' Lotte pulled up the picture of the four men talking together as their kids ran riot. 'He was certain the little girl was me. Do you remember this?'

'That's not you,' her father said immediately. 'That's Eelke's daughter. She's about the same age as you. Seeing her made me miss you a lot.'

Lotte noticed that Maaike squeezed her father's hand in a comforting gesture, and she thought about saying that he needn't have missed her if he hadn't slept with this woman behind her mother's back. But when you were a responsible grown-up and not a stroppy teenager, you didn't come out with things like that. You might still think them, you just no longer said them. She shouldn't have come here alone on a whim. She should have come tomorrow evening with Mark for dinner and then everything would have been easier.

'I told Wim that it wasn't me and he didn't believe it.' She felt vindicated. 'Do you remember what she's called?' she asked out of idle curiosity.

'I'm not sure, it was a long time ago,' her father said. 'Sandra? Saskia? Something like that, but I honestly can't remember.'

'It doesn't matter,' Lotte said.

'How's Wim holding up? I googled what happened to his son after you called me yesterday. It's tragic.'

'I saw him and Rick's widow earlier tonight. That's why I'm here.' She took a gulp of her water. 'He's having a tough time, I think, and I don't blame him. He's drinking quite heavily, from what I could tell,' she had to make an effort not to stare at those filled-up wine glasses, 'and Rick's widow was angry about that.'

'Because it was a drink-driving accident?' Maaike said.

'Because Rick had been sober for a while,' Lotte corrected her, 'and then got legless again and hit a child with his car before crashing into a wall.' She looked at the photo again, at the police officer fathers and their three kids. 'I saw this man's dead body,' she pointed out the eldest child, 'two weeks ago.'

'Barry Simmens' son?'

'Yes. Teun Simmens drowned in a pond at the back of the building he was squatting in.'

'Oh my God.' Her father reached for his wine glass in shock. His other hand held on to Maaike even more tightly. 'And you think those deaths are related? Is that why you asked for the name of this girl?'

'I'm sorry, Dad, I didn't mean to scare you.' She should have broken this news differently to a man who'd had heart problems in the past. 'Their deaths are related, I think, but they're not suspicious. Rick and Teun were friends, and I think Teun's death hit Rick hard. I also asked Rick to give Teun's ex-wife more bad news: Teun had late-stage cancer when he died. That was really rough on Rick, and I should have gone myself.'

And she would have gone herself if he hadn't come to see her with that stupid photo and told her they were friends. Now she didn't even know if he'd talked to the widow before his death. She should check that. It was a mess and it was deeply sad.

'Rick first stopped drinking after he got in trouble during

the lockdown riots,' she said. 'He beat up a protester and apparently it went viral.'

'Do you remember how *you* got beaten up during the coronation riots?' Maaike smiled at Piet. 'That's how we met,' she told Lotte. 'There was a huge clash with squatters on one side and riot police on the other.'

'And I got caught between the two sides.' Piet cut short the anecdote. 'She rescued me.'

Lotte thought back to that footage of former squatter leader Gerard Klaasen on the barricade, being mowed down by a tank, bricks flying from one side and batons flailing from the other. It was disturbing to imagine her father being involved in that.

That was why she had no desire to look at the YouTube clip of Rick van Buren laying into a rioter. She had known there was going to be trouble as soon as she'd seen the government's announcement of the new lockdown rules. If you banned football supporters from the grounds and cancelled all fireworks on New Year's Eve, the people for whom those were the only outlets were bound to go berserk. Plus, it had seemed a petty ruling. Those were outdoor events that even at the time seemed safe enough. It had caused people to go out on the streets in their thousands, the protests as big an outdoor crowd as at a football match, and it had inevitably ended in violence and scores of arrests.

'They stuck us in Amsterdam for a month during the coronation riots, and I was so naïve at the time,' her father said. 'I had no idea what was going on.'

Chapter 20

10 April 1980

As Piet stumbled back through the despair-laden streets of the Red Light District, he fitted right in. Ten minutes ago, he had been elated because he had correctly identified the club that Leon frequented, and more to the point, he had done that all by himself. He had been the smart kid with the sharp mind again whom teachers praised. It had taken only one wink from his boss to turn him back into a stupid idiot with half a brain.

The worst thing was that the boss wasn't wrong.

It was laughably dumb to have gone to a sex club by himself. And how stupid did you have to be to think that you should put in an expense form for money you'd given to a prostitute? He'd been lucky to bump into van Merwe, because it had rescued him from getting an official reprimand.

A dealer emerged behind him with the unerring instinct of an experienced salesman. Nobody had tried to sell him anything on his way here, but now that he was a failure again, the man followed in his wake like a shark smelling blood. He kept out of Piet's eyeline and was no more than a disembodied voice from behind his shoulder. 'Do you need anything?' he whispered. 'It's good stuff, it will make you feel better.' Piet neither turned his head nor broke his stride and the man veered off. At least the dealer had kept the pick-pockets off his back.

When he got back to the hotel, he had a quick look in the bar, but none of the others from his team were there. He went upstairs and listened at Wim's door. It was all quiet. In his own room, he put the last twenty-five-guilder note back in his wallet and took his police badge out of the drawer. Had he done a policeman's job? He could have arrested that dealer trying to sell him drugs, but he'd done nothing. All he had to show for his evening was a girl's business card edged in pink swirls. He could have found that in any phone box. He wished he could talk to someone, but the thought of telling Hilda that he'd spent fifty guilders in a sex club made him wince. In his head, he could imagine the prolonged silence that would follow. He had to make up some excuse for the money. If he had Maaike's phone number, he might have called her to tell her that Leon's upstairs neighbour was right and he'd found the club.

But that wasn't really what he wanted to talk about. He wanted to say to someone: I saw my boss in a sex club and he winked at me.

There was nobody he could share that with.

All night he tossed and turned more than he slept. He got up early and dressed in his police uniform. In front of the mirror, he made sure he looked the part. Last week he'd looked so little like a police officer that riot police had attacked him. Last night he'd looked so little like a police officer that a dealer had tried to sell him drugs. Now everybody could see what he was. He buttoned up his uniform jacket and it felt reassuring.

He went downstairs, grabbed a seat in the breakfast room and asked the hotel manager for some coffee and white toast. There were no other guests and so there were no staff either. The manager brought him his order a few minutes later, along with an orange juice and a newspaper. As it was all paid for, Piet didn't complain. The front page had pictures of the riots and a countdown to Princess Beatrix's coronation. Nineteen days to go until Queen's Day. That was Queen Juliana's birthday, but Princess Beatrix had already announced she'd keep that date as the national holiday. Her own birthday was in January, and nobody wanted a day off when it was cold and miserable, or a parade in front of the royal palace when it was freezing.

The door to the breakfast room opened and Barry came in bleary-eyed. 'Lots of coffee, please,' he said to the hotel manager. He drew back the chair opposite Piet. 'You didn't sleep well either, then?'

'I had too much going on in my head,' Piet said. 'You?'

'I talked to my wife till late. Our son, Teun, finishes primary school next year. He's really clever and she thinks he should go to a different secondary school than all his friends. He's not happy about that.'

'I thought it was going to get easier. My daughter is at kindergarten.'

Barry shook his head. 'It never gets easier,' he said. 'I promised to talk to him over the weekend.'

'Maybe it's important to let kids do what they want to do,' Piet said, sounding strangely like Maaike.

'Nah, he's young enough to do what I tell him to,' Barry said with a grin.

Piet had been the same age that Barry's son was now when he'd planned to be held back for a year to look after his brother. What would his father have said, Piet wondered, if he'd told him? He was pretty sure that his mother had known, and he'd felt her approval. Even now, he remembered the warmth of her hand on his shoulder after he'd beaten up Robbie's bullies.

If he and Hilda had a second child and that child was slow like Robbie, he wouldn't want Lotte to sacrifice herself. He knew that deeply and instinctively. Hilda might think differently, because mothers and fathers were not the same. Mothers were protective, like Patricia Martens, who was selling her house purely to keep her son away from the Red Light District. Maybe Lotte was smart enough to one day go to university. Like Leon.

'That missing student,' he said to Barry, 'is going to a sex club regularly. Meets the same girl. I've got her card.'

'I forgot to tell you at dinner,' Barry said as he buttered his toast. 'Sergeant Bouma talked to me and Eelke yesterday afternoon and said we should step back from that case.'

'Why?'

'He said it's all in hand. He implied they've gone higher up.'

A weight Piet hadn't realised he was holding fell from his shoulders as he connected the dots. It all made sense. Leon's parents were exactly the kind of well-to-do people who pushed things up the ranks; they had clearly gone to the head office where his boss was located. They'd wanted someone more senior to investigate their son's disappearance; not some Officer Plod in uniform like him, but someone important like Inspector van Merwe.

He nodded to himself. 'My boss is working on it,' he said. Now that he was dressed in his uniform again and had sorted out this conundrum, all was well in the world.

'Your boss?' Barry asked. 'Are you sure?'

'Yes, I saw him in that sex club last night and I wondered why he was there. Leon's parents must be happy that they have someone more experienced looking for their son.'

Barry put more sugar in his coffee and concentrated on stirring it really thoroughly. 'You're a decent guy, Piet,' he finally said, 'but give me that girl's card. I'll call her.'

'Didn't Bouma say to drop it?'

'I'm not a fan of Bouma,' Barry said.

The hotel manager came over and filled their cups again.

'How much did you pay?' Barry asked when the man had left. 'A snipe?'

The snipe had only adorned the hundred-guilder banknote for a few years, but already the bird's name was common parlance.

'Half that,' Piet said.

'You did well.'

Piet blinked. He wasn't told that very often.

Barry took his wallet out and gave him two twenty-five-guilder notes. 'I'm used to paying informers,' he said as Piet hesitated. 'Don't worry about it.'

Piet accepted the money with deep relief that he didn't have to explain to Hilda where those fifty guilders had gone.

Barry looked at the girl's card. 'Katinka. Real name probably Karin. She'll be asleep right now. I'll arrange a chat with her after our shift today. You should come with me.'

Piet hesitated. If van Merwe was working on this, he didn't want to interfere with his investigation. 'I can't today because my boss is giving me a ride back to Alkmaar. And isn't it all in hand? Wasn't that what Bouma said?'

'Okay, when you're back next week then. It's fine if another team is searching for the guy as well.'

He was relieved. He didn't want to get in Inspector van Merwe's way and mess up. 'I also asked the police at the Warmoesstraat to keep an eye out.' The desk sergeant there had agreed that he would look for Leon this morning.

'I still don't like it.' Barry pocketed the card. 'Don't tell the others about this. And definitely don't tell your boss.'

Chapter 21

'I came from a smaller city police force,' Lotte's father said, 'and had always worked with the mindset that I was responsible for the people in the area I patrolled.'

'You'd walked the same beat for years,' Maaike said. 'And then they threw you into the deep end in an unfamiliar city, at the worst time in Amsterdam's history.'

'The city was at a crossroads. I would say even the entire country was at a crossroads. What were we going to do about the housing shortage, about having too many cars on the roads, about the influx of hard drugs?'

'I saw it happen with my own eyes,' Maaike said. 'Within five years of heroin arriving, the Red Light District went from mildly criminal to a complete no-go area. And the people in power thought: oh well, it's only a small section of Amsterdam, as long as it stays there, we can ignore it. It was almost as if they tried to quarantine heroin in that area.'

'The drugs only became an issue after the Vietnam war, remember, when the Chinese had lost the rich market of American soldiers for their heroin and needed another outlet.'

'And found Amsterdam,' Lotte said, to interrupt her father and Maaike filling in the details of each other's story.

'Right, but as Piet said, the country was at a crossroads. We could have turned conservative – you know, go for the war on drugs, or the right to buy on housing – but luckily we turned left.'

'Too far left,' Piet said.

'Maybe so, but all these things are choices. We chose to treat addiction as a disease and housing as a fundamental good, no different from water or food. We made the decision that children should be safe cycling to school.'

'It's important for her to get on her soap box every now and then.' Piet winked at Lotte. 'Her parents wanted her to fight for nuclear disarmament.'

'And instead I became an estate agent and married a cop. But seriously, property shouldn't stand empty. Do you remember that huge squat on the Keizersgracht?'

'I thought I was going to get attacked outside there on my first day in Amsterdam.'

'After the riots, Amsterdam's council bought the property and turned it into rent-controlled accommodation for young people. They could have sold it to the highest bidder, but instead they used common sense and made it available to those who needed it.'

Lotte thought that Maaike sounded remarkably like Gerard Klaasen. He was wealthy, as he owned the big property on the Singel where Teun Simmens had died, but had also given her a lecture about housing as a human right.

'The last thing they wanted,' Piet said, 'was for anybody to die during the coronation.'

That reminded her of Klaasen too. 'One of the former squatter leaders told me the other day that if you were afraid to die, you shouldn't get in a car.'

Piet grimaced. 'I hope you didn't repeat that to Wim.'

For a moment Lotte had forgotten that Rick van Buren had died in a car crash. 'He hit a child,' she said, 'before he hit the wall. A child on a bicycle.'

'That's terrible,' Piet said.

'Do you think,' Lotte said, 'that we'll ever treat alcohol in the same way as drugs?'

'Have you been to the Westerkerk?' Maaike asked. 'The memorial plaque for Bols, the distiller, is ten times as big as that for Rembrandt's son.'

'But that was the seventeenth century,' Lotte said, 'and times change.' She should really control the reflex to disagree with everything that Maaike said. 'Did Wim van Buren already drink a lot back when you worked together?' she asked her father.

'Yes,' Piet said. 'He was always going somewhere by himself after dinner, and most mornings he smelled of booze. He got an official reprimand for that.'

Maaike stared at her half-full wine glass. 'I think I've had enough for the evening.'

Piet got up with a smile and carried both their glasses back to the kitchen.

It flashed into Lotte's mind that these two were good together. She'd never appreciated or accepted that before.

'Listen,' Maaike said, 'your father says I shouldn't bring this up, but the daughter of a friend of mine is looking to rent a place in Amsterdam. It will only be for one year. I was thinking about your flat. How long has that been empty now?'

Lotte welcomed back her far more familiar annoyance with her stepmother. 'It isn't empty,' she said.

'You're not living there. You're living at Mark's place.'

'Are you going to report me to the council? There's a handy website for that.'

'Of course not. I'm just saying that it's a really good short-term let. The woman lives in Boston and she's only coming back to the Netherlands for a year for work.'

'It's still my flat.'

'She's got no kids, no pets, she would keep the place tidy. It shouldn't stand empty, Lotte, that isn't right.'

Maaike now definitely sounded like Gerard Klaasen.

Her father came back in. 'Leave it.' He threw Maaike a glance that definitely said: I told you she'd refuse.

Yes, Lotte thought, I am that predictable. She checked her phone. It was well past eleven. Nearly time to go. She pulled up the other photo, the picture of the team chatting while there was a riot going on. 'What about this, Dad?'

'Wim showed you that as well?'

She nodded. 'He had a newspaper cutting of it.'

'A student had gone missing,' her father said, 'and we got a tip-off that he'd been spotted somewhere.'

'That he was hurt,' Maaike added.

'Yes, and so we rushed to find him.'

'You're not really rushing in this picture,' Lotte said.

'We didn't know this was going on. There was no social media to tell us that the anarchists had organised a big demonstration. We had no GPS to help us when we didn't really know our way around Amsterdam, apart from the sector we were working in. We just got there and were stuck behind these rioters.'

'So, what? You had a chat about the best route?'

'Exactly. And then the reporter took that photo.'

'Did you at least find the guy?'

'No,' her father said. 'We never found him. After the coronation, Amsterdam calmed down and we went back to our original locations. The case just sizzled out.'

She put her phone away. 'I'd better head back,' she said. 'Work tomorrow.'

She said her goodbyes and got in her car for the drive home.

Why was she so adamant that she didn't want to give up her flat? she wondered as she drove along the empty motorway. She answered her own question. Because if things went wrong with Mark, she'd have no place to stay. She knew it was unfair as well as irrational. She was happy with Mark. There was no reason why they couldn't be like Maaike and her father: still content together in their seventies. Not every relationship ended because someone cheated.

Plus, if they did break up, she could easily rent another place somewhere. She could sell the flat, even with a sitting tenant, and just buy a new one.

She overtook a silver car with a broken tail light before slotting back into the right-hand lane.

Her flat was more than just a safety net, though. It was the place she'd bought with the money from her divorce. She'd part-funded her ex-husband's start-up company, and at the divorce she'd taken what she was entitled to, despite the bitter words from his family, who were keen to point out that, with a baby on the way, her ex and his pregnant lover needed the money. The flat was a symbol of having gone through that extremely painful time and come out at the other end still standing.

Both Maaike and Gerard Klaasen would say that it wasn't a symbol, but a place for someone to live.

She knew the rules, of course. For the first two years she could rent it out as a short-term lease, and any tenant wouldn't have rights. Maaike's suggestion was a sensible one.

It was coming up to midnight by the time she hit Amsterdam's ring road. Mark was normally asleep by now. It was a good thing that he hadn't been with her tonight. Between Maaike and Mark there would have been no way for her to refuse to rent out her apartment, not without hurting her partner by admitting that she wanted to have a bolthole for when they split up. *If* they split up.

She didn't go to Amsterdam Zuid, but turned instead towards the canals and parked outside her flat. She didn't want to think how long it had been since she was here last. Much longer than six months. She opened the door to the communal area with the black and white tiles. A pile of mail had collected in her mailbox. She grabbed it all and clambered up the stairs to the third floor. When she opened her front door, the inward movement made the layer of dust from the floorboards fly up and then drift down in a low-hanging cloud. Grime covered everything, and the dead plants in the front room showed how long the place had been empty. She hadn't realised what abandonment did to an apartment.

She stood in the doorway and considered turning around and going home to Mark's. But she'd told him that she was planning to stay at her father's place, so he wasn't expecting her back. If she went to his house now, she'd wake him up and probably freak him out. So she just closed the door behind her and rolled into bed. And even though the duvet was dusty, her old bed welcomed her back and she slept deeply.

The next morning, she got up early. It was annoying that she'd taken all her clothes to Mark's house, because now she had nothing clean to wear. In a desolately empty cupboard under the sink, she found a new toothbrush but no toothpaste. The towel smelled disgusting, so she didn't take a shower. There was no shampoo anyway.

Dressed in yesterday's clothes, she scanned through that ridiculous pile of post. At least she had a sign on her mailbox that said *No Leaflets*. She turned the pile over and went through it in reverse chronological order, sorting it into letters she had to deal with and items that could go directly into the recycling. It was lucky that all her bills were online or she would have been in trouble.

Trouble had found her anyway. A white sheet of paper with large printed letters was close to the bottom of the pile. It must have arrived recently.

BITCH YOUR NEXT!

Chapter 22

11 April 1980

Piet spotted the bulldog face of van Merwe from across the canal. The man was scanning the area whilst leaning against his blue Citroën 2CV. Barry's words were in his head: that he shouldn't tell his boss that they had Katinka's details. He couldn't understand why Barry had said that. Van Merwe had been in the same club anyway, because he knew that Leon had been going there. But he would do what Barry had asked him and keep his mouth shut.

Van Merwe clocked Piet and raised his hand in a greeting. Piet still had a whole bridge to cross with the inspector's eyes on him. Those eyes made him feel stupid even though he hadn't made any mistakes. Yet.

The boss opened the boot of the car as Piet approached and locked his suitcase away. Piet got in and pulled the door behind him with a clank that reminded him of a prison cell being shut. He put his seat belt on and was tied inside the metal box on wheels with a man who made him feel small.

'The Red Light District is quite something, isn't it?' the boss said as he started the engine and smoothly reversed the car out of the tight parking spot along the canal. 'An area like that comes up in every investigation. We got a tip off that some IRA guys are based right opposite Casa Blanca.'

'The IRA?' Piet remembered Bouma telling them that special forces were dealing with the terrorist threat and they should stay well away from it. He looked at his boss with renewed respect. 'Did you find them?' He was in awe that van Merwe had been included in that operation.

'Yeah, we did. The first floor of that club gives us a perfect view and they're now under constant surveillance. Can you imagine if they assassinated Prince Charles during the coronation?'

'That would be a disaster.'

'Not least for him,' the inspector joked. 'What were you doing there?'

'I was looking for a missing student.'

'Any sign of him?'

Piet shook his head. 'No, none. But he used to go there.' He'd been wrong to think that his boss was working on Leon's case. Still, Bouma had said that it was all in hand, so there must be someone else higher up who was involved.

'Poor bastard, I bet Casa Blanca really fleeced him,' his boss said. 'He buys that girl a drink and she'll order the most expensive thing on the menu. The punter will drink a few beers, the girl will drink whisky – which is really cold tea – and before the poor sod knows it, he'll have run up a bill of hundreds of guilders.'

'I know,' Piet said, 'but nobody has seen him in two weeks.'

'If he's got any sense, he's abroad by now. Hopped on a bus to Spain or something. If you're stuck, I can help. I have to go back to that club anyway for those IRA terrorists.' Van Merwe tapped the steering wheel. 'We're all in this together for the next couple of weeks,' he said, 'and then it won't be our problem any more.'

'Thanks,' Piet said. Maybe his boss could find out for him who was now working this case. But not until he'd talked to Barry about that. He owed his temporary colleague that much. 'Will this help with my promotion?' he asked. He was nervous bringing the subject up, but he'd promised Hilda, and he hadn't told her that he'd chickened out of raising the subject on the trip back to Amsterdam last Sunday.

'Promotion?'

'I want to study for the exams,' Piet said.

'You? You want to study?' Van Merwe burst out laughing. He threw a sideways look at Piet and noticed that he was serious. 'You can try,' he said. 'It's a free country.'

'But will it be in my favour that I was in Amsterdam for a month?'

'It depends on how you do. Keep me posted if you hear anything about this missing guy.'

'Yes. Thanks. I will do.' His boss was finally showing an interest in his career and Maaike had offered to help them find a new house; Hilda would be pleased with him.

On his arrival back home, his welcoming committee mobbed him just like last Friday. Robbie, Hilda and Lotte told him the details of their past week all at the same time as he lugged his suitcase through the door. Stories about trucks, the cost of chicken, and bears living on a boat collided until the words were just a cacophony that bounced against the walls. He nodded and took nothing in other than a general sense of what he was supposed to sort out over the next two days. Apart from maybe the bears, because he was pretty sure his daughter didn't think they were his problem.

He took his suitcase up to the bedroom with all three accompanying him. Hilda insisted on unpacking his bag for him and wanted to check out the bruise on his arm, Robbie pushed three leaflets into his hands with pictures of trucks, and Lotte was adamant that he had to read her a story after dinner plus watch her favourite cartoon with her tomorrow. He was only rescued by the sound of a beeping clock when the roast chicken was ready. It wasn't easy to talk and eat at the same time, and so he had a better chance of hearing what his family wanted to tell him.

As though by agreement, after dinner Hilda and Robbie left him alone for long enough that he could read Lotte her bedtime story. When she fell asleep, he crept down the stairs and met two sets of staring eyes.

'About being a truck driver . . .' Robbie said.

'About your promotion . . .' Hilda said at exactly the same time.

'Later,' Piet said.

'What do you mean, later?' Hilda asked. 'We need the money.'

'I meant about Robbie being a truck driver.'

'Robbie? Robbie?' Her voice rose. 'Why did you answer him first? Why not me first? You haven't told me what your boss said on Sunday. I've been waiting all week. You haven't called once.'

Piet suppressed a sigh; that was why he'd told Robbie that he'd discuss things with him later. 'I can't talk to two people at the same time.'

'I've been by myself all week. I've had nobody to talk to apart from a small child, and now you're home and you only want to talk to your brother.'

'Shh,' Piet said, 'don't wake Lotte.'

'Don't you shh me!' she hissed. 'I've been cooking all afternoon, I've unpacked your suitcase and am washing your clothes, and you're telling me to be quiet? You come swanning back and think you can decide who to talk to?'

'Do you want to draw straws?' Piet tried to lighten the mood.

'It's okay,' Robbie said to Hilda. 'You can go first.'

'That's not up to you,' she whipped at him. Then she visibly stopped herself from saying more and took a couple of deep breaths. 'I'm sorry,' she said, slumping on the sofa. 'I'm being unreasonable. It's just that my period started this morning and I'd hoped I was pregnant.'

'Oh!' Robbie said. 'I didn't know you wanted another baby.'

Piet stared at them. It wasn't that they wanted more of him, he told himself, they just had to cram both their needs into smaller periods of time. This was his other job, he knew. It was his responsibility to look after his family as it was his responsibility to sort out their arguments. 'Fine,' he said. 'Shall we talk about what Hilda wants to discuss for the first hour, and then Robbie gets the next hour? If that's not enough time, we'll do it again tomorrow. I'll get a stopwatch.'

'Now you're just being silly,' Hilda said with a glimmer of a smile. 'Robbie, you first.'

'Can I take him for a walk,' Robbie said, 'if I promise to bring him back in exactly an hour?'

As if Piet was a dog or something.

But at Hilda's generous nod of agreement, Piet was just as quick as his brother to grab his coat and escape the house.

The evening was closing in and the sky was dark grey with threatening rain. Piet lit a cigarette.

'That's bad for you,' Robbie said. 'You should give up.'

'Can't I have one bad habit?'

'I want you to live a long life,' Robbie said.

Piet smiled. 'I'll do my best. Do you still want to be a truck driver?'

'Can I?'

Piet thought of Maaike's words that everybody should have the freedom to do what they wanted as long as they didn't hurt anybody. He still didn't quite agree with her. Some people hurt themselves or others and didn't know they were doing it. But what Robbie wanted wasn't like that. Piet had to trust the driving instructors and the examiners to decide whether it was safe to let Robbie get behind the wheel of a sixteen-ton vehicle.

'It's not up to me,' he said. 'It's your responsibility to renew your licence. You'll need to get a few lessons, because you haven't driven a truck in ten years. Money is tight at the moment, but if you pay for that yourself, I can't stop you.'

'I don't want you to say you can't stop me,' Robbie said. 'I want you to approve.'

Piet rubbed the back of his hand over his eyes. He'd been

on his feet for most of the day and he was just so tired. 'Later,' he said. 'Let's talk more about it later.'

The deep disappointment in his brother's eyes hurt physically. Robbie turned around and walked back home, and Piet followed him. Neither spoke.

Hilda took one look at him when he came through the door and said they could talk in bed. He was grateful, and fully intended to listen to her, but the sound of her voice lulled him to sleep. That night he had a disturbing dream: he got a promotion and it didn't solve a thing.

Chapter 23

'That guy Gerard Klaasen really hates the police,' Lotte said when she came into work. She chucked the *BITCH YOUR NEXT* note over to Thomas. This was clearly a threat from the former squatter turned property magnate that he was going to report her flat as empty.

Thomas thankfully didn't comment on the fact that she was wearing the same clothes two days in a row. He wore a freshly laundered and ironed peacock-blue shirt and made her feel grubby in comparison.

'What's this?' He frowned as he unfolded the piece of paper.

'I found it in my flat this morning. Klaasen already threatened to shop me to the council last time we met.' Considering the sad state of the place, maybe she should just rent it out. Sometimes it was good to have your hand forced.

'Are you sure this is from him?'

'Well, he didn't sign it, but yes, I'm pretty sure.'

He put the note carefully in front of him on his desk. 'You should take this more seriously.'

'It's what I used to get on my social media feeds all the time. Especially after I was a special guest on that true crime podcast.' She counted them off on her fingers. '"Bitch, you should die for what you did", "I'll come to your house and smash you up", "I'll kill you", "Someone should rape some sense into you". Stuff like that. Some more graphic. You know, with extra details.' Talking about those messages made her hands shake, and she turned on her computer to hide it.

'I had no idea you got that level of abuse,' Thomas said.

Some of the messages were lurid descriptions of what exactly they were going to do to her. Most of these hadn't been in Dutch. As if a foreign mob had discovered a perfect female target to threaten and abuse. On the worst day, she'd received forty-seven messages in two hours. That was the day she'd packed up all her belongings, and her cat, and finally moved into Mark's house after months of him asking.

'I've shut all my social media accounts down. I wasn't using them much anyway. I only posted pictures of my cat, and now I send those to my mum directly. She's conflicted by it, because she likes the messages but hates the cat.' She tried to keep her voice light and made a joke to dispel the growing unease.

'This isn't some idiot posting something on social media. This is a threat that came through your letter box. This person knows where you live.'

'Ah yes, they said that all the time too: "I know where you live".'

'Did you report them?'

She shrugged. 'In the beginning I did. But it turned out it wasn't one person cyberstalking me. The messages came from different accounts all over the world. I guess they were using VPNs to pretend to be somewhere else. There was no point in taking it any further. The angry mob moved on to another target.' She looked at the note again. 'It's odd,' she added, 'but compared to that barrage, this letter doesn't feel all that threatening. Maybe because it's not going into any details.' But she recognised that considering renting out her flat was a similar response to shutting down her social media and moving to Mark's house. 'Do you know what's funny?' she said. 'Someone might have threatened me months ago and I had no idea. I haven't been to my flat in ages.'

'This isn't recent?'

She thought about the pile of mail again. She'd opened the oldest letters first. This note had been near the bottom, but then perhaps everything had got mixed up. 'Fairly recent, I think, but I couldn't tell you if it was a day or two weeks old.'

'Your immediate reaction was that it was Gerard Klaasen's work.'

'Everybody has been on at me to rent out my flat. I went to my father's house last night and my stepmother gave me the name of a perfect tenant plus a lecture on how property shouldn't stand empty.'

'She isn't wrong.'

'Don't you start. But I wonder how good Gerard Klaasen's spelling is. I want to get a red pen out to correct the note.'

'Stop joking,' Thomas said. 'I really don't like this. At least have it dusted for prints.'

'There's no point: I've touched it, and so have you now. We most likely smudged whatever good prints there were. Plus, nobody is going to stick a note through a cop's letter box and not wear gloves. Everybody watches so many police dramas, they all have a basic understanding of how this stuff works.'

'Humour me,' he said.

She got her phone out and stared at that picture of the four policemen and their children. She held it out to Thomas. 'Look at this,' she said. 'Teun Simmens, Rick van Buren . . . "bitch your next"?'

He took the phone. 'Are you sure? That doesn't look like you.'

'Everybody else thought it was.' Apart from her and her father. Now Thomas had joined the select group of people who knew her well enough not to misidentify her. She didn't think she could pick *him* out of a childhood photo.

He enlarged the picture and shook his head. 'This girl is smiling and happy,' he said. 'There's no way that's you.'

'I'm impressed,' she said. 'You're an arse, but I'm impressed.'

He burst out laughing. 'I didn't know you were so gullible! You told me yourself, remember? You came in complaining last week after you'd had lunch with Rick that he thought you were his childhood friend but you really weren't. You were going on and on about it.'

She rolled her eyes and took her phone back. She pulled up the police database and looked for an Eelke Wieringa who'd been an officer in 1980. It wasn't hard to find him, and from there it was child's play to find the details of his daughter, Chantal. She was a surgeon who worked part of the time in a hospital in Utrecht and the rest in Amsterdam. The hospital's website usefully offered a work email address. Lotte sent a message identifying herself as Piet Huizen's daughter and attaching the photo, and asked her if she wanted to meet up. This might be pointless, but at least she was doing something.

She looked again at the photo of the three children and four fathers. 'I don't like this,' she said.

'I'm not surprised,' Thomas said. 'Nobody likes being threatened.'

She stared at him, but couldn't find any hint of sarcasm in either his tone or his face. 'It's all your fault for taking it seriously.'

'You want to look into Rick van Buren's death more,' he said. He really did know her well.

'Does it seem crazy to you?' She doubted her own judgement, because she'd been threatened. Yesterday when she'd met with Rick's widow, she hadn't even considered that his death was anything more than an accident. Even when his father had told her that it was suspicious, she hadn't accepted that. After all, Rick was a former alcoholic who had started drinking again. That was all there was to it, however tragic it was. Now she stared at that picture and was concerned, not necessarily for herself but that they'd overlooked something.

'We can ask a few questions,' Thomas said. 'Just see it as something to do during our lunch break. I bet Rick went to a bar, initially just for one. We'll find it.'

Her eyes suddenly burned at his solidarity. 'Fine,' she said, 'and I'll have this note dusted.'

When she came back from dropping the piece of paper off with forensics, Thomas already had the name of the bar where Rick had spent his last afternoon and early evening.

'It's out of the way,' he said, 'in Eastern Docklands. That's not anywhere near his work.'

'It's on the other side of Amsterdam from where he lived, too.' Now yesterday's visit to Amy came in handy. 'I guess he didn't want to bump into anybody he knew.'

When Lotte had arrived at the police station this morning, she hadn't been nervous at all, but now, after Thomas had made her dust the note, she was hesitant to leave the safety of their shared office. She told herself not to be stupid and didn't check around her all that much as they walked to the car park to get into Thomas's car for the drive to Eastern Docklands.

The bar was easy to find and there was plenty of parking right outside. As Lotte got out of the car, she threw a quick look over her shoulder, but of course there was nobody following her. She gave herself a mental shake. Focusing on work was more productive than worrying all the time.

The place was a trendy wine bar with large windows and metal tables. 'Here? This is it?' She had imagined a basement dive where Rick had drunk anonymously. Here everybody was visible. It was a bar for after-work drinking with your colleagues, not for getting drunk by yourself because you were upset about the death of your friend.

It was completely empty and waiting for the first people to arrive at lunchtime. The woman behind the bar was dressed in a black shirt tucked into black trousers, as if to indicate that the selling and drinking of wine was a serious business. A white name tag identified her as Emily.

'I already spoke to your colleagues,' she said after Lotte

and Thomas identified themselves. 'I showed them the footage too.'

'Do you still have it?' Lotte asked.

The woman hesitated.

'We'd like to have another look at it,' Lotte urged her.

'When I gave your colleagues a copy, I made myself a copy as well. Was that wrong?'

'Just show it to us,' Lotte said.

'It's just that I was working that day,' Emily said as she opened a door to the back, where it was chaotic with bits of paper and half-torn cardboard boxes everywhere. 'Afterwards I wondered if I could have stopped him.'

'Stopped him drinking?'

'Driving. If I could have stopped him from getting in his car. Sorry, our office is such a mess,' she said. 'We never have time to tidy up here. It's out of sight so it's always the last place that gets cleaned.' She opened a white laptop that had black finger marks all over it and started the footage from the camera behind the bar.

Rick was clearly visible. He was sitting by himself at a small table and staring at nothing that Lotte could see. Then he gestured and Emily came into view. She returned a couple of minutes later and put a glass of wine in front of him. He hesitated for a few seconds and then drank.

'He ordered two large glasses,' she said, 'and then a bottle.'

'Was he by himself all the time?' Thomas asked.

'Yes. He arrived alone and just drank for two hours. Shall I fast-forward it? One of my colleagues brings him a second bottle an hour later.'

'If there's nobody else with him,' Thomas said, 'we can skip to the part where he leaves.'

She found it immediately. 'Right, here it is. As you can see, I'm busy with this other table, so I never noticed him leaving.' She must think they were here to hold her responsible, Lotte suddenly realised. That was why she knew exactly the time stamp when Rick left. That was why she'd made a copy of the security camera footage.

Lotte didn't blame her for doing that. It had come in useful.

Rick had drunk by himself and staggered out of the bar by himself. Even if it was unpleasant to watch him drink himself into oblivion, a weight lifted from her shoulders. This had just been an accident. 'Thanks for showing us,' she said.

'Do you want a copy?'

She shook her head. 'No, it's fine.'

Thomas thanked the woman for her time and they got back in the car. 'I feel better after that,' he said.

'Yes,' Lotte admitted, 'so do I.' She now felt stupid that she'd emailed Chantal Wieringa about meeting up. She'd overreacted, and was relieved that there'd been no response yet. Maybe Chantal was too busy at work to check her emails, or maybe she thought Lotte was some weird person who should be avoided. Or perhaps the email had gone into her spam folder and she'd never seen it. That was the best alternative, Lotte decided, because then she didn't have to explain to Chantal why she'd emailed her.

A ping announced the arrival of a new email, but it was from forensics about her note. As she had expected, there were no prints other than hers and Thomas's. 'Unless you're the one threatening me,' she joked to him, 'and you handled the note just to cover up that fact.'

'Nah, I'd just say it to your face,' he said. 'Plus, I know you don't live there any more.'

It suddenly occurred to her that Gerard Klaasen knew that as well. He would have stuck the note through Mark's letter box.

She shelved that thought, and when they were back at the police station, she called Maaike to tell her that she would rent out her flat to her friend's daughter for a year. Her stepmother was pleased. Lotte wasn't sure whether it was because now a flat no longer stood empty or because she had taken her advice to heart. She didn't tell her it was because of a threat that someone had posted through her letter box.

She didn't mention the note to Mark either when she arrived home that evening. He was sitting on the sofa with Pippy on his lap and neither had any intention of moving. 'How was your dad? Did you have a nice evening?'

She took off her coat, hung it over the back of one of the dining-room chairs and sat down next to him on the sofa. 'I've decided to rent out my flat and to stop drinking.' She stroked Pippy's head, and the cat at last deemed her worthy of a glance and half a purr.

Mark grinned. 'Sounds like you had a good time. So Maaike told you about the perfect tenant?'

'Wait, you knew about that? She told you before she told me?'

'Maybe?'

'Oh God, was that why you said we should make this

official? Because Maaike has a tenant for my flat? I feel so manipulated.'

'We manipulated you into doing the right thing.' He hugged her with one arm without disturbing the cat. 'And I'm happy you're doing it.'

Lotte pushed any thoughts about the real reason why she was renting out her flat to the back of her mind. She didn't want to think about threatening notes; she just wanted to enjoy her evening at home.

That pleasant feeling lasted until she got ready for bed. She'd just undressed when her phone pinged with an email from Chantal Wieringa, who wrote that she was on a late shift tomorrow, so if Lotte wanted to talk, she was at home until midday. She gave her address in Utrecht. She also wrote that she'd called her father about that photo and was curious to meet Piet Huizen's daughter. Her dad was always reluctant to talk about that time and Chantal hoped that Lotte could fill her in on all the juicy details.

Lotte didn't actually have any juicy details to share. All she had were assumptions about her father's time in Amsterdam, and they were guesses she didn't enjoy dwelling on. All in all, it was a friendly, chatty email and she knew she would have looked forward to tomorrow's visit if the two other children in the photo hadn't died. Even though she had ascertained that Rick had been drinking before he got behind the wheel of his car – nobody had spiked his soft drink or anything like that – she still felt uncomfortable. It was purely a premonition based on a random photo plus a threatening note, she told herself firmly, but the unease settled like a stone on her heart and didn't lift.

Chapter 24

16 April 1980

Back in Amsterdam, they were busy with an endless stream of burglaries and pickpockets, another robbery, three fights and four stolen bicycles. Piet kept an eye out for Leon, but there was no sign of him. On Wednesday, as the team handed over to the relief, Barry sidled up to him not unlike last week's drug dealer. 'I'll knock on your door in fifteen minutes,' he said softly. 'I've set it all up. And don't wear this.' He indicated Piet's uniform.

At the door to the hotel, Barry told Wim that he was tired and was going to have a kip before dinner. Could they eat later? Six thirty, maybe? Wim joked about some people getting old before their time and added that he was going to have a heart-starter in the hotel bar if anybody wanted to join him. There were no takers.

Piet changed into his jeans and was just lacing up his trainers when Barry's knock sounded. He grabbed his coat and followed Barry out via a back entrance he hadn't even discovered yet. To his surprise, they didn't go east towards the Red Light District but headed west. They had only crossed two canals when Barry entered a small café on the corner of a bridge. He said it was Katinka's choice of venue. They sat at a table at the back from which they could see the door and Barry ordered them a couple of beers.

When Katinka entered five minutes later, Piet immediately recognised her. She wasn't quite as young as she'd been painted, but this was the pretty girl whose picture adorned Casa Blanca's outside wall. She wore jeans so tight he could see the shape of her hip bones and white high-heeled shoes of the kind Hilda wouldn't be seen dead in. Permed blonde hair and large gold hoop earrings bounced with every step she took. All eyes were on her and a couple of eyebrows were raised when she scanned the bar and joined the two men at their table.

'As I said on the phone,' she started before Piet could even tell her his name, 'I'm interested in a deal. I'll tell you when I saw Leon last and how much he owes us if you tell me where he is as soon as you find him.'

'You don't know where he is, then?' Barry asked.

'If I knew that, I wouldn't be here. Not a fan of coppers at the moment,' Katinka lit a menthol cigarette and blew the smoke in their general direction, 'but needs must. Fucking Leon's done a runner.'

Fucking Leon. Piet felt as if ants were crawling down his spine. He was as angry as he'd been when he'd seen Robbie bullied all those years ago. 'Aren't you worried about him?' he asked.

'Worried? Why should I be worried about someone who stole from us?'

'He stole? What did he steal?'

'He owes us five grand,' she said, 'and now he's run away without paying us.'

Piet nearly choked on his coffee. That was almost five months' salary for him. 'How did he get that deep into debt?'

'His mama's allowance didn't stretch to paying a prostitute on a regular basis. He was at the club most afternoons while he was supposed to be at lectures. The only time he could escape from his mother, he said.' She took a deep drag of her cigarette.

Piet knew he was being stupid, but he couldn't help himself. 'You spent a lot of time with him and now he's disappeared. He's a person, however deep in debt he is.'

'Sure, he was one of my regulars. But listen, copper, I'm not doing this for fun, or out of affection. I'm doing it for money. And Leon spent a lot of dough.'

He stared at her, this pretty girl, and understood that Leon had been a gold mine for her. Someone who lived a sheltered life must be easier to fool. After going to the Red Light District, Piet had no rose-tinted view of what Casa Blanca was like or what the girls there did for a living, but Inspector van Merwe's words sprang to mind: that they had fleeced Leon for all he was worth. And clearly then some.

'When did you see him last?' Barry asked.

'Monday last week.'

That was the day before his mother reported him missing.

'Not a sign of him since,' Katinka continued. 'I wouldn't have talked to you lot otherwise. I hate the fucking cops.' She stubbed out her cigarette in the ashtray with an angry gesture. Her lipstick left a pink stain on the filter. 'I know his parents are good for the money. Just tell them to pay up.' She grabbed her handbag and stormed out of the door.

'Well shit,' Barry said. 'Everybody hates us these days.'

'Maybe she and Leon are in it together,' Piet wondered out loud. He wanted to believe that Wim had been right all along and this was simply Leon's bid for freedom.

'You're a decent guy, Piet.' There was more of an edge to Barry's words than when he'd said the same thing the other morning. 'But you've watched too many movies.'

Barry went back to the hotel, but Piet didn't feel like having dinner with the rest of the team. He went for a walk, planning to grab some fries with mayonnaise at McDonald's. As he came past the Martens apartment, he saw that the lights were on. All those light bulbs he'd screwed in the other day were clearly being put to good use. He came this way most evenings. It was on his route, but he also hoped that Leon might have returned. With two weeks to go before the coronation, he really wanted to see a good ending to this case. He stopped on the bridge and lit a cigarette. When people went missing, it was the uncertainty that was so difficult for the families. He hoped Leon had just run away from those soaring debts to the wrong kind of people. Maybe he was holed up in a squat somewhere until it all blew over, as Maaike had speculated.

The lights went out in the apartment and Piet waited to see who was going to leave. Katinka had said that the parents were obviously good for the money. She must have checked that they were well off, because she wouldn't have taken Leon's word for it. What if the heavies from Casa Blanca had come looking for him, he'd run away and they had cleared out the flat as a down-payment on his debt? The bouncers Piet had seen were big enough to lift a couple of sofas out of an apartment.

The front door opened and Leon's father came out. He had been aggressive towards Wim and Piet when Leon first went missing and refused to speak to them. But nonetheless Piet flicked his cigarette into the canal and called out, 'Mr Martens! Can I talk to you for a minute?'

The man turned abruptly. 'What do you want?'

'I'm Piet Huizen. I'm a police officer. I was here the day your son went missing.'

'Ah yes, I remember you.' He relaxed and extended his hand. 'I'm Allard. I don't think I told you my first name.'

As Piet shook Allard's hand, he could only think about Katinka's words that the parents should pay up. Why hadn't this guy cleared his son's debt? 'Have you heard from Leon?' he asked.

'Not yet,' Allard said, 'but I will soon.'

'That's good.' It struck Piet that normally he was the one comforting the parents, not the other way around.

Allard stood next to him and rested his hands on the railings of the bridge. 'Once she's taken all my money.'

All his money? Piet suddenly realised that he had misjudged these people; five thousand guilders must be as hard to find for Leon's parents as it would be for him. 'We can help,' he said, feeling more sympathy towards the father than he'd done before. 'I talked to her earlier today.' He fished out his packet of cigarettes and offered Allard one.

Allard accepted. 'It's hardly a matter for the police.'

He must think that paying back his son's debt was a

private matter. 'As long as Leon's all right,' Piet said. 'And she doesn't fleece you too much.'

Allard shrugged. 'I see you're married.' He indicated Piet's wedding ring. 'Do you have kids?'

'A daughter.'

'How old is she?'

'Almost five.'

'It's easier at that age,' Allard said. 'They don't take sides yet.'

Piet had no idea what that had to do with running up debts in a sex club. He took a drag from his cigarette.

'You said you talked to her earlier?' Allard asked.

'Yes, just before I came here.'

'I guess she had to apologise.'

Apologising had been the furthest thing from Katinka's mind.

'I'm sorry too,' Allard continued. 'Especially with all the riots, it's crazy. What was she thinking? I had no idea she was going to the police.'

Piet suddenly twigged that Allard wasn't talking about Katinka at all. His wife, Patricia, had alerted the police, but what reason did she have to apologise? 'Your wife knows where Leon is,' he said, because that was the only logical conclusion.

'I assume she told you that earlier.'

Piet thought it best to hide that he'd spoken to another woman altogether.

'And she must have insisted you keep Leon's whereabouts from me,' Allard continued. 'Look, that she cleared out the apartment is one thing, but she shouldn't have involved our son in our argument.'

Piet took a deep drag from his cigarette to buy time so that he could figure out what Leon's father was telling him. Patricia Martens had emptied her own apartment?

'Her son is all that matters to her. She couldn't have cared less about me, until I found a bit of companionship somewhere else. Then it was suddenly a problem.' Allard blew a plume of smoke into the evening air. 'I was only sleeping with the woman, a bit of fun, there was no need to make such a big deal out of it. Suddenly insisting we move; it was just crazy. I've got my job here, Leon is at university, but no, we couldn't live downstairs from Anna any more.'

Finally the pieces fitted together. 'You had an affair with Anna?'

Allard turned to him. 'Patricia didn't tell you? She loves telling everybody else.'

'Are you sure that's what happened?' Piet thought that Patricia had been far too upset that afternoon to have staged this. 'Your son has run up a huge debt at a sex club.'

'He's what?' Allard snapped.

Piet frowned. 'You didn't know?' Katinka had implied she'd talked to the parents.

'Is that why he's run away?' Allard said. 'Not because of my affair?'

'The people at the club think he legged it to avoid paying them,' Piet said. 'Haven't they chased you for the money?'

'No, this is the first I heard about it. Maybe they went to Patricia for the money, but she never told me. I haven't spoken to her in days. Shit, I thought she'd cleared me out.

Hired a removal company just to spite me, sold the lot and given Leon the money to go on holiday. I thought she wanted to steal my son from me as well as all my stuff. I'm just waiting for the divorce papers to drop.'

Piet imagined that if Hilda ever caught him cheating, she would react like that. Throw him out of the house immediately, take Lotte, take everything that mattered. It was a good thing he had no intention of cheating on her, because he could only imagine the lengths she'd go to. 'Was there a removal company?' he asked. 'Did anybody see a truck and removal men?'

'I don't know, it was a stupid idea of mine.' Allard grimaced. 'I can't believe Leon was going to sex clubs.'

'The same club all the time, as far as we can tell,' Piet said. He also remembered that Anna from upstairs was the one who'd told him that Leon was going to the Red Light District. Was it weird that she hadn't told her lover this? They probably had other things to talk about. He shook his head to get the image out of his mind. It was more likely that she hadn't seen Allard since his son disappeared, especially as that seemed to have coincided with his wife finding out about his affair. He was lying low and not sneaking up the stairs to meet with his conveniently located mistress.

None of this was his business, Piet told himself, unless it had something to do with why Leon was missing. 'Did your son ever come to you for money?' he asked.

'No,' Allard said. 'This is a total shock.'

'It's possible that Leon himself cleared out your apartment

to pay off his debt,' Piet said. 'Or that the club owner did that to recoup his money.'

Allard stubbed out his cigarette on the railing. 'I bet Patricia knows more about this. I've been avoiding her calls as I thought it was about the divorce. What a mess.' He stormed off.

'Call me,' Piet shouted after him. 'Let me know what she says.' But Allard didn't turn around.

Piet stayed behind and finished smoking his cigarette whilst looking out over the water of the Singel. Only after Allard had crossed the bridge and disappeared from sight did it strike him as strange that he'd never asked for the name of the club.

Chapter 25

Lotte drove over to Chantal Wieringa's house in Utrecht the next day. Mark had complained that she'd taken half a day's holiday for this, but she saw it as a social call. It wasn't work. Meeting Chantal, finding the third child in that photo, was about tying up a loose end. Lotte wasn't a big fan of loose ends, especially not when people stuck threats through her letter box. She had to admit that she was curious to see how that happy child had turned out.

Chantal's house was on a quiet street, and Lotte noticed a couple of net curtains twitch as the neighbours kept an eye out on who was coming to visit. When Chantal opened the door, Lotte saw that she still had the brown curls she'd had as a child. It was almost exactly the same haircut.

She came across as one of those people who were happy in their own skin. She was dressed in a bright purple T-shirt with green trousers, a combination that made Lotte blink. On Chantal it was a happy splash of colour, but Lotte would look like a clown wearing something like that. Inside, a photo of two women in wedding dresses took pride of place on the mantelpiece, flanked by photos of two teenage children.

'It was a surprise to get your email,' Chantal said. 'I called my dad and he clearly remembered working with your dad.'

'Is he well?'

'Old, of course, but still fit. He cycles everywhere. He also plays the guitar. He took that up after my mother got her diagnosis.'

'Her diagnosis?'

'Cancer. But that was almost ten years ago, and she's beaten it now. She's fine – apart from hating my father's guitar playing.' Chantal was surprisingly open with someone she'd never met before. 'She says that's the worst side effect of having been ill. He had to find something to do while she was in hospital all the time. What about your parents?'

'Both alive and kicking,' Lotte said. 'Do you remember meeting my father?'

'I have a few photos. Hold on a second, my dad made me copies some years ago.' She showed Lotte the same images that Wim van Buren had shared with her. 'I remember the photos more than the actual events, if that makes sense.'

Lotte nodded. She was only too aware of how pictures could replace memories. She put the photos on the table in front of her. 'Rick and his father were both adamant that this girl was me,' she said.

'But you weren't there, were you?'

'No, my parents were divorced by this point, and I'd lost touch with my father.'

'That's tough.'

'I later found out that he'd wanted to see me all along but my mother blocked any visits.'

'That's why you joined the police: you didn't know what

you were getting yourself into. I saw the hours my father worked and was adamant that I was going to have an office job where I worked nine to five.' She laughed. 'It didn't work out like that, of course.'

'So you're a surgeon.' Suddenly those green trousers looked like hospital scrubs. She was pretty sure they weren't. 'You work crazier hours than I do!'

'Nah, it's fine. I mainly do joint replacements. That's something that can be scheduled long beforehand.'

'Thanks for meeting me on your morning off.'

'When I talked to my father last night, neither one of us could figure out why you wanted to see me. Unless this is purely social?'

Lotte shook her head. 'Not entirely. Your father isn't in touch with the others any more, then?'

'No, he said that the last time he'd seen them was when this photo was taken. He thought that was 1981. Has something happened?'

Lotte pointed at the photo on the table. 'Teun Simmens died a month ago. Rick van Buren died two weeks ago.'

Chantal's hand flew to her mouth.

'There was nothing suspicious about their deaths,' Lotte quickly explained, 'but it made me curious about the other person in the photo, and about our fathers working together.'

Chantal picked up the photo and touched Rick and Teun's faces with a tender finger. 'I hadn't seen them in decades, not since we were kids, but their deaths are still a shock. So sad. And their poor parents.'

'I saw Wim a couple of times after his son died. It's been really hard on him.'

'I can imagine. Can I ask how they died?'

'Teun was living rough and drowned behind the building he was squatting in. He was an alcoholic and we think he just fell in. Rick died in a car accident. He crashed his vehicle whilst many times over the limit. Neither death is being treated as suspicious; Rick drank because his friend's death hit him hard.'

'I'm going to stop drinking,' Chantal said. 'My wife has been telling me for a long time that we should cut down.'

'I'm having a dry April,' Lotte said.

Chantal reached for her handbag under the chair. It was a beautiful black bag with a circle in green stones on the front. She got a packet of chewing gum out and offered it to Lotte. She caught Lotte staring at the bag. 'Do you like it?' she asked. 'Lucy is a handbag designer. This one is made from recycled plastic bottles with a motif of sea glass.'

'It's beautiful,' Lotte said honestly.

'She makes them by hand and they're all unique. She's talented. Let me give you her card. It's got her website on it.'

Lotte took it, but she couldn't afford a hand-made bag, not even if it was made out of recycled plastic and bits of glass found on the beach. But when her flat was rented out, she would have some extra money. Actually, the environmentally friendly angle of the products would appeal to Maaike, and *she* had plenty of money. She stuck the card in her pocket.

'I hope you don't think,' Chantal said with an impish grin, 'that I'm so upset that those two couldn't remember me that I killed them?'

Lotte narrowed her eyes. The change of topic took her by surprise. 'This isn't a joke,' she said.

'Sorry, sorry,' Chantal said. 'I've watched too many episodes of *Midsomer Murders*. It's my father's favourite.'

'My dad loves that too. Probably because it's so far removed from reality.'

'Ha! Our fathers should get together to watch that show.' She looked at the picture again. 'I've often wondered what they're talking about so seriously. Do you think they were friends?'

Lotte thought about her relationship with her team. Thomas and Charlie knew her well. 'Close colleagues,' she said. 'And colleagues are important.'

'They're the only ones who really know what we're going through; it's the same for me.'

'Did your dad tell you anything about that time?'

'He's tight-lipped about it. He doesn't like talking about work much anyway. For you it must be different, because you're a cop as well.'

'I don't like asking him about it,' Lotte said. 'That was when he met the woman he left my mother for.'

'Really? While he was stationed in Amsterdam for a month? Right. I'm going to call my father and ask for all the details.'

'Don't.'

'Why not? Aren't you curious? I would be.'

'I've got a decent relationship with both my parents, and I'd like to keep it that way.'

'What's she like?'

'My mother?'

'No, the other woman.'

Lotte paused. 'She's nice enough,' she said, to be fair to Maaike. 'They're still together.'

'And your mother?'

'She remarried too. But only fairly recently.'

'I see. She was the injured party.'

'My stepmother also has a lot of money and my mother had none.'

Chantal leant forward. 'This story is getting more interesting by the minute. Your father managed to hook up with a rich woman? Did he meet her as part of an investigation?'

'She rescued him from a riot.'

She laughed. 'That's priceless. I can't believe you never asked for all the details. It sounds as if it would be a great story.'

Lotte was taken aback by that. 'I'm genuinely curious: if *your* dad cheated on your mum, would you want to hear all about it?' She waited for Chantal's response with her heart racing, as if the surgeon was an oracle with all the answers.

'I see your problem. It's complicated.'

Lotte was disappointed with the non-committal response. That it was complicated was blatantly obvious. Then she gave herself a mental shake. Why was she expecting a solution to her personal issues from a woman she'd never met before today? She was relieved when that train of thought was interrupted by the ringing of her mobile. It was Thomas, who told her that he'd just got off the phone to Teun Simmens' widow. Rick van Buren had indeed arranged to talk to her but had never turned up.

The appointment had been for the day he died.

Chapter 26

17 April 1980

The next morning, at 8.30 a.m. on the dot, as if she'd waited for opening hours, Patricia Martens came storming into the police station. Piet was unlucky enough to be cleaning the floor in front of Bouma's desk. He'd have preferred not to encounter her with a broom in his hands.

'Why did you speak to my husband last night?' She pretended to be calm, but her hands were gripping her bag so tightly the tendons stood out. She blinked rapidly as if the pale morning light irritated her. 'I made it clear I wanted someone more senior working on this.'

'I bumped into him,' Piet started to defend himself, but Barry quickly came over and joined them.

'Have you heard from Leon?' he asked.

Patricia Martens was as perfectly put together as she had been on that first day. Piet didn't know much about women's clothes, but he could tell that what she was wearing was expensive. It wasn't the same outfit she'd worn when she first came to report Leon missing. Everything she'd owned had been stolen two weeks ago. Katinka had been right, they must have plenty of money if she'd bought new clothes like these. He should check with Maaike if the apartment on the Singel had sold. He reprimanded himself for not getting the phone number of someone who'd turned out to be a useful contact. That was Policing 101. Oddly enough, the voice reproaching him in his own head sounded just like Inspector van Merwe.

'I haven't heard from him at all,' she said, 'in case you think I'm hiding him. That's what my husband and that slut upstairs seem to think.'

'Leon has run up huge debts,' Piet said. 'Are you aware of that?'

'I knew that he was going to the Red Light District about a month ago. I found out he was skipping lectures.'

'How? Did the university call you?' Actually, Piet would be surprised if universities did that. When he'd skipped classes in secondary school, nobody had cared.

'Of course not. They don't keep an eye on their students. That's why they're all out protesting right now instead of studying. No, I have a copy of his lecture schedule, of course, and I was waiting for him to walk him home. When he didn't appear, I went inside and checked if the lecture had been cancelled.'

Maaike's words came to mind, how embarrassing it must be to have your mum accompany you all the time. The guy was twenty-one years old. He was an adult and his mother was checking on him. 'Do you think Leon minds? That you keep such a close eye on him?'

'I'm his mother. I protect him.'

Piet nodded. He felt the same way about Robbie. 'Was he bullied at school?'

'I'm glad you understand.' Patricia seemed to mellow a bit. 'If I hadn't been with him all the time, he would have been.'

'You were with him all the time?'

'I always watched him, especially during break time. I worked at his primary school, and when he went to secondary school, I got a job there. I needed to know what he was doing.'

'And when he went to university?'

'I applied for a job there, of course, but my qualifications aren't high enough.'

'That was the first time you weren't with him all day.' Piet understood.

'Exactly! And it showed I'd been right to stay with him so closely. Whatever my husband now says, as soon as my back was turned, Leon abused my trust, skipped lectures and spent all his money on that prostitute.'

That prostitute. 'You know where he went,' Piet suddenly realised.

'Yes, I followed him the next day.'

'You followed him?' He frowned.

'I had to take a day off work,' Patricia said. 'I waited outside until he left at around two p.m. I followed him there and back. He was clever about it. He was back at the UvA by six, exactly the time his lecture was supposed to have finished.'

Piet had a hard time imagining the extremely smartly dressed Patricia Martens in the Red Light District. 'Were you okay?' he asked.

She shrugged. 'I was pickpocketed, but that hardly

mattered. I wasn't carrying much cash. It's what you do for your child.'

'Did you report it?' Barry said.

'That I was pickpocketed?' She laughed. 'They weren't all that interested at the nearest police station. And neither were they willing to help me keep Leon away from that club. I tried to talk sense into him, and he promised me he'd stop going. I wanted to trust him, but it turned out I couldn't. Like an addict, he went back the next day. And like an addict, he got really good at hiding it.'

'Why didn't you tell us this straight away?' Piet asked.

'My son is just going through a phase,' Patricia said, 'and I didn't want anybody to know about it. I was looking after him. I'm still looking after him,' she corrected herself, 'and that's why I'm going to file a complaint at the central police station. You're not taking this seriously. You think it's all my fault, just like my husband does.'

'We're doing our best—' Barry started.

Patricia cut him off. 'Don't talk to my husband,' she said, 'and don't talk to that slut upstairs.'

'Talking to the neighbours is a key part of any police investigation,' Barry said.

'Yes, but only when it's a proper investigation and not a couple of idiots from out of town, one of whom is half drunk when he arrives. Don't think I didn't notice that.'

Wim had reeked of alcohol that day when Patricia had first reported Leon missing. Piet remembered it all too well.

'Anyway, I'm just here to tell you that. Oh, and one more thing,' Patricia said on her way out. 'I'm getting a different estate agent. Someone who doesn't let the police into our house without our knowledge. You can tell that woman she's fired,' she said to Piet, 'if you see her before we do.'

Barry raised a quizzical eyebrow, but didn't comment until after Patricia was out of sight. 'What's all this about an estate agent?'

'She rescued me when I got caught up in a clash between the riot police and the squatters last week. I bumped into her on the Singel and helped her put the light bulbs back to get the apartment ready for the sale. That's when I talked to the upstairs neighbour and found out about Leon going to those sex clubs. She's really helped me a lot,' Piet said. 'I feel bad that I've lost her this sale.'

'Ask if she wants to come for dinner with us one evening. We can expense it: it's the least we can do for such a useful informant.'

'I doubt she'll come,' Piet said. 'She's not a real fan of the police.'

But he thought he should tell her that she'd been fired. If only he had her number, because then he could have called her. Now he had no choice but to inform her in person.

Before he could put that plan into action, Desk Sergeant Bouma came storming in. 'You two,' he pointed at Barry and Piet, 'with me. Now!'

Piet was on his feet immediately and followed Bouma to a small room off the main corridor.

'Did I or did I not tell you to stay away from the Red Light District?' the sergeant barked as soon as he'd shut the door behind them. 'So why do I hear that you've gone to a sex club?'

'We're investigating—' Barry started.

'And I told you to stop investigating Leon Martens' disappearance. I explicitly told you it's all in hand.'

'Yes, but—' Piet said.

'You're interfering with an ongoing investigation. You're only seconded here; you have no idea what's going on and that's why you need to listen to me.'

'We have a lead now that we know which club he was going to,' Barry said.

'I don't give a fuck what you've got.' Bouma slammed his hand on the desk. 'There's an anti-terror operation going on in the Red Light District. That's what matters. We need to safeguard the royal guests who are arriving in just over a week. That's a priority. Not some missing student who's done a runner from his overprotective mother and is going to crawl back home in a couple of weeks.'

With a sick feeling in his stomach, Piet remembered van Merwe telling him that they were watching the IRA, who were in the building opposite Casa Blanca. He should have stayed away.

'We're not interfering with anything,' Barry challenged Bouma, 'and this missing guy has run up a large debt. His parents' apartment was stripped bare.'

'And the guy's mother has just filed an official complaint to say that one of you was clearly drunk whilst on duty. I got a call from a very angry chief inspector at the main police station.'

Piet quickly suppressed the thought that Bouma should be shouting at Wim van Buren rather than them.

Bouma stabbed a finger at Barry. 'Whatever your fucking rank or job is back at home, here you're on my turf and you do what I say.'

Chapter 27

'I was curious about why Rick van Buren went to that particular bar,' Thomas explained on their way back over to the Eastern Docklands. 'It seemed such an odd choice because it wasn't close to his house or his work. I wanted to know why he'd driven out here, so I chatted to his colleagues. They had no idea either. Then I remembered you were pissed off that he hadn't got back to you and that you'd asked him to speak to Teun Simmens' family. I looked up her address and found that Teun's widow lives right around the corner from that bar. She claims he never turned up.'

His choice of words made her stop typing a message to her father to ask if he and Maaike wanted to come over for dinner. That was probably a dumb idea anyway. 'You don't believe her?' This upcoming interview suddenly demanded her full attention.

'She probably has no reason to lie.' Thomas turned into a wide street with large houses. 'But you wanted to talk to her anyway, so it's worth a chat.'

'True.'

'I can imagine that Rick decided to have a drink to

steady his nerves. And didn't stop drinking. Or he was upset afterwards and stopped at that bar.'

Lotte could also imagine these options. She wished she hadn't asked him to talk to Teun's family.

Teun's widow, Vicky, was in her sixties with short-cut white hair. She wore a black silk shirt tucked into black trousers, showing off her trim figure. It reminded Lotte of the sommelier's outfit in the bar where Rick had been drinking. She'd matched the black clothes with a pair of green shoes with kitten heels studded with sparkling stones. She showed her visitors to the sitting room at the back of the house and introduced them to her son, Marco. He was a large guy in his early twenties, rosy-cheeked, with thin brown hair. He wore a suit and tie. Lotte wondered if he was an estate agent, but she'd probably just made that assumption because everything these days seemed property related.

Anybody involved with property would love the sitting room, which was mainly constructed out of glass to give a great view over the water. Maaike might have something to say about how a glass wall wasn't a great idea with rising temperatures, but the view was stunning. A few rowers were training on the water and startled the ducks that were drifting peacefully, minding their own business.

'What can I do for you?' Vicky asked Thomas. 'Over the phone you mentioned Rick van Buren.'

'You spoke to Rick after Teun died?' Lotte asked.

'Yes, I informed him of Teun's death. I thought I ought to do that. Then he called me a few days later but never turned up.'

'That didn't surprise you?'

She shrugged. 'Rick was always unreliable. And he was a weird guy. He and Teun got legless together all the time, but when Teun's life spiralled out of control, he was nowhere to be seen. You'd think that having a cop friend would be useful when you're going to jail. But nope.'

'He told me he was jealous of Teun,' Lotte said.

'Yes, jealous when Teun's life was great and then he went AWOL when things got rough. Not what you'd call a good friend,' Vicky said.

'My father told me that friends should stick together through thick and thin. That's why he didn't leave his mate. They met in prison and had squatted somewhere together ever since,' Marco added in an attempt to smooth out the edges of his mother's visible annoyance. His voice was higher than Lotte had expected given his size.

'His mate who he squatted with?' Thomas asked. 'Do you mean Daan?'

'That's the one,' Vicky said. 'You met him? He has some in with that guy Gerard Klaasen, who gives him a heads-up whenever a property of his is empty.'

'My father told me that they were like guards. They kept an eye on the property, called Klaasen if anything was broken or if anybody tried to rob the place. I guess that was his new job.'

'Isn't that what a building manager does?' Lotte exchanged a look with Thomas. Gerard Klaasen again. That might be worth following up on. He gave her a small nod of agreement, as if he could read her mind.

'He tried to make it sound more important than it was,' Vicky said.

'How long had Daan and Teun been living in Klaasen's properties?' Thomas asked.

'Two years, I think. It started after my father's second stint in prison. That was also when he refused to meet anybody from his past, including me,' Marco said. 'But he was still my dad. I wanted to keep in touch.'

'Rick met your father a few times at the squat on the Singel.' Lotte tried to bring the conversation back to their former colleague.

'I'm surprised,' Vicky said. 'He dropped Teun like a hot potato earlier.'

'He must have done what I did,' Marco said, 'and bumped into my father in the street. I saw Dad around town every now and then and talked to him. I didn't give him any money. Maybe I should have.'

Lotte didn't correct Marco. It was hurtful to say that Teun had met his childhood friend but kept his son at arm's length. It made her wonder if Rick had given Teun money. Not if he thought it supported his drink habit, though. More likely that he'd brought food. 'Rick had stopped drinking with help from AA,' she said.

'It's part of their process, isn't it, to apologise to the people you've hurt,' Vicky said. 'Teun was clearly on that list.'

Rick had told Lotte he should have apologised to her for messing up that case years ago.

'We wanted to talk to you about something that showed up in Teun's post-mortem,' she said.

'Was there anything other than that he drank himself to death?' Vicky's voice was harsh.

'Did he tell you he had cancer?'

She shook her head. 'I hadn't talked to him in years.'

'He didn't tell me either,' Marco said. 'I tried to stay in touch, but he wasn't interested.'

'Teun wasn't really into being a dad,' Vicky added. 'His job was much more important to him than his family, and once he no longer had a job, after prison, he filled that void with his new best friend. He had no time for his son, not even when Marco tried so hard to help him.'

Lotte looked at Marco. 'I wanted to tell you that the post-mortem showed that your father had late-stage bowel cancer. It can be hereditary.'

'Do you think he killed himself?' Vicky asked.

'There's no evidence of that,' Lotte said. 'All I know is that he must have been in a lot of pain, and I can imagine he was drinking more and more to make it go away.'

'I'm sure I'll be fine,' Marco said. 'My grandparents are still going strong even though they're both in their eighties.'

If he didn't want to take it seriously, that was his choice. She had done her duty in telling him.

'You're the girl in the photo, aren't you?' Marco suddenly sounded like a kid. 'My dad told me about it the last time I saw him.'

'That wasn't me.' Lotte had said the same thing dozens of times now. 'But yes, my father worked with your grandfather.'

'I heard so many stories,' Marco said, 'about the total mess the police were back in the days.'

'We try to do a better job now.' Thomas cut him short, ruining any opportunity Lotte might have had to ask about those stories.

'There's someone here to see you,' the desk sergeant said to Lotte a few days later. He pointed in the direction of a woman in a purple top. It was Chantal Wieringa. Lotte waved, pleased to see her. She'd liked the surgeon when they'd met a week ago. Maybe it was the connection of their fathers, but she felt she'd made a friend.

'What brings you here?' she asked with a smile.

'I'm probably imagining things,' Chantal said, 'but my wife said I should talk to you.'

The smile disappeared from Lotte's face. This wasn't a social call. She was immediately concerned.

'I haven't got much time.' Chantal checked her watch. 'I have a meeting at the VU hospital in about an hour.'

'I understand. Come on through.' Lotte led her to a quiet corner near reception that had a sofa. It was normally occupied by people coming to report burglaries and robberies, but luckily it was empty. Chantal put her handbag beside her and checked her phone.

Lotte waited until the surgeon stopped texting before she asked, 'Have you received threats?' She thought of the note she'd got through her letter box. There hadn't been any since. She'd gone to her flat a couple of times just to check. She didn't want Maaike going to the apartment to sort stuff out before her tenant moved in and accidentally finding one.

'None as such,' Chantal said, 'but I keep thinking I'm

being followed. Though when I turn around, I don't see anybody.'

'When did this start?'

'The day after you came to see me. That's why I think I'm imagining it. That I'm spooked because you told me of the possible connection between Teun and Rick's deaths. I was fine at first, but that evening I began to feel unsettled. I talked to my father and he said he couldn't imagine anything linking us.' Chantal grinned. 'He's adamant that it's all in my head. He said I shouldn't have read up about how Rick died. That poor child he hit is still in hospital.'

Lotte wished she could agree with Chantal's father, but she had a bad feeling about this.

'Also,' Chantal continued, 'I only get this feeling on the days I'm working in Amsterdam. Not in Utrecht.'

Lotte grabbed her notebook. 'Which days were you here?'

'Hold on, let me check my diary.' Chantal got her phone out. 'The day after you came, I did two back-to-back operations in Amsterdam in the afternoon and we went out with the team for a bite to eat afterwards. That was Tuesday. That evening in the restaurant was the first time I sensed it. You know, that prickling along your spine?'

'What's the name of the place?'

'My colleague suggested it and I just followed him. I'll ask him.'

'Text me the details later.'

'Sure. Then I was here yesterday as well, and today of course.'

'There isn't much we can do at this stage, not when

you haven't received any threats, but I want to look into it a bit more.'

Chantal smiled. 'Thanks at least for not thinking I'm crazy.'

Without that note through her own letter box that said *BITCH YOUR NEXT*, Lotte might have thought that. 'Be careful,' she said.

'Sure. And just in case something does happen, I'm not suicidal and I've stopped drinking.' Chantal's phone beeped. 'I have to go,' she said. 'I'll text you all the details.'

She must have asked her colleague for the name of the restaurant as soon as she got to the hospital, because the details came through half an hour later.

'What exactly are you going to do with that?' Thomas asked when she showed it to him. 'You can't just pull a restaurant's CCTV because someone feels as if she's being followed.'

Lotte was just about to go to the canteen for a coffee later that afternoon when a call was put out for assistance at a major collision on a busy main road dissecting Amsterdam. Traffic had to be diverted and the Elandsgracht police station happened to be the one closest to the pile-up's location.

'We owe traffic police one for getting us the report on Rick van Buren's accident,' Charlie said.

She was supposed to be having dinner with Mark that evening and gave him a quick call to let him know that she would probably be late, these things always took a while. Then she shrugged on the police jacket with the fluorescent stripes that Charlie handed her and together they went down to the car.

He drove them to the location, fast and competent as befitted a former traffic cop. 'It's a total mess.' He filled her in, speaking loudly over the sound of their blaring siren. 'Someone jumped, and a delivery van hit a tram and then a few other vehicles. It's selfish, don't you think, to do that? That poor driver.'

Lotte had seen it a few times: people jumping in front of a train during the height of rush hour, or from a tower block onto a crowded school playground. 'It's about being noticed,' she said, 'in their last moments.'

'If they want to be noticed, they should just live-stream their suicide for the sick people who want to watch that kind of stuff and not make everybody else's life hell.'

Hell was a strong word, but as they turned the corner, she saw utter carnage. A red delivery van blocked the tramline, and three vehicles were concertinaed behind it. The white and blue tram was stationed a little distance back. The tram driver must have been far enough away that he had almost come to a stop before hitting the van and had reversed away from the site. An empty ambulance stood next to the van. There was no sign of the person who'd caused the accident. They must have been carried off already. Mayhem ruled and Charlie had no choice but to park up on the cycle path, which drew curses from two girls cycling past even though he still had the siren going.

Lotte got out. She was about to start directing the traffic and help the stream of cars go around the pile-up when she saw a handbag abandoned in the gutter.

It was a black bag made from recycled plastic. There was a circular pattern on the front made out of green sea glass. She wanted to believe that there was more than one of those, but Chantal had told her that all the bags were unique. This one had been custom-made just for her. She kneeled by the bag, dusted it off and picked it up. She felt her heart beat fast, the thrumming rising to her mouth and up into her eyelids as disbelief and grief combined. Then she rose and strode towards the red van.

'She came out of nowhere,' the driver was saying. He was a middle-aged man with the big gut of someone who made a living sitting in a vehicle all day. He rubbed his hands over his eyes as if that could make the image of the woman disappear. 'I'm okay, I'm okay.' He waved away the paramedic who was checking him over. He was lucky to have got away scot-free.

He was being watched by a traffic cop Lotte recognised. Arnaud Groot, who'd worked with Charlie, greeted her with a nod. She didn't particularly like him, because he'd once said that he thought Charlie was as thick as a plank of wood, but she went over to talk to him.

'How's the victim?' She squished up the handles of the black handbag.

Arnaud shot the driver a quick glance, then steered Lotte away, out of earshot. 'DOA. We just got the call,' he whispered. 'The poor guy's in bits. She jumped in front of his van.'

Chantal wouldn't have jumped, Lotte immediately thought, and even though she was holding Chantal's bag in her hands, hope flared inside her. Only three hours ago, the woman had declared she wasn't suicidal. Or had that been a weird thing to say and purely to draw attention from what she was about to do? 'Was there a dashcam?'

'Yeah, I've got the van's footage here,' Arnaud said. He held out his iPad.

Lotte watched the clip. The woman was no more than a flash bouncing off the right-hand side of the vehicle, but she saw a hint of curly dark hair.

'Hold on a second,' he said, 'it's much clearer from this one.'

She didn't want to have a clearer view of someone she liked getting killed.

'This is the footage from the vehicle behind the van.' He swapped the van's SIM card for another one.

Lotte wanted to stop him but couldn't tear her eyes away from the screen. She hugged the bag to her chest. It was depressingly easy to identify Chantal in this recording. Any hope Lotte had was stripped away. For a second, the surgeon was clear to see as she waited on the edge of the busy pavement amongst a crowd of people. Then she suddenly flew into the road with her upper body forward, striking the van head-first and at speed. Only after the impact did the driver hit the brake and swerve left.

Chantal had never stood a chance.

And to be fair, neither had the van driver.

Then a thought came to Lotte. Head-first, not feet-first. 'Let me see that again,' she said, and swallowed down her nausea. 'Look at the angle: she was pushed.'

Half an hour later, she stood on the pavement with Charlie and watched the tow truck drag the delivery van off the tramline. 'She came to me this morning and told me that she thought she was being followed.' At least Lotte had taken that seriously. She knew exactly which restaurant Chantal had been at, and there was now a good reason to pull the CCTV from that place.

'We've looked at the clearest footage six times now,' Charlie said, 'and it's impossible to identify who was behind her. Either way, the delivery driver isn't to blame. He couldn't have stopped.'

Lotte scanned the street for security cameras. There was a camera on the traffic light, but that was too far down the street. 'Have you got the footage from the tram?'

'The tram arrived after the crash had already happened,' Charlie said.

'Sure,' Lotte said, 'but we're no longer investigating an accident. This is now a murder inquiry, and I think the same person killed two people before Chantal.'

'Seriously?' Arnaud said. 'Someone has pushed more people?'

'Not pushed.' She thought about Teun Simmens, who'd drowned, and Rick van Buren, who'd crashed his car into a wall. 'Anyway, two earlier deaths are linked to this one, and I suspect he isn't done yet.'

'He'll kill someone else?' Arnaud said.

'He'll try.' Lotte grimaced. 'I think he'll try to kill me.'

Chapter 28

17 April 1980

Armed with a bunch of flowers and a bottle of wine, Piet went to Maaike's apartment that evening. He felt terrible that he'd caused her to lose a deal and wondered how he could make it up to her. After Bouma's tirade, Barry had just glared at the man. When Wim and Eelke had asked him what it was all about, he'd said it was nothing. Piet thought it best to follow his lead. He didn't even dare ask him what exactly his rank and job were. Instead of burning with questions he shouldn't ask at the team dinner, he'd come here, to Maaike. Apologising was the lesser of two evils, he told himself.

Before he could even ring the bell, however, the door swung open and an elderly lady with a purple rinse stared at him.

'How are you doing?' she asked, as if he was a long-lost acquaintance.

'I'm fine,' Piet said. He wanted to skirt around her, but she made that impossible.

'Are those for Maaike? You should thank me too. I'm the one who noticed you in our doorway.'

'You are?' Piet adjusted his assumptions about her. 'Thank

you so much,' he said. He held out the flowers and the wine. 'You can have one of them,' he said. 'You choose.'

'Don't be daft,' she said. 'Give them both to her upstairs. She's a good girl.'

'I'm grateful to you for rescuing me,' he said with a mock bow.

'Have you got any cigarettes? I'd prefer those over flowers.'

He put the bottle of wine on the ground and dug in his pocket for his tobacco and Rizla papers. 'This is all I have left. Just roll-ups. I hope you understand that this is a greater sacrifice than the flowers.'

She laughed raucously and reached for the offering. 'You should stop, smoking is bad for you.'

'For me? What about you, then?'

'I'm old. It doesn't matter any more. You still have some living to do, I reckon. Ah look, there she is.' She gestured with her head to where Maaike was walking down the street. 'I've kept our new friend company for you,' she called.

'Did Betsy steal your fags?' Maaike said. 'She always does that.'

'She did it for my own good,' Piet said, 'so that I'll stop.'

Betsy laughed, shook the tobacco in his direction and retreated inside her ground-floor flat.

'Come in,' Maaike said. 'You should have called.'

'You should give me your number.'

'I'm in the phone book,' she said as they went up the stairs.

'I don't know your last name.'

'It's Glimmer. At least you remembered the address.'

'I've got a good memory for locations. It's a useful skill for a police officer.'

'And for an estate agent.' She unlocked her front door and let him in. 'Grab a seat,' she said. 'You know where everything is.'

'I'm really sorry,' he said. 'I've come to apologise.' He tried to push the flowers and the bottle of wine in her hands.

'For what?' She held her hands by her sides as if reluctant to take his gifts before she knew why he was saying sorry.

'Patricia Martens told me she was going to fire you as her estate agent.'

'Oh, is that all?' Maaike took the flowers with an expression of total uninterest. She filled a vase with water and plunked them in. 'They're pretty,' she said. 'I'll do them properly later.' She took the wine and checked the label with raised eyebrows.

'I know nothing about wine,' he said.

'Do you want a glass?'

'Sure,' he said, and then was mortified when she reached for another bottle in the cupboard and opened that. 'It wasn't the bottle I found in my desk,' he said.

'In your desk?'

'Yes,' he said. 'When I got to the police station, I found a bottle of cognac in the drawer.'

'You've got to love that the police leave evidence of their corruption behind so blatantly.' She poured the red wine. 'You bought this in a shop, right?' She pointed at the bottle he'd brought.

'Yes,' he said. He was embarrassed to admit that he'd asked for something a woman would like. He had a sneaky suspicion that Maaike wouldn't be too impressed with that. 'I feel responsible for you losing that sale.'

'You do?' Maaike settled herself in the comfortable chair near the window. 'Why are you responsible?'

'Patricia got annoyed because you let me in their apartment without her knowledge.'

'If anybody's responsible, it's her, not you.'

'But if it hadn't been for me—'

'Plus, I found them a buyer this morning and we verbally agreed on the sale.' She brought the glass of wine to her lips with obvious delight. 'The buyer offered the asking price, so if those people think they can worm their way out of paying me my commission, they've got another think coming.'

He felt weird being so easily stripped of the guilt he'd laden himself with. 'What time was this?'

'I called Allard around ten this morning.'

'You talked to Allard, not Patricia?'

'Oh yes, he's much easier to deal with. He didn't mention firing me.'

'You don't seem upset.'

'I've got the sale plus some flowers and free wine. I've done well out of it.' She smiled at him. 'Sorry, I was messing with you. Allard Martens called me an hour ago and apologised for what his wife had said, if I'd already heard. Which I hadn't at that point. He said she was understandably upset about their son's disappearance and had no real intention of cutting me out.'

He tasted the wine. It was surprisingly pleasant. He had never seen himself as a wine drinker, but this was much better than what he'd had in the past. Not as sweet. 'I don't think I've ever liked wine before.' He swirled the red alcohol in his glass and wondered if that made him look sophisticated. Probably not.

'Buy more expensive stuff,' she said. 'It makes all the difference.'

'You must think I'm really stupid.'

'No, why?'

'I don't know anything about wine, and I came here because I thought I'd made you lose a deal.'

'Not knowing anything about wine doesn't make you stupid.'

'It's okay,' he said. 'Everybody thinks it.'

'How interesting,' Maaike said.

'What is?'

'Your choice of words. You didn't say "I'm not all that smart" or something like that. You said "everybody thinks it". That means *you* don't think it.'

'I'm included in everybody.' He tried to swipe her scrutiny away.

'No, you were really saying that everybody thinks it. But I know better.'

It was odd how a lump formed in his throat at her words. He clearly wasn't going to get all emotional here, so he took a gulp of wine.

'With wine,' Maaike went on, 'you get what you pay for. Pay more money, you get wine of a higher quality. There's a huge difference between something cheap and nasty and a bottle that's mid-price and pretty decent.'

Piet was happy enough to follow her change in topic. 'I have no money,' he said. 'My wife would kill me if I spent it all on wine.'

'I'm not saying spend a lot. Buy less wine but better quality. Better to have one glass of decent stuff than two glasses of cheap plonk. Trust me.'

'I don't think I'll turn into a wine connoisseur any time soon. My wife wants to have another baby.'

Maaike gave him that look again that said she was weighing him up.

He thought about his choice of words. 'That's her right,' he said, 'to want a baby.'

'I didn't say anything.'

'You were looking at me as if I'd said something revealing.'

'See?' she said. 'You're not stupid at all.'

'Did Allard mention Leon?' He changed the subject. 'Has he come home?'

'No,' Maaike said. 'He's still missing. Why did you think he'd come home?'

He shrugged. 'His father didn't know that he'd run up a large debt. I just assumed he'd gone to pay it off last night.'

They stopped talking about Leon and finished their wine with companiable chat about the weather and the upcoming coronation. Without mentioning riots and squatters.

But the student didn't leave his mind, and as Piet walked back to the hotel, he couldn't stop thinking about him. The parents had money; even Piet with his limited knowledge of fashion and real estate knew that. They could write a cheque for Leon's debts. Patricia hadn't told her husband what was going on because she tried to keep their son's image clean, but once Allard had found out last night, nothing should have stopped him from paying up. This was the life of their only child they were talking about. If you had the cash, you paid.

As he strolled along the canal in the evening light, Piet thought that maybe the family *had* paid. But what if the club had demanded more cash than Leon owed? The quickest way to his hotel from Maaike's place obviously wasn't via the Red Light District, but still he found himself heading there. He went on a hunch, which was weird because he had never seen himself as the kind of police officer who acted on hunches. He was much more the guy who made sure people kept their windows shut so that burglars couldn't get in; or who broke up fights and subsequently brokered peace between those involved. That was what two glasses of wine did to you, he thought. It made you follow your instincts. Or maybe it was someone telling him he wasn't stupid.

He was back in the Red Light District against Bouma's instructions and walking the dirty cobbles of this square kilometre of misery again. Hadn't van Merwe told him on the first day that he looked like a tourist, and wasn't this one of the reasons tourists came to Amsterdam? He had a perfect disguise.

Already the users, dealers and prostitutes were less shocking than they had been the first time he'd seen them. He took up a position in the one doorway that wasn't occupied by someone shooting up and watched Casa Blanca. He cursed the fact that Maaike's downstairs neighbour had taken his tobacco, because he could really do with a cigarette right now. It would round off his disguise as a potential punter perfectly. Someone who was working up the courage to go into a sex club or a brothel would have a smoke, he thought.

The windows of the house opposite Casa Blanca were dark. He wondered if those IRA terrorists were aware that the police were watching them from the club and were taking extra precautions. The street wasn't wide enough for two cars to pass each other, and it was easy to see from that house into the club. This wasn't his area of expertise, but he wondered at the choice of location for the stake-out. It seemed too close.

Just then the bouncers opened the door to Casa Blanca to let a punter leave. The man who came out was Inspector van Merwe. Another man followed him. He was wearing a shirt with the top buttons undone to display a heavy gold chain. He handed van Merwe a thick envelope, which the inspector tucked into the inside pocket of his jacket. The man held out his hand and Piet's boss shook it.

Piet's stomach somersaulted, because he didn't doubt for a second what he was witnessing. There was no way his boss was here for a stake-out. He probably hadn't been here for that reason last time either. The man with the gold chain must be the pimp, the owner of Casa Blanca.

He pushed himself as far into the doorway as possible and prayed that van Merwe would turn left so that he wouldn't see him. Unfortunately, he turned right and clocked Piet watching him. This time he didn't wink. He flinched. He halted his stride as if he was going to stop and brazen it out, but then changed his mind, turned and quickly left. Piet was frozen to the spot, unsure how to act. More than ever, he was dying for a cigarette. He wondered what the hell he was going to do now. Before he'd come up with any kind of solution, the door opened again and Katinka came out. She wore a thick dressing gown over a skimpy outfit. She took a packet of menthol cigarettes out of her pocket. Then she spotted him in his doorway and came over.

'Have you got a light?' she asked.

Maaike's downstairs neighbour at least had left him that. Piet fished his lighter out of his coat before he could question whether this was a good idea. He lit the cigarette she held out.

'That guy is so disgusting,' she said. 'And he refuses to use a rubber. I've got half a mind to tell him I've got a disease, but then he'll revoke my licence for a month.' She took a deep drag. 'It's probably worth it.'

Tomorrow was Friday and his boss was going to give him a lift back to Alkmaar. The idea of sitting in a car with the man both scared and revolted him. Also, when this was all over and the coronation had taken place, they would both be back in Alkmaar and van Merwe would have the desk next to Piet's again. They had to continue to work together.

Piet was screwed.

Chapter 29

Lotte stuck the photo of the three children and the four fathers onto the whiteboard at the police station. 'Teun Simmens, Rick van Buren, Chantal Wieringa. They all died accidental deaths. Which now don't seem like accidents any more.'

'Did Chantal get any death threats?' Thomas asked.

'No. I asked her specifically and she didn't.'

'But *you* got one. That's an important point, don't you think?'

'That I should be dead but I'm not?' Lotte pointed at the photo. 'But that isn't me.'

'So the murderer thought it was you originally, sent you a threat and then found out they were wrong? That links the murder directly to the photo.'

'I know it's weird, but what else could it be?'

Thomas shook his head. 'If we go with that, it means the killer was aware of the photo, they were aware of the assumption that this was you, and then they became aware that it was actually Eelke Wieringa's daughter. Who did you talk to about this?'

Lotte thought. 'My father, Wim and Amy van Buren. And Chantal herself, of course.'

'What about Teun Simmens' family?'

'Good point. I told them it wasn't me, remember? When we met with Vicky and Marco to ask if Rick had been there.'

'Chantal died three days after you told them that. Has anything happened to you since Rick's death? You didn't get pushed, suddenly tripped, had your drink spiked or anything like that?'

'Nothing. There's been nothing.'

'Nobody's followed you?'

'Not that I'm aware of. I think I would have known. Chantal did.'

'Right, she sent you the list of places where she'd been, didn't she?'

'Yes.' Lotte got her phone out. In a way, it was a good thing she'd received that threat. Without *BITCH YOUR NEXT*, she wouldn't have taken Chantal's statement that she was being followed so seriously. Might even have thought that her death was a tragic accident too. But she had heard her say that she definitely wasn't suicidal. 'They went to Café Koetsier last Tuesday from seven p.m. Actually, that's before we went to see Vicky and Marco.'

'Interesting. But we only have Vicky's word for it that Rick van Buren didn't meet with her. Well, that's as good a place to start as any,' Thomas said. 'Come on, Charlie, let's go.'

'You and Charlie?' Lotte asked. 'What about me?'

'You're number four in this sequence. You're staying here.'

As if she was going to stay home and be wrapped in cotton wool. 'Don't be an idiot,' she said. She pushed the thought to the back of her head that both her father and Mark would disagree with her. They would say that Thomas was being sensible. 'I'm coming with you.'

'Fine,' Thomas said, 'if you insist. But if you get killed, don't forget I told you so.'

She rolled her eyes at his poor attempt at a joke. 'Charlie,' she said, 'you talk to Arnaud Groot again, and look at Rick van Buren's accident report. See if you can find out his whereabouts before he started drinking. He was going to meet Vicky and then changed his mind. Or maybe he did meet with her.'

'It's going to be hard,' Charlie said, 'because it's a couple of weeks ago now. But I'll see what I can find on the traffic cameras.' He was good at traffic footage.

Lotte put her coat on.

'At least wear a bulletproof vest?' Thomas suggested.

'Nobody's been shot! There's no sign that this person has a gun. I'll stay well away from water, cars and pavement edges. And I've stopped drinking.'

'Not funny,' he said.

'Trust me, I know. But I can't sit here and do nothing.'

'I'm not saying you should do nothing. I'm saying you should take sensible precautions. Don't be an easy target.'

She didn't wear the vest, but she did feel better after she'd strapped the holster with her gun around her waist. She also knew that Thomas was watching her back.

Café Koetsier was a large establishment along the Singel opposite a bridge. They were just preparing for the dinner crowd when Lotte and Thomas arrived. They still had the footage of last Tuesday and the proprietor found it for them. From the camera behind the bar, Chantal's table was barely visible. She was only caught on film a few times. But they weren't looking for what Chantal had been doing that evening. Lotte thought it was actually easier to watch the screen whilst the surgeon herself wasn't in the picture. Their main aim was to see if there was anybody who was obviously watching her. Anybody they recognised.

Thomas spotted it before she did. 'Oh fuck,' he said out loud.

Then Lotte saw it too. On the footage, someone had come into the café and was looking around before going up to the bar. Even though he didn't stay long, he was easy to identify; there was no mistaking the long tied-back white hair and the pencil moustache. He was wearing the same Arafat scarf he'd had on when they'd spoken to him after Teun Simmens' death. The death he had called in.

It was Gerard Klaasen.

Chapter 30

18 April 1980

Friday came too soon and worry burrowed in the pit of Piet's stomach. Especially after Inspector van Merwe had called in the morning to confirm the exact time he was going to drive him home. The boss's dislike of Piet was audible in every syllable he uttered and it made the call feel like a threat. Piet was being invited to get beaten up and still couldn't refuse. He worked on autopilot all day and hated that he was busy because it made the time go fast. As he crossed Amsterdam with his suitcase, he thought he should turn and take the train back to Alkmaar instead. He didn't do it. He kept going.

When he got into the car with his boss, it was like being with someone who had a heavy cold: you were inevitably infected by their proximity. But refusing the ride was impossible. Van Merwe stayed pointedly silent as they drove through Amsterdam's streets, and the silence grew so thick it filled Piet's lungs with every in-breath.

'I don't know what you think you saw.' The boss started talking as soon as they hit the motorway, as if someone could have overheard them while they were in the city. 'But you have no idea what was going on last night. It's all part of that terrorist operation.'

Piet huffed involuntarily. He heard the disbelief in the sound he made. How stupid did the boss think he was?

'It's highly confidential, so it's important you keep silent about it.'

Especially with your wife, he thought.

'We're only in Amsterdam for another week and then we're back in Alkmaar.'

Then Piet would be back to sitting next to his boss, who now revolted him.

'Listen,' van Merwe said without taking his eyes off the road. 'If you keep quiet and don't screw up our operation, I can help you with that promotion. You must be worried about the exam, I know studying isn't your thing, but I can give you the questions in advance.'

Piet wanted to open his mouth and shout that he wasn't an idiot. That he didn't need his boss to spoon-feed him answers and that he didn't for a second buy the story that taking a bribe was part of an operation. This wasn't just a hunch; he knew what he'd seen.

But he couldn't say any of that, so he looked out of the window and watched the fields go by.

Van Merwe didn't feel the need to say anything else all the way back to Alkmaar and gave a little demonstration of how easy it was to keep silent. He pulled up outside Piet's house and waited for his subordinate to get his suitcase out of the boot. Then he pushed the window down and leaned his elbow on the door. 'We'll talk more on Sunday,' he said, making the ride back to Amsterdam sound like a dangerous expedition. 'Don't mess this up for yourself. Don't destroy your career.'

As the boss drove away, Piet's front door opened and Hilda and Lotte came rushing towards him. Someone was missing from his weekly welcoming committee. 'Where's Robbie?' he asked. Even inside the house, he couldn't see his brother anywhere. Had he kept Robbie too close all his life, like Patricia Martens had done with Leon, and now he'd run away too? For a second, he had the weird sense that failing to find the student was the reason Robbie wasn't here right now. 'Where's Robbie?' he repeated.

'He's out with his friends,' Hilda said.

Piet put his suitcase down and pulled a hand through his hair. Normally he would have wondered out loud whose money Robbie was spending, but now he just felt relieved.

'Come, sit down. Unpack later,' Hilda said. 'Let's have dinner.'

The smell of roast chicken wafted from the kitchen. He wanted to shower first, because he was contaminating the house with the nearness to van Merwe still clinging to him, but Hilda steered him towards the table. He knew better than to upset his wife, who'd gone to all the trouble of cooking. He sat down and she put the chicken in front of him.

The house was quiet and dull, as if arguing with Robbie, being frustrated with him, was the entertainment he provided for all of them, and Piet was glad when he could use his electric carving knife, which buzzed as easily through silence as through chicken. He divided the meat between their plates, giving Lotte a bit less than himself and Hilda.

His daughter finished hers quickly and then relayed to her

parents exactly what had happened in the last episode of her favourite TV series. Piet had never been so happy to hear the minutiae of the problems that bears had on their boat.

After dinner, Lotte sat down to watch the latest episode, where more problems arose but were also resolved in the ten-minute duration of the show. If only real life was like that. Afterwards, Hilda got her to go to bed and Piet read her a story. His wife watched him from the doorway and he noticed she had a notebook in her hand. He read slowly and did all the voices. When Lotte wanted to hear it again, he humoured her for once. Then his daughter's eyes closed and he followed his wife down the stairs.

She went into the kitchen and opened two bottles of Heineken, pouring them into the matching branded glasses. 'It's a special occasion,' she said, and handed him his.

He gulped half of it down in one, then switched the radio on. The station played 'Una Paloma Blanca'. He'd heard this exact music that first time he'd seen van Merwe in the sex club, but even this song was better than silence. He remembered that the girl he'd talked to had told him that Katinka was busy. The boss hadn't been there to shadow and monitor IRA terrorists that time either.

He'd been such an idiot, Piet thought, to have believed that obvious lie.

Hilda took a dainty sip of beer before she put the glass down and got her notebook out.

'Van Merwe said he'd help me with my promotion,' Piet said before she could run the numbers by him.

She dropped the notebook on the floor and put both hands in front of her mouth in silent excitement. 'Oh my

God, Piet,' she said, with a clear effort to keep her voice down and not wake Lotte. 'That's such great news.'

He reached for her hand. 'We need to talk about this,' he said. 'I don't know if I should take it.'

She nodded so vigorously that her curls went flying. 'Of course you'll take it.'

He should have told her the story the other way round. He should have begun with seeing his boss at the club, not with the promotion she wanted so badly. He took her other hand. 'Listen to me,' he said.

Her smile faded when she realised that he was serious. 'Okay,' she said, 'tell me.'

'Van Merwe is taking backhanders,' he said, 'and I saw it.'

'Your boss? You must be wrong.' She tried to pull her hands back, but he held them in place. 'He's not that kind of person.'

'I saw it, Hilda. He was outside a sex club and received an envelope full of cash from the guy running the place.'

'What were you doing there?'

'I was working.'

'How do you know he wasn't?'

'That's what I thought the first time. That he was there for a stake-out. But when I saw him the second time, it was clear he wasn't.'

'And he saw you too?'

'Yes. On the drive back this evening, he implied that if I keep my mouth shut, I'll get that promotion.'

'I see,' she said. 'Do you have to do anything else?'

'Like what?'

'I don't know. Be part of whatever he's up to.'

'I don't think so. I just need to not tell anybody what I've seen.'

'That's not too bad,' Hilda said. 'If he wanted you to do something illegal, that would be different. Just not talking, that's okay, isn't it? Plus, nobody would believe you anyway.'

He stared at his wife. He could tell that, as she was talking, she was rationalising it for herself. But this wasn't the response he'd expected. This wasn't the response he'd wanted.

'There's nothing wrong with keeping quiet.' She nodded to herself as if she finally had everything sorted out in her head. 'You need that promotion.'

'I don't know.'

'Piet, what are you going to do otherwise? Rat him out?'

He didn't think he could do that. He also realised he didn't have any evidence. 'I could do nothing,' he said, but even to himself he sounded lame.

'Exactly. Do nothing. That's all he's asking for.' The smile came back onto her face. 'If you're going to do nothing anyway, you might as well get promoted for it, and then all our problems will be solved.' She nestled next to him, and rested her head on his shoulder. 'Isn't this perfect?' she murmured with her lips against his neck.

He downed two more beers in quick succession to give himself an excuse to go to bed, immediately turn on his side and pretend to fall asleep.

Pretend, because he couldn't sleep at all. He felt like stupid Piet again. There was something wrong with what Hilda had said, but he couldn't put his finger on what it was. There had to be a flaw in her argument, because this felt all wrong.

Beside him, Hilda began to snore softly.

He shouldn't have drunk those beers so quickly, because now he needed the bathroom again. He removed her arm from around his waist, careful not to wake her, and slid out of bed. From the hallway, he threw a glance into his daughter's bedroom and saw her peacefully asleep. He crept down the stairs, avoiding that third step that always creaked.

He took a leak, but the unease in the pit of his stomach remained. In his pyjamas, he sat on the sofa, with only a small light to pierce through the darkness and enveloped by the silence of the house. He looked at the clock. It was only just after eleven. The long night stretched out ahead of him. Maybe he should do what Hilda did and write things down. That might sort out his thoughts.

He went to the coat rack and got his notebook out of his inside pocket. He opened it to an empty page and grabbed his pen, but no words came out. Writing wasn't going to do the trick; he needed to talk to somebody. Had Robbie been here, they could have tried to work it out in whispered tones, his brother functioning as much as a sounding board as anything else. He should just wait up for him to get home. No, he thought, he couldn't tell his brother what Hilda had said, because it would only cause another argument between the two of them. He had few friends. Barry Simmens came to mind, but he shouldn't talk about this with a colleague. His eye fell on the open notebook. Maaike had given him her phone number the other day. She was enough of an outsider, because after his stint in Amsterdam he would never see her again. This was perfect.

He picked up the phone by the side of the sofa and dialled her number. Just when he thought it was crazy to call her this late, she picked up. He heard noises in the background; maybe the TV, or maybe she had guests over.

'It's me, Piet,' he said. 'Can I run something by you?'

'Did something happen?' she asked. 'Is it a police matter? Is it urgent?'

'I'm sorry, it's not urgent and it's only partially a police matter,' he said. 'But I need to talk to someone. Is that okay?'

'Are you in Amsterdam?' The background noise was silenced. Either she'd switched off the telly or she'd shushed her guests.

'No, I'm at home in Alkmaar. I'm back in Amsterdam on Sunday.'

'Can it wait? Come and talk to me when you're back in the city.'

He was clearly disturbing her in the middle of something. 'Yes, it can wait,' he said reluctantly. 'I'll be there around six or so,' he said. 'I need to drop my stuff in the hotel first.'

'Fine,' she said. 'Just pop round.'

'Thanks, Maaike,' he said. 'I'll see you Sunday evening.'

'Go to sleep, copper,' she said, and disconnected the call.

He smiled and put the phone down. Now that he had someone to discuss this with, the unease in his stomach settled a little. Or maybe the alcohol was going down after all.

He got up and saw Hilda standing in the doorway.

'Just who the hell were you talking to?' she hissed.

Chapter 31

'I've been reading up on it and this was the exact spot where the police were first violent with the squatters. It was all happy-clappy up to that point,' Thomas said as he parked his car outside the former squatter's home. 'The Kinkerbuurt was cleared by riot police in 1978, two years before the coronation riots.'

'What's your point?' Adrenaline raced through Lotte's veins and she wasn't in the mood for a history lesson.

'It's interesting that Gerard Klaasen picked this place to live. All the houses were pulled down and this area was newly built. For someone who says that police are still triggering for him, to have bought a flat exactly here says something about him.'

'That he's now part of the establishment?'

'Or that, even after the redevelopment, ordinary people should live here.'

'The man's a millionaire now, Thomas, hardly ordinary.'

He paused with his hand on the car door. 'We can go back,' he said, as if he'd picked up on her nerves. 'I told you we should just pull him in for questioning.'

'For what? He went to a restaurant on a Tuesday night,

that's all we got. It's not a crime. With someone like Klaasen, with his background of police violence against him, we should be open-minded.'

'Not if that endangers your life.'

Lotte sensed his frustration, but she couldn't get the image of Klaasen on that barricade, being mowed down by a tank, out of her head. 'If Klaasen was the murderer, he'd have killed me instead of Chantal. He would kill a cop before a surgeon.'

'Maybe that was his plan but something went wrong,' Thomas said.

She got out of the car. 'I know he was in the restaurant,' she said, 'but I can't see him for it. I don't understand why he would have killed Chantal. Teun, sure, we know he was often aggressive whilst drunk. They could have got in a fight; Klaasen could have pushed him in or held him under. Rick could have been an accident too, but Chantal . . . It makes no sense.'

'I see your point, trust me, but that doesn't mean you should deliberately put yourself in harm's way.'

She went up the stairs to Klaasen's flat first, but when she reached the top, Thomas pushed past her to ring the doorbell. He was putting himself between her and the door, and even though she understood his intentions, it was annoying.

Gerard Klaasen opened the door with greater reluctance than last time. Lotte felt protected by the weight of her gun sitting heavily on her hip but still was relieved when the look on Klaasen's face was more one of worry than aggression. He didn't try to run at the sight of the two police detectives on his doorstep. Speaking to him in his house was the right thing to do.

She followed him into the flat and down a corridor, checking the rooms on either side to ensure there was nobody there who could jump her. Her heart was beating way too fast for what was really a conversation with an elderly man. Thomas scooted past her again and placed himself between her and Klaasen. That he felt he needed to guard her only added to her anxiety.

'Take a seat,' Klaasen said. He plopped down on the large sofa. 'I guess you've found him?' He ran a hand over his head and down the thin white ponytail. He looked tired.

Lotte frowned. 'Found who?'

Klaasen propped himself up. 'Isn't that why you're here?'

'We're here,' Thomas said, 'to ask you about Chantal Wieringa.'

'Who's that?' Klaasen looked confused. Lotte had interviewed a lot of people and she didn't think he was pretending.

'Chantal Wieringa, who was killed yesterday,' she said. 'A surgeon.'

'I've never heard that name,' Klaasen said.

Lotte got a picture of Chantal out and put it on the table in front of the former squatter. 'This woman.'

He shook his head. 'I've never seen her before.'

'Where were you yesterday afternoon?' Lotte asked.

'I was at the building on the Singel late afternoon. We've got people interested in renting the space and I joined the building manager to show them around.'

'What time was this?'

'We met at four and I spent an hour or so there.'

Lotte and Thomas exchanged a glance. That was the exactly the time that Chantal was pushed into the road.

'And there are people who can vouch for that, I guess?'

'Yes,' Klaasen said. 'Julie was there, and I can give you the names of my clients, even though I'd prefer you to check with her first. Being called by the police puts off even the keenest prospective tenant.' His tone was sarcastic.

'We'll do that,' Thomas said. 'But you were following Chantal on Tuesday night.'

'Following her? I have no idea what you're talking about.' His tone was definitely more defensive.

'What were you doing on Tuesday night?' Lotte asked.

'Nothing much.'

'You went to Café Koetsier.'

'Is that a crime? Why are you keeping tabs on where I was? I thought we were allowed to go wherever we wanted.'

'Chantal Wieringa was there at the same time. She was with a group of colleagues,' Lotte said. 'She told me she was being watched by someone. And two days later she was killed.'

Klaasen looked again at the photo on the table. This time he seemed to study it more closely. Then he looked at Lotte again. 'I'm sorry, I don't remember seeing her.'

'You didn't stay in the café long.'

'Am I suspected of anything? Because if I am, I want my lawyer.'

'Of course, it's your right to contact your lawyer, Mr Klaasen, and we will follow up on your alibi for the time of

Chantal's death,' Lotte said. 'But we're here because there's a link between Teun Simmens and Chantal Wieringa.'

'There is?'

Lotte got her phone out and showed Klaasen the photo of the three children together. 'Teun Simmens, Rick van Buren and Chantal Wieringa.'

'Really?' he said. 'I thought that was you.'

Lotte's heartbeat raced. 'You've seen this photo before?'

'Yes, Teun showed it to me. You say this is Chantal, but it had your name on the back.'

'My name?'

'Well, the names of the policemen and the names of the three children. Your name.'

'When did he show you the photo?'

'When Daan complained about Teun's mate coming to see him so often.'

'You mean Rick van Buren?'

'That's right. I don't like the police, Daan doesn't like the police, so Teun had some explaining to do. Teun said we were overreacting and that they were childhood friends. Rick had given him this photo.'

'Rick had given him the photo with our names written on the back?'

'That's right.'

'And then Teun showed that photo to you and Daan?'

'Yes.'

Lotte recalled that Teun's wife had told her that Daan had some in with Gerard Klaasen. 'What's Daan's surname?'

Klaasen narrowed his eyes. 'Why are you asking about him?'

'Daan and Teun were friends,' she said. 'That's what Teun's widow told me.'

'They met in prison,' Klaasen said. 'And I helped them with a place to live every now and then.'

'And his surname?' she asked again. She would pull his records and see what he'd been in for.

'Ter Aar.'

'Where *is* Daan?'

'Gemma called me on Tuesday because she hadn't seen him in two weeks.' He rubbed his hand over his head. 'That's why I was in Café Koetsier. I was looking for him.'

'Why would *you* know where he was?'

'Because I know his mother.'

'Was she also in the squatter movement?'

'No, not really. I lived in a squat opposite the place she worked.'

'What's her name?'

Klaasen hesitated.

'You can tell me, or I can look it up in five minutes back at the police station,' Lotte said.

'Katinka. Katinka Fledder.'

'Was this during the 1980 riots?' Lotte wondered if this was what linked Klaasen to the policemen in the photo.

'Yes. I was there for almost a year, but it wasn't a good place. It was right in the middle of the Red Light District and there were too many junkies around. Lots of nasty stuff was happening and the police didn't do shit.'

Chapter 32

20 April 1980

'I shouldn't have called you so late on Friday,' Piet said. He probably shouldn't have called her at all, but in Maaike's relaxed flat, he could already feel his tension starting to unwind. Tension caused by an extremely fraught weekend. Hilda had given him the silent treatment for a morning while he tried to explain that she had the wrong idea, that he'd never cheated on her and that Maaike was purely a friend. Even though he'd told her that she was someone who could help them get that bigger house she wanted, it had taken most of Saturday before she was appeased. She'd talked to him again after lunch when Robbie had stumbled out of bed with a hangover and she'd turned to Piet in exasperation to sort him out. Annoyance with his brother clearly trumped her anger at her husband.

'What was so urgent?' Maaike asked.

'I need your advice. I need a second opinion,' Piet said, as if he was at the doctor but a kind one who was willing to listen. Maybe a therapist more than a doctor. 'I didn't know who else to talk to.'

'You must have some friends. Why did you call me?'

Piet shook his head. As Hilda had pointed out, she'd been suspicious not just because he had never had any female friends before, but because he actually hardly had any friends at all. He'd had a good friend at primary school, but they'd lost touch when his friend went to secondary school and Piet was held back a year. Then he'd always been together with his brother. At the time when other people made friends at school, he'd been so close to Robbie that there was no room for anybody else.

Maaike was the first friend he'd made in a while.

That was a scary thought.

'What about colleagues?' she asked.

'God, no. Them least of all.' Even though that wasn't what she had asked him, he didn't see his colleagues as friends. Never had done. They sometimes talked about their lives as they walked their beats, but he didn't socialise with any of them outside of work. He spent his free time with his wife, his daughter and his brother. It was only now that he realised how tight, how insular and claustrophobic, their little group really was.

'Your wife?'

'I talked to her . . .'

'But you didn't like what she had to say.' Maaike finished his sentence.

'It's not so much that I don't like it, more that I think she's wrong.'

'That's the same thing,' Maaike said.

'I'm not sure it is. She could have been right but I could still not have liked it, if I didn't want to hear the truth.'

'That's deep.' She laughed at him. 'I'll give you an opinion too and you can dislike mine as well.'

'I promise you that if you agree with my wife, I'll do what you both say.'

'The responsibility weighs heavily on my shoulders. I might need a glass of wine to cope with it. Do you want one too?'

He nodded. It reminded him of drinking beer with Hilda. This seemed to be a topic of conversation that demanded alcohol. He watched her open the bottle. It wasn't the one he'd brought with him last week. That was probably such bad quality that it wasn't worth drinking and she'd thrown it out.

'After I saw you on Thursday,' he started his story, 'I went back to the Red Light District.'

'Do I even want to hear this?' she said as she put a glass of wine in front of him.

'As someone who dislikes the police, you're the perfect person to tell me what to do.'

'Not dislikes,' she said, 'distrusts.'

'Even better.' He picked up his glass just to give his hands something to do. 'After I told Leon Martens' father about his son's debts, I assumed he'd immediately paid them off. If my brother was in financial difficulties and I had the means to bail him out, I would do it in an instant. But then you said that Allard had told you his son was still missing, and I thought I'd check at the club if his debt had been paid.'

'Right.'

'I was explicitly told by my superiors that I shouldn't go there. Because there was an operation going on.'

'An operation.'

'That's all I can tell you. When I went back, I was curious about the place they were staking out. It looked like a normal squat to me. You know, like the place down the street, boarded up. I watched it for a bit. And then I saw my boss.'

She leaned back on the sofa. 'I don't like where this is going.'

Piet nodded. 'I saw him accept a thick brown envelope. From the guy who runs the club.'

'Please tell me he didn't see you.'

'Yeah, he saw me.'

'That's not good.'

'I know, and it gets worse. One of the girls came out. She indicated that she'd just serviced my boss. She said he was disgusting.' Piet took a big gulp of wine. 'I know his wife. He goes to our church.'

'Did he say anything to you afterwards?'

'Not immediately; he just walked away. But he drove me back to Alkmaar on Friday, as he's done every week. He said that if I kept my mouth shut, he'd make it worth my while. I'd get a promotion.'

'You need to tell someone about this,' Maaike said immediately. 'Report him.'

'No, listen,' Piet said. 'I think—'

'Is that what your wife said too? You said that if I agreed with her, you'd do it.'

'She said I should take the money. The promotion.'

Maaike raised her eyebrows. 'She did? And you don't want to do that either?'

'She's right: I need the promotion because we need a bigger house. She wants to have another baby and it's my responsibility to support them, to provide for them.' He ticked the reasons off on his fingers. He'd once made a decision that was detrimental to him but saved his brother. He could now make a decision that he didn't like but that meant there was finally enough money for all of them.

'You have two choices,' she said. 'You either report him or you take his bribe.'

He looked at her. 'I don't want to do either.'

'The problem is that your boss knows that you know he's crooked. If you don't take the promotion, you're implicitly refusing to keep quiet. Don't you see, to him you'll be a ticking bomb that can go off at any moment. You either have to take his side or he'll make your life hell.'

Piet stared down at his wine glass, hoping to get a better answer from there.

When van Merwe had pulled up outside the house that afternoon, Piet had been surprised. He'd half expected him to not show up, to demonstrate how easy it was for him to fuck him over. The boss had hardly talked. He didn't mention the promotion again. It was an uncomfortable journey that gave Piet a good understanding of what was to come in a week's time when the secondment was over.

'He makes my life hell anyway,' he said. 'That means that nothing will change.'

'Piet, you can't take the bribe. You'll be just like him.'

'That doesn't matter. I can carry on with my job. And it's not a bribe, it's a promotion.' He closed his eyes for a second, because he wanted it all to go away. It didn't.

'Report him, or leave.'

'Just because I saw him, *I* have to leave? I didn't do anything wrong.'

'Then report him.'

'I can't do that!' His response was immediate. As if it was that easy. He didn't have any evidence, so it was the boss's word against his. As Hilda had said, nobody would believe him. He rested his face in his hands. 'All I was doing was looking for Leon. I was just trying to do my job. I didn't want to stumble on something like this.'

Maaike lifted her glass to her lips and gave him a searching glance.

'I can't leave the job,' Piet said. 'We'd have no money coming in. I'm not like you, I don't have a good education.'

'Fine, you do what your wife wants you to do. You'll have the satisfaction of making your family's life better. Don't worry, I won't tell anybody. I'll keep quiet whatever you choose to do. Thank you for trusting me enough to tell me about this.' Her words had a finality to them, and an edge of disappointment.

Piet finished his glass of wine and left. He didn't think he'd come back here.

He wandered along the dark canals. What a mistake it had been to come to Amsterdam. If only he'd refused the secondment, because then he wouldn't have this problem. Part of what Maaike had said was right: if he didn't take the promotion, van Merwe would be impossible to work with. She was astute to understand that.

He had no choice but to do what his boss wanted.

This was a positive thing, he told himself. It was a great

opportunity that had fallen in his lap. Hilda would agree with that entirely. He was going to get a higher salary and they could get a bigger house so that even if they had another child, Robbie could live with them for as long as he wanted to. There was no downside to this decision.

The water of the canal was black and cold but oddly tempting. He could swerve and fall in and everybody would assume he'd just lost his footing. He understood why people chose to do that.

He shook his head.

His life was on the up and he was going to be happy about that.

Chapter 33

Back at the police station, Lotte checked Daan ter Aar's details. Teun Simmens' widow had told her that they'd been in prison together. She pulled up his records. Daan had been arrested during the lockdown riots for breaking and entering a shop. Then he'd resisted arrest and beaten up a police officer and was found to be in possession of more drugs than were acceptable for his own personal use. Drug dealing, violence, theft – it was quite something to have achieved during one single day of rioting.

Then a small detail stopped her in her tracks.

Arresting officer: Rick van Buren.

Rick van Buren, who'd beaten up a protester during the same lockdown riots. His father had told her that there was a video uploaded on YouTube that showed the violence and she hadn't wanted to watch it. Now she had to, because she had a really bad feeling about this.

As he'd said, it wasn't hard to find. Rick van Buren, dressed in uniform, laying into a man with his baton, hitting him until his colleagues pulled him away. She recognised the protester immediately.

'We need to find Daan ter Aar,' she said out loud to

Thomas and Charlie. 'We need to find him as soon as possible.'

She wondered what it was like for Daan to find out that the friend of his best friend, the guy he'd lived with for years, was the cop who had arrested him. Klaasen had told her that Teun had had some explaining to do for having a mate who was a cop. He hadn't said that it was the cop who'd beaten Daan up. Had that led to an argument between Daan and Teun, and was that why Teun had died? Was that why Rick had died? It was hard to believe and somehow really easy to believe at the same time.

But why Chantal? They were still missing something.

'Daan ter Aar,' Thomas read from his screen, 'was taken into care as a child. In and out of prison for years. Look at this: given a higher social security payout after an official diagnosis of FASD, which caused his lack of impulse control.'

'FASD?' Charlie asked.

'Foetal alcohol spectrum disorder,' Lotte said. 'Mother drinking heavily whilst pregnant.'

'This diagnosis happened a month after Rick van Buren beat him up. It smells like unofficial compensation to me.'

'I'm not surprised,' Charlie said. 'Anything else useful?'

Thomas scanned through the document on his screen. 'Ah,' he said, 'he used to be a car mechanic.'

Lotte got up. 'Let's go back to that shelter in Amsterdam Noord,' she said. 'Maybe he's still there. Charlie, can you check if you can spot Daan anywhere near Rick van Buren's car?'

'We know he's after you, so you stay here,' Thomas said. 'Someone has to look at the CCTV footage and it makes much more sense if you do that. Charlie and I will find Daan, and we'll put out a general alert too.'

She was too slow to protest, and Thomas and Charlie were out of the door, leaving her to stare at the screen. Her head was spinning. Killing both Teun and Rick in what might have been a red mist she could understand. But why threaten *her*? Why kill Chantal?

Surely Daan hadn't pushed the surgeon into the road because she was in a photo that Teun had in his possession? That made no sense.

Maybe it wasn't the photo but what had actually happened in 1980. Something involving these four policemen.

There was only one person, Lotte thought, who could throw any light on it. She needed to talk to her father. She considered calling him but knew that wouldn't do; she wanted to see exactly how he reacted without having to stare at a small screen. If she was going to have this conversation with him, it had to be face to face. She had to drive north to Alkmaar and ask the questions about the period in her parents' marriage that she'd spent all her life not talking about. It now was no longer possible to avoid it. She owed it to Chantal to find out what had happened in 1980. Maybe she also owed it to Teun and Rick. To the three children who were in the photo that she should also have been in.

She went down the stairs and left the police station. She unlocked her bike and was about to turn towards Mark's house to pick up her car when she thought better of it. Rick had crashed his car. Gerard Klaasen had said that if you were worried you were going to die, you shouldn't drive. Well, that was the answer, then: she was worried she was going to die and so she was going to take the train. She turned the other way, towards Amsterdam Centraal.

The station loomed large as a cathedral at the end of the road. All the work on it had finished and the outside was restored to its original stately beauty. She locked her bike in the triple-storey racks and tapped her public transport card onto the reader. A steady stream of people flowed through the station. Commuters, students, tourists mingled in the main corridor in a way they'd never mingle anywhere else. She scanned the departure board for the train to Alkmaar and saw that it left in six minutes, right from the other side of the station.

She took the human obstacle course in record time and went up the stairs. The platform was packed. Within minutes, the train would arrive from Maastricht to carry all these people north. It would be standing room only, she could tell. The pressure from the crowd behind her brought her further to the front, closer to the platform edge than she liked. Her heart sped up. She looked around but didn't see anybody she recognised. She should have driven, she thought. It was safer than standing here. She wanted to go backwards, away from the platform edge, but there was no space. Instead she planted one foot forward to be more stable and secure. Just in case.

The headlights of the yellow double-decker train were the first signs of its approach. As it came nearer, she hoisted her bag higher up her shoulder, ready to board as soon as it arrived. Everybody moved up just a little bit, the shuffling of all those feet wanting to be the first on board vying with the sound of the coming train.

And then there was a push in the small of her back. A sharp, sudden, violent push that shoved her forward.

Chapter 34

23 April 1980

At dinner on Wednesday evening, a despondent air hung over the team. They were exactly a week away from the coronation and the end of their secondment. This time next week, the coronation would have taken place and then they'd go back home. Once Princess Beatrix was queen, the dignitaries would leave and the terrorist threat would be gone. All the riots that were so focused on the coronation would end, the eyes of the world would no longer be on them, Amsterdam's police force could return to their normal jobs and Piet would be back to walking his beat in Alkmaar.

When you were this close to the finish, things always felt hard, he thought. Plus, it didn't feel as if they were actually going to finish a single thing. He worried that they were going to leave Amsterdam without Leon being found.

'I can't wait to go home,' Eelke said. 'Sleep in my own bed. Back to my wife's cooking instead of restaurant food.'

'I'm looking forward to not having to talk to you guys every evening,' Wim joked. 'Sitting next to my old team again. Even if my temporary partner turned himself into a top navigator.' He clapped Piet on the shoulder. 'I appreciate the work you put in walking those streets every evening. Now that we're nearly done, you can finally go for a drink with me.'

Piet took a gulp of his beer to wash the apprehension down. He no longer walked to learn Amsterdam's geography but instead carried Leon's photo in the faint hope of spotting him somewhere. He didn't think anybody else was looking for him. Not the police, but not the club boss either. The apartment on the Singel was lit up every evening, but only because the new owners were about to move in. 'It wasn't what I expected,' he said, 'but I know a lot more about Amsterdam.'

Barry looked at him from across the table and nodded. 'Keep focused for the last week. You never know what might happen.'

The bruise on Piet's arm was only just beginning to fade as a physical reminder of what could happen when you got in the way. He took another deep gulp of beer and, judging by the look on his face, surprised Wim by accepting a second drink. The alcohol made thinking less necessary, and Piet didn't want to think this evening. He didn't want to think about going home and all the decisions he had to make. He wanted to enjoy the company of the team for these last few days.

'Just as you're going home, you're starting to drink a decent amount,' Wim said. 'We should all meet up again this time next year. Bring the family. What do you think?'

'That's a good idea,' Eelke said. 'Have our kids play together on Queen's Day, because they'll have the day off school anyway. Unless you think your son will hate it,' he added to Barry. 'He's a bit older than ours.'

Piet superstitiously thought it was premature to talk about next year with such a crucial week ahead of them. The others didn't seem to share that feeling, because at the talk of their kids and this future reunion, the mood around the table lifted.

'Teun loves telling others what to do, so he'll happily boss your kids around,' Barry said. 'My wife says he's destined to run his own company.' He sounded proud.

'My daughter is currently obsessed with playing doctors and nurses,' Eelke said. 'She cut open her best friend's top with a pair of safety scissors when the teacher wasn't looking. Luckily nothing was harmed apart from a T-shirt. She'll probably become a nurse.'

'Or a surgeon,' Barry said.

'Either way, you'd better get your kids to wear old clothes.'

'My Lotte is only into this cartoon about bears living on boats,' Piet said. 'What does that say about her future career plans?'

'She's going to work in a zoo,' Wim said, 'and become a wildlife conservationist. Specialising in bears.'

'Or work on a boat. Maybe she'll sail around the world one day,' Barry said.

Piet rubbed his eyes with the back of his hand. That second beer had made him all maudlin.

Wim slapped him on the shoulder. 'What's got into you? You don't want her to sail a yacht?'

Piet thought about his boss and the decision he had

coming up. 'As long as she doesn't become a cop,' he said, 'she can do whatever she likes.'

'My kid is definitely talking about wanting to catch the bad guys, and I encourage him,' Wim said. 'But you're right, it isn't really a job for a girl. Maybe she'll work in a pet shop.'

'They're all so young, who knows what they'll end up doing,' Barry said. 'I wanted to be a farmer at that age. Or a fireman.'

'I grew up next to a farm,' Eelke said, 'and I loved seeing the piglets. They were so funny and adorable. And then they were all slaughtered and I'm still having nightmares about that.'

A shiver ran down Piet's spine.

'But you became a policeman instead?' Wim burst out laughing.

'Well, I haven't killed anything or anybody,' Eelke said. 'Not even any animals. Apart from flies. And ants.'

'Mosquitoes?'

'Those too. I've killed nothing apart from insects.'

'I want to be like that,' Piet said. The words came out slightly slurred. 'But I once killed a mouse.'

'Why are we talking about killing?' Barry asked. 'Maybe it's time to head back to the hotel.' He asked for the bill and settled up.

'I'm going to miss the free food,' Wim said. 'Anybody up for another drink?'

Barry shook his head. 'Let's keep it tidy.'

Wim didn't heed him and walked off in the opposite direction to the hotel to find himself an open bar.

'I don't know how he does it,' Piet said. His room was calling him and he couldn't wait to roll into bed.

In the hotel lobby, a man was waiting for him. 'Ah, shit,' he muttered under his breath. It was his boss.

'We need to talk,' van Merwe said.

Barry shot him a concerned glance, but Piet knew he had to get this over and done with. 'I'll see you guys tomorrow,' he said, and followed the inspector out.

They walked in silence along the canal in the direction of the Elandsgracht, where van Merwe was stationed.

'Are we going to your office?' Piet asked. The evening air had sobered him up a little.

'Don't be stupid for once,' his boss replied, and immediately Piet felt like the kid who'd flunked a year at school. They turned into a narrow alley. This must be around the corner from where van Merwe had worked these past weeks. They went into an empty café. Even on his many evening walks, Piet had never found this place.

He didn't protest when his boss told him to sit down and ordered two beers. The barman disappeared into the back after van Merwe slipped him a banknote.

Piet folded his hands around the cool glass but didn't drink.

'I thought you'd get in touch with me,' van Merwe said with a smile that only half lifted his jowls. 'But I had to come looking for you.'

'Sorry, boss,' Piet said. 'It's been busy.'

'Not too busy for you to go out with the rest of your team.'

'Sorry, boss,' he said again. He stared at the foam on top

of the beer, how it slowly sank and disappeared as time went on.

'I talked to the people in charge,' Inspector van Merwe said, 'and they agreed to your promotion. I'll give you the questions they'll be asking beforehand so you'll pass. Also,' he grabbed something from his inside pocket, 'I know that money's tight with your family and I want to help out.' He pushed a brown envelope across the table. It looked fat, exactly like the envelope that the inspector had received the other day from the guy running the sex club.

Maaike's words jumped into Piet's head. He would be no better than his boss if he accepted the money.

And so what? he said to himself. He could be just like his boss. He didn't have to be any better than him. Sure, he'd be in his pocket for the rest of his years in the police force, but he would make his way up the career ladder and get a little backhander every now and then. What was so wrong about that? Wasn't that what everybody was doing? You had to compromise with your conscience sometimes.

He reached out and put his hand on the envelope. His fingers fitted around it easily, as if this money was supposed to be in his hand. The envelope was warm from sitting inside van Merwe's jacket. From being close to his boss's heart.

You'll be just like him.

You'll be just like him.

You'll be just like him.

The words echoed in his head, and however much he knew he ought to take the money, make his wife happy, support his brother and keep his career on track, he couldn't do it.

He pushed the envelope away. The movement came automatically and instinctively.

'Keep it,' he said. 'And your beer.' He grabbed the glass and poured the alcohol into the nearest plant pot. He didn't want anything van Merwe had bought him. 'And keep your fucking promotion.' He didn't meet his boss's eye as he got up and left.

He walked back to his hotel and tried hard not to think about what he had just done.

Chapter 35

Lotte threw out an arm. Her hand hit the chest of the large man next to her and her fingers found just enough purchase on the lapel of his jacket to keep herself upright.

'Jesus, woman, what the hell are you doing?' he barked.

'Sorry, sorry,' she said. Now fully turned the other way, she couldn't spot anybody who could have shoved her on purpose. The man right behind her was absorbed in his smartphone. A tourist with a huge backpack and a tiny skirt stood to his right. Maybe this girl had bumped into her by accident.

The train pulled into the station and the doors opened. Lotte rushed up the stairs and fell into an empty seat by the window. Sitting down felt safe. Her hands were shaking as she undid the zip of her coat. She rummaged through her bag and found her phone. She had to concentrate on steadying her fingers as she drew the pattern to unlock it and called Thomas. 'I think someone tried to push me under the train.' Now that she'd said this out loud, it felt surreal.

A woman in the opposite seat gave her a funny look.

'Can you pull the CCTV footage? Platform 11.'

The elderly woman to her side loudly shushed and

gestured with her finger to her lips, then pointed at the sign that said she was in the quiet carriage. Even if someone had attempted to murder her, she should move to another carriage to notify her colleague of this fact.

Thomas said he'd check it.

Lotte disconnected the call and texted her father to tell him which train she was on. She would have fallen on the tracks if she hadn't half anticipated that push. If she hadn't put her foot forward to brace herself and if the man next to her hadn't been that solid, she could have died. Like Chantal had.

For the next fifteen minutes she stared out of the window, watched the flat landscape go by and tried to calm down. The tulip fields formed colourful squares like sections of an enormous quilt. If she had died, she'd never have seen this again. Never kissed Mark again. Never had the chance to ask her father what exactly had happened with his divorce.

They pulled into Alkmaar and Lotte got up. The woman opposite her followed her out. 'Are you okay?' she asked. 'I heard what you said about someone trying to push you under the train.'

'I'm fine. Thanks for asking.' Tears pushed into her eyes at the stranger's kindness. Just an after-effect of the adrenaline.

'I'll wait at the doors as you get off. I'll keep an eye out.' She put her hand on Lotte's arm. 'I bet you know who did it. Was it your ex?'

Lotte shook her head. But she was pretty sure she knew who it was. She thanked the helpful woman and got off the train.

Her father was waiting for her outside the station. 'Have you eaten?' he asked. 'I thought we could go for lunch.' He pointed at the Indonesian restaurant opposite.

She hadn't thought about food at all, but why not? 'Sure,' she said, 'let's eat.' She was nervous about the conversation coming up, but the brush with death at the station had made her appreciate that time wasn't endless. There was no better moment than right now to ask the questions she'd avoided all her life. She needed to do this if she wanted to know why her parents had got divorced. And if she wanted to get to the bottom of who had killed Teun, Rick and Chantal, and possibly tried to kill her less than an hour ago.

At the thought of her own death, adrenaline pumped through her body again. She pushed her shaking hands deep inside the pockets of her coat to hide them from her father's watchful glance.

They went into the restaurant. Only a few tables were taken. Lotte indicated one as far away from everybody else as possible and her father nodded his agreement. She threw a glance at the menu to make sure they had her favourite, but then every Indonesian restaurant had babi pangang and nasi goreng. Her father ordered the same thing. She would normally have a beer, but Dry April called for a glass of water instead. She shouldn't blunt her reaction speed either. Just in case whoever had pushed her was intending to have another go.

'I think I have no choice,' she said, 'but to talk to you about what happened in 1980. You said last time that you were looking for a missing man, that it was a mess and that you were naïve.'

'I saw something I shouldn't have seen,' her father said, 'and when I refused to take a bribe, it all blew up.' He told her about seeing Inspector van Merwe in the sex club when he'd been there to find Leon Martens. 'When my boss offered me the cash and I refused it,' he said, 'I knew what the fallout was going to be: my job became a nightmare and Hilda was livid.'

'Mum knew about it?' Lotte was shocked.

'Yes, I told her that van Merwe had offered me a promotion. She wanted me to accept it. Do you remember your uncle Robbie?'

She shook her head. 'I remember little of that time.'

Her phone beeped with a message. It was from Thomas. It had been so crowded at the station that it wasn't obvious if someone had pushed her. He could just about make her out, he said, but not anybody else.

'Are you busy?' her father asked. 'Do you need to make a call?'

'No,' she said and stuffed her phone in her handbag. 'It's nothing.'

'Your uncle died too soon,' her father said. 'He was going to retire, but he kept doing just one more trip. He had a stroke, but luckily he managed to pull into a lay-by. Because he was in the middle of nowhere, when they got to him it was too late. Maybe it's what he wanted; I don't know. Anyway, he lived with us back then. Three adults and a child living in a two-bedroom house. Your bedroom was no more than an extended cupboard. Your mother wanted us to get something bigger, and I didn't blame her for wanting that. I still don't,' he added quickly.

She thought he was trying too hard to be fair. She suddenly remembered what her mother had said: that she'd have preferred it if her husband had been on the take. Only now did it dawn on Lotte that she had meant that literally. 'You refused the bribe, you argued and that was why you got together with Maaike?'

'I don't want to speak badly of your mother,' her father said, 'not after all these years. I just want you to know that I never cheated on her with Maaike.'

Lotte found it hard to process that she had been unfair towards the woman for almost forty years. She was saved from immediately responding by the waiter bringing their food. 'You did meet her a few times during that month,' she said when the man had disappeared again.

'Yes, I met her and she helped me a lot. Your mother knew and was pissed off about that too. But it was mainly the money. That I refused it.'

'You're saying that you got divorced because you didn't take a bribe?'

Her father nodded.

Lotte felt her world rock as everything she'd thought she knew about her parents' divorce turned out to be wrong. She had always seen her mother as the injured party. That she had wanted her husband to be a corrupt cop purely so that they could buy a bigger house was appalling. 'You didn't take a bribe; you didn't mess up—'

'We did mess up. But that was because we got caught up in the riot.'

'And Wim van Buren was drinking.'

'Yes, he was drinking heavily all the way through. We were lucky in a way. He was always driving and I became the navigator; he must have been over the limit most days. To be honest, I should have stopped him. I deserved my reprimand just for that.'

Wim van Buren shouldn't have driven a car. His son had died in a car crash from getting behind the wheel drunk. Lotte remembered that the woman at the wine bar had also said that she should have stopped him from driving. 'And you never found the missing student?'

'No, Leon is still officially missing. I heard that he was on that list that circulated in the prisons a few years back. Do you remember? They printed pictures of missing people on a calendar so that the inmates would see them. They hoped that somebody would be willing to speak up because the statute of limitation had long passed on most of these cases.'

'I remember. We only got a couple of results from that. Even after all these years, inmates aren't keen to turn informer.' It suddenly struck her that Teun Simmens must have seen that list. She wondered if he knew his father had worked on the case of the missing student. 'Did you meet someone called Gerard Klaasen during that time?'

Her father frowned. 'Klaasen? I don't think so.'

'He was a big shot in the squatters' movement.' She thought back to what else he'd told her. 'He lived for a while in the Red Light District. Were you part of the riot police teams that cleared out some of those squats?'

He shook his head. 'No, we didn't get involved with that at all. Our job was to do the normal work whilst

Amsterdam's police force suited up in riot gear.' His voice was hard.

She looked through her notes of the interview with Klaasen for anything that could jog her father's memory. She rattled off the facts. 'He had a friend called Katinka. He—'

'Katinka?' her father interrupted her. 'Katinka Fledder?'

'Yes,' Lotte said. 'That's her.'

'I knew her. She worked in the sex club that Leon Martens frequented. I talked to her because Leon always asked for her.' He paused for a second. 'And so did van Merwe, my boss.'

'Your corrupt boss had sex with this prostitute? As did the missing guy?'

'Yes.'

'She's the mother of Daan ter Aar. He squatted with Teun Simmens.'

And Teun and Daan had been in jail together around the time the photo of Leon Martens was circulated.

After lunch, they went back to the station. Her father said he'd come with her to the platform, as there was still ten minutes until the train arrived. She'd normally refuse; would say that it was a hassle that he had to check in and out with his public transport card, but now she was grateful for the extra pair of eyes. It wasn't busy and nobody approached them. When the train arrived, she took a seat upstairs and waved at her father until she couldn't see him any more.

At some point she had to talk to her mother about what he'd told her. That point wasn't now. Another dreaded conversation to put off as long as possible. But thinking about mothers made her decide that she should pay Daan ter Aar's mother a visit. Not only because her father had met her, but also because Daan could well be with her.

Katinka Fledder lived in a small flat in Almere. There were enough officers trying to locate Daan in the normal places where the homeless hung out. Thomas and Charlie had checked or called every shelter by now. Even social services knew that the police wanted him. With that many people looking for him in Amsterdam, Lotte and Thomas could go to Almere. He didn't tell her not to be stupid, that she shouldn't go, that she should stay in the police station. One look at her face and he nodded. He only insisted he'd come with her.

'I would never live in Almere,' Lotte said on their drive there, to break the silence and calm her nerves.

'Why not? What don't you like about it?'

'There something wrong about land that's younger than I am.'

'Didn't they reclaim Flevoland in the sixties? You're not that old.'

'The first house in Almere was finished around the same time I was born.'

'And what's the problem with that?'

'I don't know. Building a whole new city purely to deal with Amsterdam's overflow. It doesn't seem right.'

'Talking about population overflow,' Thomas said, 'what's happening with your flat?'

'Someone's moving in on Monday.'

'You'll be packing this weekend, then.'

'No, my stepmother's dealing with all that. She's hired a removal firm.' Maaike had been very excited to do it. It had made Lotte wonder if she didn't secretly miss her previous job.

The sat nav took them to a small block of flats on the edge of the city. The buildings were painted yellow and pink to bring cheer to a grey morning. 'That's another reason I wouldn't want to live here. Who wants to live in a pink house?'

'Says the woman who lives in a posh house in Oud Zuid and rents out a flat on the canal.'

'What does that have to do with the colour of the house?'

'Some people have choice,' Thomas said. 'That's all I mean.'

They rang the doorbell and an old crone of a woman opened the door. She was deeply wrinkled and had straggly grey hair. She sucked her top teeth as if her dentures hurt her. Her cheeks were sunken and large liver spots marked her skin.

'Come in,' she said. A cigarette dangled between her fingers.

'Is Daan here?'

She shook her head. 'Haven't seen him in two weeks.'

'Is that unusual?' Thomas asked.

'I thought he'd come yesterday, but he didn't.' Katinka fell rather than sat into a big chair with armrests that shone from years of sweaty hands rubbing over them. 'He helps me out with money most weeks.'

'He gives you cash?'

'Since they added that disability allowance.'

This miserable person opposite her was the reason he had FASD in the first place. Unless it was purely a payment to compensate for what Rick had done, as Thomas had suggested.

'It's not my fault,' Katinka said as if she'd read Lotte's mind. 'We didn't know any better in those days.'

Lotte raised her eyebrows but didn't correct her.

'It could have been worse. I only drank.' She waved the cigarette around. 'And I smoked, but so did everybody else.'

Lotte hadn't asked her for a health update.

Katinka gestured towards her fallen-in cheeks. 'I didn't always look like this,' she said. 'I was really beautiful. They painted my portrait on the wall of the club. I was the advertisement.' She cackled. 'Can you believe it?'

'You worked at a sex club.'

'That's right. I stupidly thought having a kid would give me a reason to clean up. Instead, he only made everything harder. Cried so much and didn't stop, and I drank more and more to get some sleep. When the booze didn't do it any longer, I moved on to the hard stuff. He was taken into care when he was just a year old. He wanted to meet with me when he was twelve. I was shocked when his foster parents called me, to be honest. They meant well, but I have no idea what they were thinking. They couldn't cope with him and they thought he'd calm down when he met his mother? As if that miraculously made things better. He asked me all these questions about his father, and what was I going to say? That I spread my legs for a living and it could have been any number of men?'

'What *did* you say?'

'I told him a story. It was a good story.' She took a deep drag from her cigarette.

'What story was that?'

'That Leon Martens was his father.'

'Was he?'

'Who knows? Those were pre-AIDS days. Some guys refused to wear a rubber and it was extra money.' Katinka shrugged. 'And sometimes it wasn't worth the fight.'

'Why him?'

'If I was going to make up a father for my son, shouldn't it at least be a decent guy? I always joked with Leon that he was my first. My first of the day. Not many punters came at lunchtime.' She chortled. 'He did, because he skipped lectures so that his mother didn't find out. University student who fell for a whore. It's really Cinderella, isn't it? I always hated fucking Cinderella. Plus,' she took a deep drag of her cigarette, 'unlike my other punters, I knew Leon was never going to come back to tell Daan it wasn't true.'

Lotte understood what the woman was telling her. 'Because he's dead.'

'That's right. Long dead. Dead before Daan was even born. Hell, probably even before he was conceived, if I did the maths right.'

'What happened to him?'

'I'd be mad to tell you. I'm not going to go to prison for this.'

'The statute of limitation expired years ago,' Thomas said. 'You can't go to prison for something that happened in 1980.'

She stubbed out the cigarette.

Lotte waited. She knew Katinka was going to tell them. Get the secret off her chest and out in the open. At long last.

'Leon Martens owed us a lot of money.' The woman coughed, a hacking noise that screamed she should have quit decades ago. 'The boss let him run up a huge tab as he had followed him a couple of times and saw that his parents were good for the cash. They had this lovely apartment on the Singel and they seemed the kind who'd bail out their kid when push came to shove. But it took some time and the boss felt that pushing and shoving was in order. He roughed Leon up a bit when he came that day. That was all. Just a couple of kicks and punches.' She lit another cigarette. 'He must have broken one of his ribs and punctured his lung. That's what we thought afterwards. Anyway, the guy died. We took his keys and six of us cleared out the parents' apartment before his mother came back from work.'

'What did you do with his body?'

'The boss had a couple of paramedics on his payroll and they let us know the next time a junkie OD'd. We dumped Leon's body in with the junkie, buried both corpses at once and nobody was any the wiser.'

Lotte thought about what her father had told her about bribes. 'Your boss paid off paramedics? What about cops?'

'Sure. The nearest desk sergeant was one of his. But then it was the riots and a total mess because these new guys came in from out of town. All the ones the boss had been paying off were suddenly beating up the squatters instead. But there's always one, isn't there?' She winked. 'One who can't keep his dick in his pants. One you can blackmail to do what you want and clean up your mess. Fuck knows, maybe that guy was even Daan's biological daddy. I hope not. Filthy fucker.'

'What guy?' Lotte's stomach was in her mouth. 'Piet Huizen?'

'Nah,' Katinka said. 'Huizen was a decent enough guy. For a cop, at least. He tried to help me a few times afterwards. I bumped into him when I was heavily pregnant and he put me in touch with social services. I was in a bad state then. I wasn't earning any money, of course.' She flicked her grey hair back in what must once have been a coquettish gesture. 'I told Daan this when he came here two weeks ago. He had a photo.'

'This?' Lotte held out her phone.

'Piet Huizen once showed me that photo too. He was still looking for Leon, the poor sod. It was at least a year after the boy died. Anyway, he showed me that and told me he'd got divorced and was upset that the other guys had their kids there and he didn't. He probably thought that if he told me about his kid, maybe I'd tell him what I hadn't told him before. I could have told him,' Katinka closed one heavily crusted eyelid in a nightmarish wink, 'that he should have asked his own boss about Leon instead.'

'You told Daan that this girl was Eelke Wieringa's child?' Thomas asked.

'He didn't believe that a cop could be a decent person, but Huizen never crossed the line,' Katinka said. 'Daan was pissed off and said I'd ruined his plan.'

Lotte wanted to laugh and cry at the same time. It had never been about the photo. The reason he hadn't killed her was because her father had once been decent towards a prostitute.

'So Daan thinks these four,' Thomas pointed at the picture on Lotte's phone, 'were responsible for Leon's death.'

'What was I going to tell him? That I was upstairs getting fucked by some other punter while my pimp beat the shit out of Leon? That we could have called an ambulance and he would probably have been fine? After he'd seen Leon's photo in prison, realised he was still missing, he became obsessed with him. He read that these four had been punished for failing to find Leon during the coronation. It was that picture that did the damage: the photo of the four of them standing there dithering while all hell was breaking loose.'

'Yes,' Lotte said. 'I've seen that picture.'

'Leon's parents talked to the press afterwards too. According to them, Leon was still missing because of these four officers. Everybody liked that version a lot. But his bitch of a mother came to the club and refused to pay. I was shocked. She had all this jewellery and could have solved her son's problems in an instant, but she refused. I think she was jealous that Leon would rather spend time with me than with her. Such a weird woman. And then there was Huizen's boss. It couldn't have worked out any better for him, could it?'

Whatever her father was going to say, after getting an official reprimand he was never going to be believed. 'Did you ever tell Huizen any of this?'

'Of course not! You think I'm crazy or something?'

'Do you know where Daan is?' Thomas asked. 'Give us his number.'

'He doesn't have a phone.'

'You know what he's done,' Lotte said. 'He's killed three people. How do you think he's going to feel when he finds out that you've been lying to him? That it wasn't these guys,' she indicated the picture on her phone, 'but *you* who was ultimately responsible for the death of Leon Martens? And that Leon wasn't his father at all?'

'You wouldn't.' The old woman suddenly looked scared.

'We'll tell everybody who knows Daan,' Thomas said. 'Gemma, Gerard Klaasen, I think they'll all be really interested in the true story.'

'Yes,' Lotte said, 'we can definitely do that, but don't you think it'll be quicker to put out an official statement in the press? Piet Huizen is my father. He should be properly exonerated. I know! There's that woman who does those true crime podcasts. I should call her too. We should give as much air time to this story as possible.' She turned and faced Katinka. 'Give us a few days and the truth will reach Daan. He'll be really angry, don't you think?'

'You fuckers,' Katinka hissed. 'You wouldn't do that.'

'Try me,' Lotte said. 'I'm not a decent person like my dad.'

Chapter 36

25 April 1980

That Friday, Piet didn't go to the usual meeting place with his boss but turned left out of the police station and lugged his suitcase to Amsterdam's Centraal station. At the entrance to the station, he passed a surprisingly unvandalised phone booth. He stopped. It was almost 5 p.m. and he should let Hilda know he was going to be home later than the previous weeks. If she burnt the chicken, the weekend would get off to a bad start. Robbie answered the phone and Piet told him what train he was going to be on. On an impulse he told his brother to meet him at the station so that they could walk home together.

He crossed the chaos of the central hallway. As he approached the platform where the trains to Alkmaar left from, junkies filled the space. Close to the back entrance, with easy access to the Red Light District, a man sat slumped in a corner. A woman was shooting up behind the stairs. On Wednesday, those addicts would mingle with the supporters of the House of Orange coming into Amsterdam for the coronation. It was going to be a mess. He wondered if his colleagues planned to sweep this corridor on Tuesday night or early Wednesday morning. Between keeping the station clear, the riots under control and the terrorists away from the ceremony, it was going to be crazy. Only five days to go.

He went up to the platform and took a seat in the train that was already there. Outside, he spotted a pickpocket working hard to steal enough cash for his next hit. He tapped on the window to warn the person on the platform that she was about to be mugged. The pickpocket showed Piet his middle digit and moved on. He could have attempted to arrest him but it seemed hardly worth the effort.

The guard on the platform blew his whistle and the train departed. Piet rested a hand on his suitcase and watched Amsterdam go by. Rain splashed the window and obscured the green fields outside. The train was busy and most seats around him were taken, yet still this was much more peaceful than being in a car with his boss.

He should have done this sooner. Van Merwe had wanted to keep an eye on him, he now realised, especially after the encounter in Casa Blanca that first time. The very next journey, the inspector had asked about the progress Piet and the team were making with Leon's disappearance.

In the distance, a church steeple raised a cautionary finger as if to tell Piet to stop thinking about this. Then the church disappeared from sight and was replaced by sheep grazing placidly. A fire-truck-red tulip field drew his eye. He could have seen all this from the motorway too, but the anxiety caused by his boss's presence must have dulled his perception. He should be worried about the fallout from his decision to refuse that promotion, but instead the world was much more in focus.

When the train pulled into Alkmaar, he saw his brother waiting for him on the platform.

'Let me take that.' Robbie held out his hand for Piet's suitcase.

Piet handed it over. He didn't always have to be the bigger and stronger brother. 'Thanks,' he said. 'How are things?'

'There's a roast chicken in the oven,' Robbie said with a grin.

Piet laughed. They left the station side by side. The rain had stopped and the sun made a brave effort to emerge from behind the thinning clouds. 'About being a truck driver . . .' he said.

Robbie was looking down at the pavement, ready to accept the rejection.

'I think you should do it. It's a good idea.'

'What?' He put the suitcase down with a loud plonk. 'Are you sure?'

'Yes,' Piet said. 'We'll rustle up the money for those lessons somehow.' He didn't want to think about the brown envelope that could have paid for all of it.

His brother wrapped his arms around him. 'I'm so happy,' he said.

'Me too,' Piet said. It felt like the right decision. If any good had come from Leon's disappearance, it was this. And maybe that balanced out the problems it had caused him with his boss. It was probably enough to mollify Hilda over having turned down his promotion.

Robbie picked up the suitcase again and talked about the research he'd done into local places that offered HGV driving lessons and the exact paperwork he needed. Piet felt a bubble of happiness inside him at his brother's obvious excitement. Without the Amsterdam secondment, this would never have happened. Between his recognition of Patricia Martens' controlling behaviour and Maaike's insistence that people should be allowed to do whatever they wanted, his eyes had opened enough to allow him to make the right choice.

He still felt that way when he went inside the house.

'How did it go?' Hilda said as soon as they came in. 'You were so cagey yesterday on the phone.'

He had called her but hadn't explained what had happened.

'Daddy!' Lotte came running down the stairs, a yellow pencil in her hand. He couldn't talk about his boss and his promotion within his daughter's earshot. Who knew what she might repeat at school?

He hugged her and hoped that she'd stay innocent for a long time. 'Daddy needs to unpack his suitcase,' he said.

Lotte kicked his bag. 'I hate suitcases.'

He stroked her hair and smiled. 'You need one when we go on holiday.'

She thought for a second. 'I'll have a small bag,' she stated, 'not a suitcase.'

'That's a good idea,' Piet said. 'A bag is big enough for a holiday.' He could get her one for her birthday, he thought, to go with the bicycle. They probably printed bags with those bears she was so obsessed with.

He carried his case up the stairs and Hilda followed him. He shut the bedroom door behind them and sat on the bed. 'It was a disaster,' he said.

'What do you mean?' Her face contorted with worry. 'What did you do?'

'I turned down the promotion.'

'What?'

'I was going to take it. I honestly was. But I couldn't say yes.'

'Call him now and tell him you've changed your mind.' The words were coming out of her mouth at breakneck speed. 'Call him.' She pointed to the phone on their bedside table. 'I'm sure it's not too late.'

'No, listen—'

'Take that promotion. You owe it to this family.'

'Hilda, I can't.'

'It's the one thing you need to do, Piet. You need to provide for us, for me and Lotte and the next child we're going to have.'

Piet felt pressure behind his eyes. He shook his head. 'I can't. I can't be like that.'

'Of course you can. What you mean is that you don't want to.'

'Maybe.'

'You're being pathetic. What good are you if you can't even do this one thing for us?'

'Robbie is going to get a job,' he said, 'so we'll be fine for money even without my promotion. Van Merwe handed me an envelope with cash, Hilda. I couldn't take it.'

'You're such a coward. You turned him down because you were squeamish about money?'

'Maaike also said I shouldn't be like my boss.'

As soon as the words left his mouth, he knew he'd said the wrong thing.

'Oh she did, did she?' She grabbed a shirt out of the bottom of the suitcase with a sharp jerk that sent his socks and underwear flying. 'If I remember right, we had a deal. You promised me you were going to take the promotion. Instead, you decide to do what another woman wants you to do? You told me last week, when you called her in the middle of the night, not to get angry with you. Well, I didn't then, but I'm really pissed off with you now. I'm giving you one final chance.' She started to cry. It scared him. 'Yes, I'll give you a chance to make it right,' she repeated. 'That's how fair I am.'

She dashed out of the bedroom, locked herself in the bathroom and only came out when the beep of the oven clock announced that the chicken was ready.

They made it through dinner because Lotte and Robbie were chatting and filled the awkward void. As soon as all the food had disappeared, Hilda went upstairs to their bedroom. He thought he heard her talking and worried about what she was doing. It was where they had their second telephone.

Robbie went out to meet his mates, and a short bedtime story was enough this evening to send Lotte to sleep. It seemed like a normal Friday night, but an undercurrent of tension tinted every word he said until it became difficult to say anything at all. Hilda went back upstairs and put a little bit of make-up on. He told himself it was purely to make herself feel brighter, and maybe it was all going to be fine. But he couldn't suppress the thought that she was waiting for something.

Half an hour later, the doorbell rang.

Piet opened up and saw Inspector van Merwe standing on his doorstep. He swallowed down his immediate fear and revulsion.

'Hi, Piet,' his boss said. 'Hilda called me. She said you wanted to talk.'

'Come on in,' Hilda said, pulling Piet out of the way. 'Thanks for coming so late on a Friday evening. Can I get you a tea or coffee? A beer maybe?'

'No,' van Merwe said. 'I'm good.' He followed Hilda inside and sat down on the sofa. He grinned at Piet and tapped the seat next to him. 'Sit down, Huizen. I'm doing your wife a huge favour, because you seemed pretty certain last time.'

Piet collapsed on the other sofa, as far away from his boss as he could. Hilda had pushed him into a corner until he had nowhere to go.

'Piet, listen,' van Merwe said. 'Hilda told me she wants to get a new house and I know some people who'll give you a good deal. With the promotion as well, you'll be all set.'

Hilda sat down next to Piet and hooked his arm through hers to make sure he wasn't going anywhere. 'Your boss knows what's best for you, darling. I don't know what some crazy woman in Amsterdam has been telling you.'

'You know what it's like, Hilda, a guy goes away from home for a bit and sometimes gets strange ideas.'

She nodded her eager agreement, as if van Merwe was wisdom personified.

Piet ground his teeth together. As a kid, he had once gone for a swim in a lake and found himself out of his depth. He remembered his panic and how water had entered his mouth as he'd screamed. Now he felt exactly the same. With every sentence either of them said, it was as if they put a heavy stone in his pocket and watched to see if this time he was going to go under.

'I'm glad you're giving him a second chance,' Hilda said. 'It makes me feel I can give him another chance too.'

He looked at his wife and understood that she was the one drowning him. She was a stranger to him. He pulled his arm free. Even though she was sitting right beside him, he felt a million miles away from her. He didn't want to be next to her any more.

How could she behave like this? He would be implicated in his boss's corruption and he didn't understand why she wanted that. Why did she want him to take this filthy money?

'I can make your promotion happen,' van Merwe said. 'Just say the word.'

'I want you to leave my house,' Piet muttered. He felt himself getting lighter, as if he'd freed himself from the weight they'd put on him. 'Get out.'

'What was that?'

'I don't want to be like you.' He was going to make it safely to shore.

'Piet, don't be rude!' Hilda snapped.

He stood up. 'I won't do it.'

Van Merwe stood up too. 'Then face the consequences, Piet Huizen. You'll see what I mean. I'm going to destroy you.' He stormed out and slammed the door behind him.

'You're pathetic,' Hilda said. 'Pathetic and stupid, just like your brother. My parents told me I shouldn't have married you. They were right.'

Chapter 37

Four police vans were stationed at one end of the path. They monitored the small structure on the edge of the Sloterplas. It was no more than a large shed and quite a step down from the substantial building on the Singel where Daan had lived a month ago with Teun and Gemma. Lotte wondered what it was used for; nobody could work in here. Maybe it was purely a storage space.

'We should have checked all of Klaasen's properties from the start,' Thomas complained.

'It's fine,' she said, 'we know now.' Daan's mother had told them where her son was. Klaasen owned the metal structure but she didn't think he knew Daan was here or he wouldn't have gone looking for him at the cafés.

'Maybe you should stay here,' Thomas said.

Her heart raced as she shrugged on the bulletproof vest that Charlie had brought her. She unholstered her gun. 'Don't be an idiot.'

'He's after you.'

'Didn't you hear what his mother said? My father is a decent guy and that's why I'm still alive. That's why he didn't kill me.' That shove in her back at the train station was just her overactive imagination.

'This isn't funny.'

'I'm not laughing.' She felt a responsibility to be here. To see this through to the end.

The head of the second team came towards her. The woman's fresh face was edged by her heavy bulletproof helmet. 'Are you sure he's inside?' she said as she buckled up her flak jacket.

'I haven't seen him,' Lotte said. 'He could be out towards the lake.'

'Is he armed?'

'He's killed three people, but there's no evidence of weapons so far.'

The woman raised her eyebrows. 'Did you watch *The Bridge*? This place looks just like the one in the first episode of the third season.'

Beside her, Thomas took an involuntary step back.

'I didn't watch it,' Lotte said.

'Basically, the main character, Saga, and her new colleague approach a trailer not dissimilar to this one. The guy who lives there has boobytrapped it, and when the colleague opens the door and steps inside: *BANG!* Just as Saga shouts *Wait!*'

Daan hated the police, Gerard Klaasen hated the police. Daan's mother could have contacted her son to let him know they were coming. 'I get your point,' Lotte said.

She thought she saw something move behind the window. 'He's there,' she said. 'He's inside.'

'Okay,' the other woman said. 'We'll take the lead. Bash in the door.'

Just then Lotte heard a thud. A thump from inside the shed. A sound she really didn't like. Before her brain was fully in gear, she was running down the path. 'We're engaging,' she heard the team leader say into her walkie-talkie. Somewhere to her left, she noticed that Thomas was following her. She was breathing heavily because of the extra gear she was wearing. Because she was getting unfit maybe.

'Lotte,' Thomas shouted. 'Lotte, wait. He's dangerous.'

But she didn't wait. She reached for the handle and yanked the door open.

Daan was dangling from the ceiling in a noose.

Lotte dashed inside, grabbed Daan's legs and lifted him to take his weight off the rope around his neck. He smelled of piss. The reek made her gag. She was struggling to hold him up. 'Thomas,' she screamed, 'come and help me.'

He was already by her side and helped her lift. Charlie climbed onto the chair to untie the rope. They lowered Daan together.

From outside, Lotte heard the team leader on her mobile. 'We need an ambulance here.'

Daan opened his eyes. He was trying to talk. Lotte leaned over to catch his words.

'You bitch,' he muttered. 'I should have fucking killed you.'

Daan sat in the interview room in complete silence, his lawyer by his side. Lotte was in the dark observation area because he had said he wouldn't talk if she was questioning him. That had been four hours ago. The clock had started ticking as soon as they arrested him.

The door opened and Thomas slid in alongside her. 'The prosecutor just called,' he said. 'He wants you to know that he won't extend the warrant past the twenty-four hours. Not with Daan's history.'

'Wonderful,' Lotte muttered.

'There's CCTV of the road where Chantal died, but it's not clear that it's Daan who pushed her. I mean, CCTV doesn't rule him out, but because he's wearing a face mask, it's impossible to identify him. Right height and size, though.'

'He says he wants to kill me, so we can let him go and follow him until he tries.'

'Lotte, I meant what I said. It isn't funny.'

She looked at him. 'I wasn't joking.'

'We should talk to Gemma,' Thomas said. 'She's still in the same shelter.'

Lotte had her coat on before he'd stopped speaking.

'Did you find him?' Gemma asked. She was sitting on the bench where she and Daan had been when Lotte first talked to her. She was turning her lighter over and over between her fingers.

'Yes, we found him,' Lotte said. 'Do you mind if I record this?'

'Go ahead.' Gemma nodded to herself. 'It's sad, but it's what he wanted. He didn't want to go back to jail.'

Lotte noticed the past tense. Gemma clearly thought that Daan had died. Lotte didn't correct her. 'You called Gerard Klaasen, didn't you,' she said, 'to tell him that Daan was missing?'

'Yes. Gerard looked out for Daan. Always had done.' She rubbed her eyes. 'I thought he was Daan's father at first, and Daan got really mad at me.'

'Did you also call him after Teun died?'

Gemma nodded.

'What happened? I thought he and Daan were friends?'

'If that guy hadn't shown up, we would still be living on the Singel. I was happy there.'

'Rick van Buren, you mean?'

'Yes. Always going on about how Teun should drink less. Daan hid when Rick was there. Didn't want to see him, but it didn't stop us hearing him.'

She should have talked to Gemma sooner. The woman was very happy to reminisce about their time living together.

'I'm sure it was hard for Daan to see the officer who'd beaten him up come to his house.'

'Right! That was all he wanted from Teun, to stop that bastard cop from coming.'

And Rick had wanted to start the friendship with Teun again, keen to get his friend to kick the booze as he himself had done.

'Rick didn't even recognise Daan. Can you believe it? We weren't people to him.'

'Was that why Daan killed Teun?'

'He didn't kill him!' Gemma spun the lighter more quickly between her fingers. 'Or maybe he did.' She turned to Lotte, eyes suddenly sharp. 'If you don't rescue someone, does that mean you kill them?'

'What about Rick? Chantal?'

'Who's Chantal?'

'When did you see Daan last?' Thomas asked.

'The day you came,' Gemma said. 'That's when he took off. He said that now he'd met all three of you, so it was meant to be. It was fate.' She shrugged. 'I don't know what that meant. He didn't tell me.'

Lotte got her phone out. 'So he'd seen this photo?'

'I did too.' Gemma pointed at each of the children in turn. 'That's Teun, Rick and you. Teun told us that.'

'Teun showed you this picture?'

'Yes,' Gemma said. 'To explain why Rick kept hassling us. Daan didn't care why. He just saw the man who'd shattered his eye socket with his baton.'

Gemma pointed to the photo again and circled the four policemen who sat talking together. 'And these are the men who killed Daan's father. The bastards.'

In the interview room, Daan looked straight ahead of him. Even though Lotte wasn't the one questioning him, he wasn't saying a word. She sat in the observation area again and watched him stay silent. Then the door behind her opened. It was Charlie.

'I've got it,' he whispered, as if anybody on the other side of the one-way mirror could hear them.

'Got what?'

'Rick parked his car around the corner from that bar, outside an office building. That building has CCTV. Look at this.' He held out his laptop.

The footage was grainy, but Daan was recognisable. He was tampering with Rick van Buren's car.

'I think he cut the brake cable,' Charlie said. 'You'd normally notice if your brakes aren't working . . .'

'But Rick was drunk.' Lotte finished his sentence. She wanted to hug him, but instead gave him a pat on the back. 'We've got him,' she said. 'Well done.'

Charlie gave her such a huge smile that she wondered if people didn't say that to him very often.

She left the observation area and went into the interview room.

'My client explicitly said he doesn't want to speak to you,' the lawyer said.

'That's a shame,' Lotte said, 'because I definitely want to talk to him.'

'He won't answer your questions.'

'He can listen, then. Isn't it really annoying,' she turned to Daan, 'that your lawyer talks as if you aren't here? That would really piss me off.'

She opened her notebook and put it down in front of her. 'What I think happened is this, but do correct me if I'm wrong. Or no, wait, you don't want to speak to me. Anyway, you were angry with your best friend because he had another friend who happened to be the guy who beat you up and put you in prison. I kind of get that you were pissed off about that.' She leaned forward. 'But I also think that afterwards you were upset.' She spoke in a much kinder voice. 'Did it dawn on you then what you'd done? Did you push him? Did he fall in and you just didn't rescue him? Either way, your best friend Teun wasn't going to come back.'

She paused to give him a chance to respond, but he didn't. 'Okay. Fine. Then, to get rid of the nasty feeling that you'd made a mistake, you doubled down and tampered with Rick van Buren's car. Cut his brake cable. Only you didn't just kill Rick, you also injured an innocent child. Collateral damage is a bitch when you're trying to get your own kind of justice. The child is eight years old, Daan, and she'll never walk again.' She spat the words out.

'That's not my fault.' His searing eyes shot to hers. 'It was down to fate.'

'Daan,' the lawyer interrupted, 'you don't have to say anything.'

Lotte sat back. Now she was getting somewhere. Someone who had no intention of talking to her had said something. 'It was fate. Right,' she said as if the lawyer hadn't spoken at all. 'You saw a photo of the four police officers you held responsible for the death of your father. Did you tell yourself that Teun's death was really revenge for your dad? Was that how you rationalised it to yourself?'

'I grew up without a father because of them. That's why my life is so messed up.'

'Really?' Lotte raised her eyebrows. 'I grew up without my father and I'm totally fine. Mate, something else messed up your life.'

'It was a test.'

'Daan,' the lawyer said again, 'don't answer her questions.'

'She needs to know,' Daan said.

Lotte could tell that he was now so keen to talk he'd ignore any advice. 'What was a test?' she asked.

'Rick. It was a test to see if I was doing the right thing. I'd been following him for days before he went into that bar.'

Rick van Buren had had a drink because he couldn't face seeing Teun's widow and giving her more bad news. Lotte wished she hadn't asked him to do that.

'Yes, I cut his brake cable,' Daan continued, 'but if he'd stopped at one drink, he'd have noticed. He didn't. He drank until he was legless. Then he died and I knew it was what I was supposed to do.'

'It was what you were supposed to do?'

'You see, don't you?' Daan frowned at her as if he was surprised at her stupidity. 'Rick had two chances to live: he could have stopped drinking and noticed the problems with his brakes, or he could have chosen not to get in his car drunk. That he died showed it was what fate wanted me to do, so I kept going.'

'With Chantal?'

'That was fate too. I didn't kill her. I just pushed her.'

'You did kill her.'

He shrugged. 'I pushed you too and you're still here.'

Her skin burst out in goosebumps and static ran along her spine as if she'd shuffled her feet across a nylon carpet.

She hadn't imagined it, and it hadn't been an accidental push. This man across the table from her had nearly shoved her under a train.

'See, you weren't meant to die,' he said. 'She was. I didn't kill anybody. I created the circumstances and let fate decide the outcome.'

'If you push someone and then they die, you killed them. You're a murderer.'

'Detective Meerman,' Daan's ineffective lawyer said, 'please watch what you're saying.'

'Fuck you, bitch,' Daan said, oddly calmly. 'I shouldn't have listened to my mother. I should have stuck to my plan. I should have killed you instead of Chantal.'

'When did you make that plan? After you killed Teun?'

'I didn't kill him. I just watched, and fate said he shouldn't live.'

Lotte held up her phone with the photo. 'And yet you claim these four men killed Leon Martens?'

He shrugged again and said nothing.

'Leon was already dead when his mother first reported him missing,' Lotte said.

'That's not true,' Daan said quickly. 'They didn't find him during the coronation and got an official warning afterwards. If Wim van Buren hadn't been drunk, they could have saved him.'

'No, they could never have saved him. He'd been dead for almost a month at that point. We now know where his body is. Do you know who told us? Your mother.'

'You're a lying bitch.'

'We'll find out, won't we, when we dig him up. We'll do a DNA test. And do you know what we'll also find? That Leon Martens wasn't your father.'

Chapter 38

Queen's Day, 30 April 1980

Even from inside the police station, the shouting was audible. It was weird to be dressed in full uniform and not go outside. Strangely, it felt as if they were in hiding. 'Shouldn't we be doing something?' Wim voiced the thoughts of the whole team to Desk Sergeant Bouma.

For Amsterdam's police force, it was the culmination of three months of riots. For the special forces, it was the day they expected a terrorist attack. For the four men on secondment, it became an easy day where they mainly sat at their desks. No walking the beat today, Bouma told them, in case it got in the way of more serious work.

'They should have sent us home last night if they didn't want us to work,' Eelke muttered. Team 3 had already gone home after yesterday's shift.

'Emergencies only,' Bouma said. 'Strict instructions from the top.'

Wim laughed. 'Fine,' he said. 'We'll just hang around and drink coffee.'

'There'll be lots of emergencies. Don't worry.'

But there were none that Bouma thought were urgent

enough to warrant them leaving the police station. They sat around and did nothing while outside it sounded as if the squatters thought that lots of screaming and shouting would bring down the monarchy.

Wim bent down every now and then to covertly top up his thermos flask. He sipped from it throughout the day and Piet was pretty sure it contained something stronger than coffee.

Now that it was nearly time to leave, he put Lotte's toy back in his pocket. He'd returned to Amsterdam on Sunday morning because the atmosphere at home was unbearable. He didn't know what he was going to do tomorrow. He couldn't even begin to imagine how he would start again with his wife. Something had broken inside him when she'd invited van Merwe to their house. He hadn't wanted to be near her all weekend. But for the sake of their daughter, he felt they should try again. Even if Hilda thought he was pathetic and stupid, even though she thought he was no better than his brother, he should continue to look after Lotte.

He opened the desk drawer to check if he'd left anything behind.

The bottle of cognac had gone.

Before he could ask Wim if he'd drunk it, Desk Sergeant Bouma shouted at Barry that there was an urgent call. Bring the team. Someone had seen Leon Martens. He was bleeding, the anonymous caller had said, in a doorway near the Waterlooplein.

'You need to go there now! All of you.' Bouma was more agitated than they'd seen him this last week. 'Look at the map,' he said. 'You can't cross Dam Square, so go along the canal and head for the Blauwbrug.'

'Shouldn't we go—' Piet started but Bouma interrupted him.

'All other routes are blocked off.'

'Finally, some action,' Wim said. The stink of alcohol came off him.

'Take two cars,' Bouma said, and lobbed him a set of car keys.

Wim caught them with a grin. 'Come on, navigator,' he said to Piet. 'We're off.'

Piet tried to grab his arm but missed. He had no choice but to follow him. 'Let me drive,' he said, but Wim got into the driver's seat.

Outside the police station, they saw people defiantly waving red, white and blue flags to celebrate the coronation of Queen Beatrix. Piet had a bad feeling about this, but that was maybe because he'd been inside all day. The sudden call-out on the back of the enforced downtime was a jolt.

The closer they came to the Blauwbrug, the more obvious it was that they were heading straight into trouble. Two army helicopters hovered low in the sky. The crowd was huge. Tens of thousands of people had congregated. Piet had never seen this many people together outside of a football match. Policemen on horseback were surrounded by protesters shouting. Across the bridge a row of military police officers held baying dogs on leashes. Bricks came flying. A riot police van was surrounded by young men dressed in leather jackets and wearing motorcycle helmets.

Piet didn't know where to look. 'Oh fuck,' Wim muttered.

They got out of the car, obvious in their uniforms. Barry and Eelke pulled up behind them. Piet remembered that squatter the first day saying he'd brought the wrong hat. He settled his cap more firmly on his head.

'What the hell are we going to do?'

'We need to find Leon,' Piet said.

'There's no way through there. Our guys won't be able to hold the line,' Wim said, as if the protesters were an invading army.

Everywhere Piet saw the myriad of banners: *My Kingdom for a House, No Location, No Coronation, 8488, 8488.*

A squadron of riot police withdrew at high speed and jumped into their van.

'This is insane,' Eelke said.

'We should help. Those fucking squatters. I've got my baton in the back,' Wim said.

Piet watched the battlefield. Saw the flying batons and didn't want to join in. Didn't want Wim with a gutful of alcohol beating up protesters. Didn't want any of them beating people up the way he'd been beaten up two weeks ago. He grabbed Wim's arm and had to use all his force to hold him back.

'No,' he said. 'Let's just find Leon.'

Wim was disgruntled but agreed. As they turned back towards the cars, Piet thought he saw a photographer pointing a camera in their direction.

One of the policemen fell off his horse and the crowd

jeered. Piet froze. Were they going to kill the man? But there was loud laughter and the protesters sang the *Ivanhoe* theme tune as they helped the officer back in the saddle.

'We can go south from here,' Barry said, studying a map, 'and then loop around.'

Route agreed, they got back into the cars, put their sirens on and drove to where Leon had last been seen. But when they got there, there was no sign of him. Piet checked the doorways. He was supposed to have been injured. There were no traces of blood.

Leon had never been here.

Back at the police station, they caught Bouma on the phone.

'You got a good picture?' he said. 'Thanks for that. Yes, yes, I'll pay you next week.' Then he clocked the team and with a wide grin put the phone down. 'Someone eternalised you making a mess of things,' he said. 'Worthy of a front page, my reporter friend told me. And I can tell that you've been drinking.' He fished a breathalyser out from underneath the counter. 'You,' he beckoned to Wim, 'blow here.'

'What the hell?' Wim said. 'You threw me the car keys.'

'Did I? I don't remember that.' Bouma grabbed him by the arm and dragged him off. Of course Wim was way over the limit. This would go on his record.

'That utter shit,' Barry said. 'He set us up. He sent us straight into that riot.'

The door to the police station opened and van Merwe came strolling in. 'Did you find your student?' he said with a grin.

He knew where they'd been, Piet realised. 'What do you want?' he asked.

'Nothing from you, Huizen. I'm here to talk to your desk sergeant. He helped me with a problem. I have to say, he's really efficient.'

The desk phone rang again. Bouma was nowhere to be seen. Piet reached over the counter and picked it up.

'Piet? Is that you? I've been calling all over the place.' It was Robbie. He was obviously in a panic. 'I tried to stop her.' His voice was thick, as though he was talking through tears. 'I tried, Piet, I really did. But Hilda's parents were there too.'

'What's happened?' Piet asked, even though his burning eyes already knew the answer.

'They came with a removal van and took all the furniture, everything apart from my clothes and yours. What are we going to do?'

'What about Lotte?' Piet asked with his gaze on this man he hated. 'Where's Lotte?' Screw his wife and his belongings. His daughter was the only thing he cared about.

'They took her with them. Piet, I'm so sorry.' Robbie disconnected the call.

'What's wrong, Huizen?' his boss asked with a smirk. 'Having some home-front problems?'

Maaike's words came to mind, that he could either report his boss or leave. Well, if he was going to leave the police force, then he could do whatever he wanted to. He could punch that smirk off his boss's face.

But Barry jumped between them and held Piet's arms

back in a bear hug. Eelke grabbed him from behind. Piet screamed in frustration at how powerless he was and fought to get free of his colleagues.

It took them all their strength to hold him back.

Chapter 39

'Hi, Dad.' Lotte greeted her father as he arrived for dinner on Wednesday evening with Maaike. She gave her stepmother an awkward hug and thanked her for her work on renting out the flat. Both these things were deeply uncomfortable. It wasn't made any better by the fact that she used to have dinner with her mother every Wednesday. That had changed after her mother got married, but Wednesdays still felt untouchable. And now she'd asked her father and her stepmother here instead. It felt like a betrayal, as if she was choosing sides. She was overthinking it, she told herself, because this dinner had been Mark's idea. He always had the good ideas, the caring thoughts.

Mark dragged Maaike off to the kitchen for a talk about something to do with architecture and new building regulations. The large table in the dining room was laid for four people.

'Thank you for this,' her father said.

'Don't worry about it. Mark's doing all the cooking.' Lotte indicated that her father should sit at the head of the table, and she took the chair to his right. That way Maaike and Mark could sit next to each other too, so that they could talk shop. She poured water for everybody: her father was driving, and she and Mark were still sticking to their Dry April.

'Food's ready!' Mark said, and came in carrying a roast chicken. It smelt wonderfully of lemon and herbs. Lotte had no idea which herbs, but she trusted that he had chosen something suitable. Maaike followed with roast potatoes and carrots. Pippy-puss weaved between her legs and tried to trip her up.

'Stop it,' Lotte said to her cat, who listened just as little as always. 'Sorry,' she said to Maaike. 'I fed her beforehand. Don't give her any chicken,' she told her father, who had the terrible habit of passing the cat bits of meat underneath the table. It was why he was Pippy's favourite person after her owners. Right on cue, the cat sat herself beside Piet's chair.

'I'll carve,' Mark said.

'Do you remember,' her father said, 'that we used to have an electric carving knife?'

Lotte shook her head. 'I don't.'

Her father looked in admiration at Mark slicing thin pieces of chicken. 'Even with that, I wasn't as good at it as you are. One of my memories of that month in Amsterdam was Hilda roasting a chicken every weekend as a special meal. Because I was eating out every night, I think she felt she had to make something nice when I was back.'

The mention of that month made Lotte think about the picture of the four policemen with their three children. The only child who was still here was the child who was missing from the photo. Daan had said that fate had decided she wasn't meant to die, but if she hadn't been concerned about being pushed after Chantal's death, she would have fallen onto the train tracks when he shoved her.

'Katinka told her son you were a decent person.' Lotte put her hand on her father's arm. She stopped herself from saying anything more.

'He is a decent person,' Maaike said. 'Always has been. Things between us weren't what you imagined.'

'We found Leon's body, Dad. Exactly where Katinka said it was.'

'I still can't believe it,' he said. 'I knew my boss was taking backhanders, but I didn't know he was covering up for a murder. The guy who was our desk sergeant during that month ended up going to prison for corruption two years later. There was a big clean-out in Amsterdam's police force, especially around the Red Light District. I didn't know at the time that he had been stationed at the Warmoesstraat for a while.'

Katinka had mentioned a desk sergeant who'd been in her pimp's pocket, Lotte remembered. 'My mother did once tell me she'd have preferred that you were on the take. I had no idea she meant it so literally,' she said.

'Money was really tight for us back then.'

'Did you feel differently about her,' Mark asked, 'because she wanted you to take the money? That promotion?'

'Something snapped in me,' Piet said. 'Especially when she begged van Merwe to come to our house. He was sitting there and he revolted me. I knew he was sleeping with prostitutes, that he was on the take, and Hilda had invited him to our house. I looked at her and thought: you're not the person I thought you were.'

Lotte glanced down at her plate. Underneath the table, Mark felt for her hand and intertwined his fingers with hers. 'What happened after that?' she asked. 'I heard you met Katinka a couple of times. That you helped her out.'

'It was just an excuse to meet up with Maaike in Amsterdam,' her father said. 'She kept me from going off the deep end when things got really rough. I don't know what I'd have done otherwise, after your mother refused visitation rights. And I still had to work with van Merwe for a while,' he added, to steer things away from criticism of her mum.

'Is he still alive?' Lotte asked.

'No, he's been dead for years. Why?'

'Just that Daan was certain that Leon Martens was his father but Katinka said something that made me think he was van Merwe's son instead.'

'You feel sorry for him,' Maaike said.

'No, I don't feel sorry for him. He killed three people. It's just . . . I don't know. He's been lied to all his life.'

'Like your mother lied to you about the reasons for the divorce?' Maaike said.

Piet put his hand on her shoulder. 'Leave it,' he said. 'It's all fine now.' He cut a small piece of chicken and surreptitiously gave it to the cat.

But Lotte thought that maybe Maaike was right. Her mother had always made things difficult between her and her father. Still, now the four of them were having dinner together, and it felt right. 'Did my tenant move into the flat?' she said.

'I had to get a cleaning company in to tidy up,' Maaike said. 'The place was a mess.'

'You should have said. I'd have helped.'

'It's fine, you had other things on your mind.'

Automatic disagreement with Maaike and defence of herself was on Lotte's lips, but she kept the words in. 'You're absolutely right,' she offered instead. 'I've been busy.'

'You can buy us lunch once a month out of the rental cheque,' Maaike said with a wide smile. Maybe she recognised that this was the first time Lotte had agreed with her on anything. 'Then poor Mark doesn't always have to cook.'

'It's okay,' Mark said. 'I enjoy it.'

Looking at those two, Lotte saw another similarity between them, apart from their professions. She now knew that Maaike wasn't a home-wrecker.

Most likely she was someone who, just like Mark, with care and love had managed to stitch back together a fractured life.

Acknowledgements

My father was seconded to Amsterdam from Alkmaar during riots in the mid-1970s and was temporarily based at the police station on the Warmoesstraat in the heart of the Red Light District. He told me many stories about that time, such as getting lost along the canals during a call-out. In this novel, I have drawn on his experiences but have taken the liberty of transplanting them to a later period.

Everything else – including the murder case – is a pure figment of my imagination.

I want to thank everybody who helped me with this book, especially my agent Allan Guthrie from The North Literary Agency, who first suggested I make this a dual-timeline novel. My editor Krystyna Green, managing editor Amanda Keats, copy-editor Jane Selley and all at Constable and Little, Brown have worked hard to make the book the best it could possibly be.

Finally, a huge thank you to you, my readers, who continue to enjoy my books.